LOVE SONGS

BOOK TWO OF THE TALIA SHAW SERIES

CHRISTINE J DARCY

To my mother who supports me endlessly. To my best friend who has always been there. To my inspirations who led me here. And to the readers. I am so grateful.

ONE

"She's holding his hand," I said. "I never noticed that before." Keanu was losing hope that anyone on the bus would survive. Sandra Bullock assured him they would and then reached out to take his hand, to comfort him. He held it tightly. It was a tiny thing in the frame, but I'd never noticed it before. Laurie reached out and held my hand. I laughed at him.

"Too cheesy?" he asked, but kept hold of it.

I had the urge to yawn but tried to suppress it. If Laurie saw he'd insist we go to bed. He'd been a little overcautious since the car accident. It had taken us too long to pick the movie. He wanted to watch a romantic comedy. I wanted to watch Speed. I won. But it was nearing midnight. The yawn beat me and came out.

"You're tired. We should go to sleep," he said, reaching for the remote with the arm that wasn't trapped beneath my head.

"No," I argued. "I'm fine."

"We can watch the rest tomorrow," he insisted. I pulled a sad face. "And, we'll watch Point Break after that."

I smiled. That would do it. "Okay."

He laughed at his easy manipulation of me and grabbed the remote to turn off the TV. I slowly rose from the couch to stand, feeling my fatigue more thoroughly. I yawned again. "Not tired, huh?" Laurie asked again.

I reached out a hand to pull him up with me. He shook his arm a little before taking my hand. "What's wrong?" I asked.

"It's numb," he answered.

I moved my hands up his arm, massaging it gently with my fingers and thumbs. "I'm sorry. Why didn't you tell me?"

"You seemed comfortable," he said with a smile. His eyes shot to the small cut on my forehead and his brows furrowed. He still blamed himself. It wasn't the best idea perhaps, after a plane crash and a car accident, to watch a movie about a bomb on a bus. I probably wasn't going to watch Flight *anytime soon, but I still loved* Titanic *and* Speed. *I had no explanation for it.*

He took the arm back and lifted me up into a bridal carry.

"Laurie," I shouted, surprised. He didn't answer. "I can walk," I insisted.

"I know you can," he answered. I didn't bother continuing. He carried me up the stairs to my bedroom, placing me gently on the bed. He started to stand back up, but I held onto him, pulling him closer by his arms. I kissed him, tenderly. He settled himself on top of me.

"Talia." A voice pulled me from my reverie. I'd been doing a lot of daydreaming over the tour. "You okay?" Vienna, my trusty makeup artist asked. My hand had stilled, a makeup remover pad trapped between my fingers and cheek.

"Yeah," I said, and continued wiping away the heavy layer of makeup. It was just after midnight in Tokyo. We were in the quiet dressing room beneath the stadium but my ears were still ringing a little. Vienna wiped the glitter from my other arm as Megan, my hair stylist, undid the knots of my updo. Once all the bobby pins were removed, she started massaging my head.

"Oh my god," I groaned as my head lolled back, "I'm going to fall asleep right here if you keep doing that."

As much as I had grown to love touring and performing all over the world, I couldn't deny that I was exhausted. We had spent a five weeks in Europe and another two in Asia. Tokyo was the last stop before we had a month long break which, as it turned out, wasn't going to be much of a break at all. Teddy and I were going to do some recording. When we weren't performing or flying to the next place or drinking with the band and crew, we were writing.

A knock sounded on the door. Sabra, my trusty young assistant, was carrying her mobile in the air. "Manny for you."

"I'm not in," I said, too tired to talk business. She nodded and held the phone to her ear.

"He says he can hear you," she said before clamping her teeth shut at the blunder.

"I'll call you later, Manny," I called across the room. She held the phone back to her ear and then hung up. "What did he want?" I asked.

"I think he was just checking in." She hadn't closed the door all the way and a sudden shouting sounded behind her.

"Who is that?" I asked, standing up.

Sabra moved back to the door. "Woah," she said, her eyes widening.

I shifted her a little out of the way and walked out into the hall. Teddy, my British opening act and dear friend, had an arm around Merrick, one of my sound mixers, holding him back from two members of my band, Lucy and Vinny. Lucy looked merely bothered, but Vinny looked upset. Merrick looked hurt and pissed.

"Just calm down, Merrick. You're acting like an idiot."

"Are you fucking kidding me, Luce?"

"What the hell is going on?" I stepped towards them. Teddy released Merrick. Leif, my hulking Hawaiian bodyguard, came running down the hall with sushi in his hand.

"Bit late, Merlin," Lucy said to Leif. Teddy laughed remembering Leif's nickname generated by the Wu Tang Clan name generator.

"Anyone?" I asked, still waiting for the explanation.

Merrick was staring daggers at Vinny. Vinny couldn't look at him. Lucy had her tatted arms crossed as she looked at both of them, waiting for one of them to speak up. When neither did, she started, "I kissed Vinny."

My mouth formed an 'o' as I tried to process that. And, Merrick was mad. The crew was gathering, watching. "Everyone inside," I said, pointedly to the band and Merrick. Teddy came too.

Vienna and Megan were packing up their things. Sabra sat in a corner and opened up her laptop. I was never sure what she was doing on there, but she typed crazy fast and everything that was supposed to be done got done. Teddy and Merrick sat on one couch and Lucy and Vinny on the other.

"Okay. Lay it out," I demanded.

Lucy started, "Merrick thinks he loves me." Merrick didn't deny it. "I'm into Vinny."

Vinny looked at Lucy surprised.

Merrick breathed fire. "You knew how I felt about her," he raged at Vinny.

"So, what does that mean? That I'm yours?" Lucy scoffed.

"I like her, man," Vinny spoke up, running a stressed hand through his bright orange locks that matched his short orange beard. Lucy tried to repress it, but she smiled a little.

Merrick shook his head. There could be no excuse.

"How long has this been going on?" I asked. How did I not

know there was an intense kind of love triangle going on there? I guess I'd been a little distracted.

"It's new," Lucy said, looking at Vinny.

"It's fucked," Merrick said, his light blue eyes flashing anger.

"Don't be so bitter, Merrick. It was never happening between us. You should've let it go years ago."

"You've gotta be a friend, Merrick. Be happy for them," I suggested. "Or try to be."

"He'll get there," Teddy said, clapping a hand on Merrick's back. Lucy looked over to him.

"Yeah sure," Merrick said, rolling his eyes.

"If we're revealing all our secrets now, I gotta say something," Lucy spoke up again.

"What?" I asked, worried.

Merrick looked a little sheepish. Vinny looked nervous. "Laurie's doing Lolla," Lucy blurted, saying my ex-boyfriend's name more quietly than the rest of the sentence, as if it might help me hear it. Lollapalooza, the music festival. In Chicago.

"Oh," I said. That was convenient timing. As soon as I returned to LA, he'd be going. And, they wanted to go with him. That made sense. They'd worked with him before me. Why should it bother me? Would they talk about me? "It's fine."

Lucy looked as if she didn't believe me.

"When do you guys go?" I asked, trying to show I was fine with it.

"Two weeks." That was soon. That was while I was recording.

"That's a little late to start crewing," I said.

Merrick spoke quickly. "We'd already signed up. None of us knew when you were recording..."

"It's okay. I didn't give you any notice. You should go if you want to go," trying to be the friend I told Merrick to be.

"I don't," Lucy said. "But I'm already contracted."

"It's really okay, Lucy," I insisted. It felt as though she was trying to make me feel better.

"I know. But I want to record. I loved recording with you. And, I've done Lolla."

"Laurie would let you go," Teddy said, though he didn't sound certain.

"I can ask him," I said and immediately regretted it.

"Really?" Lucy asked me.

I nodded and smiled. "I'll be sad to lose you boys, though, for recording." I looked to Vinny and Merrick.

"We're pretty awesome," Vinny agreed, looking at Merrick. Merrick looked at Vinny, still pissed, but not as vocal about it. That was a step.

"I need to take this off," I said, pulling at the corsetted shiny purple dress I wore. The wire was digging into my stomach and I imagined the relief of taking it off.

They got up and walked out of the room. "Sabra, can you please…" I asked, gesturing to the zip. She got up and rushed over, unzipping. I groaned. "God, that's good." She laughed.

It felt like trying to organise custody. I knew the right thing to do was to call Laurie. But I didn't know how I would react to hearing his voice and I didn't want to chance it. I texted.

Talia: Can you please let Lucy out of her contract for Lollapalooza? She'd like to record with me.

· · ·

He responded twenty minutes later.

Laurie: Hey. How are you doing? Of course, if that's what she wants. I didn't know you were recording so soon. I would've asked you.
   Talia: Thank you.

I didn't want to answer his question. He wouldn't care anyway. That I was still hurting. That touring had been incredible and life changing, but that every night when I went to sleep alone, I thought of him. That every song I'd written since had been about him.

I walked over to the desk in my hotel room, covered with bits of paper and a full notebook. Lyrics and music. I picked up my guitar and started playing, trying to figure out a chord progression that had stumped Teddy and I the night before.

Everyone was out partying, including Teddy. It being last night before the break and all. I could only do two hours before I was done. I didn't know how the crew could drink that much alcohol and sleep so little and still function. My body, my mind, everything was done. I need several hundred hours of sleep in my own bed.

I woke up the next morning to Sabra wandering quietly around my room and packing. "Sab?" I asked.

"Yes," she whispered. "Sorry."

"What are you doing?"

"Packing. Your flight is in three hours."

"What time is it?" I asked, sitting up. Three hours didn't seem like a lot.

"One," she answered. I'd slept for nearly ten hours. I hadn't done that since high school. Somehow I didn't feel any less tired.

"Why didn't you wake me?" I asked.

"I was waiting for--" A knock sounded. She ran for the door and seconds later was wheeling in breakfast on a trolley.

I took a deep breath. "That smells incredible."

I sat on the bed and started lifting covers to look at everything. Bacon and pancakes and fruit salad and french toast. "Come eat," I said.

"We need to get you packed," Sab said. "And I already ate. Breakfast and Lunch."

"Where is Teddy?" I asked.

"I think he's exploring," she said. "He should be back soon. Car is here in twenty."

"Twenty?" I asked. She nodded, nervously pushing her short hair behind her ears. Nervousness was a rarity for her.

"Okay. I'm showering." She seemed relieved to hear it. I took the plate of fruit with me.

I was clean and packed and dressed in an outfit my stylist, Ari, would surely have approved, light high waisted mom jeans, red bomber jacket, shiny stilleto boots, and a black newsboy cap. I gave myself a cat eye and a shiny lip. I'd never had much talent for makeup but Vienna had taught me some things over the last couple months.

The bellboys came to get our luggage and Sabra left to make sure the car was ready. Soon after, Leif came to get me from the room.

"Wowsa," he said, putting a hand over his chest and beating it against his chest like a cartoon character,

"Stop," I said. We walked to the elevator. "How's it looking?" I asked.

"Not as bad as London. Not as good as Malta." Each city had been it's own experience in terms of crowds. London was scary. The elevator dinged and we arrived in the lobby. I could hear the muffled sounds of a crowd. Another security guard was waiting at the door. Behind the glass was a cordoned off stairwell leading down to a car.

Either side of it, hotel workers held back hundreds of screaming girls. In amongst them were grown men with giant cameras. Those were the same in every country. I wanted to get them away from the young girls, remembering how young I was when they first started putting their cameras in my face, but I knew I couldn't. "You ready?" Leif asked as we took a moment. I nodded and he opened the door.

We crossed the space quickly. The screaming became louder. There were tears and roars and an endless clicking. People held photos out to be autographed and phones set to camera mode for selfies. But stopping meant mayhem. The crowd was pushing in. We moved faster.

I let it all blur. The screams faded to white noise and the flashing lights dimmed. Leif opened the door and gave me a gentle push in. The door closed quickly behind me. Teddy was already in there. He was drinking some kind of smoothie.

"What is that?" I asked.

"Green juice."

"Can I have some?" I asked. My speedy shower soaked breakfast hadn't quite filled me up. He passed it over. I took a sip and pulled a face. "Not good." I handed it back.

"I just signed two breasts and an ankle," he said, a smile stretching across his long face.

"Were they nice breasts?"

"Beautiful," he answered, as always. He never had a bad thing to say about a breast. I had never been asked to sign one, male or female, and I felt badly about that.

Leif got in beside the driver and we took off.

We settled in to first class, avoiding the curious looks from others in the cabin. Sabra had kept trying to convince me to fly private. Even showing me some of the larger planes we could go in. I couldn't do it if it wasn't a hundred percent necessary. I'd happily take a few selfies.

Teddy distracted me, as he usually did, during take off.

"Can you believe all that with Merrick and Lucy?" he asked. His dark red hair looked practically brown in the darkness of the plane.

"Not really. It seemed like she always knew. I didn't have a clue."

"You didn't?" he asked. "There were clues. The way he looked at her. The fact that he wouldn't hook up with any girls while she was around."

"Really?" I asked. "I thought he'd been doing well for himself." I recalled a night in Amsterdam when he went home with three Dutch girls. But then I realised that Lucy had been sick that night. Bad brownies.

"Poor guy," Teddy continued, awfully serious.

"What a punishment," I said. Teddy looked questioningly at me. "To be in love with someone who doesn't love you." And then, again, I was thinking of Laurie.

TWO

Joe, the producer of my first album, came over the day after we'd arrived home to hear the songs Teddy and I had been working on. We set up our guitars, Teddy's loop, and my keyboard in the living room and sat Joe on the comfiest couch. These songs were a little different to the first ones we'd written together and which Joe had produced. We knew each other better. We were more honest with each other. And I was more honest with myself about the kind of music I wanted to write.

Even Teddy seemed nervous as he set up. "You ready?" I asked him.

"Yeah. You?" he asked. I nodded and he started playing.

I took a breath. I hadn't warmed up my voice and it sounded a little rusty as I started singing. Soon it was warm and we found our rhythm. Joe nodded his head to the beat at some points and sat perfectly still in others. I kept looking at the hand holding one of his legs crossed on top of the other. It seemed to grip too tightly.

"There's no name for that one. Should we just jump right into the next?" I asked. Joe nodded. So, we did.

We went through the next and then the last one. It was the most upbeat of the songs and I couldn't help but start to dance during the instrumental moments. Even Teddy was bouncing a little more than he would've liked. It was a total bop. The poppiest pop.

When we were done, Joe was characteristically quiet. "What are you thinking?" I asked. I knew the songs were pretty different from the first album, which was more sad pop with a little rock, but I thought they were better. I hoped he thought so, too. Teddy looked like he knew what Joe was going to say before he said it.

"I can't do it," he said, finally.

"Can't do what?" I asked, my mouth drying out.

He threw up his hands. "Produce the album."

I furrowed my brows. "You hate it."

He threw back his head a little with half a laugh. "Far from it."

He was smiling. "Then why?" I asked.

He took a breath. "I love you, Talia. And, I love your songs. But, I can't make them what they should be."

I tried to argue but he went on. "I was hired for the Betty Coopers."

The Betty Coopers. I missed them every day without exception. If they didn't come up naturally during the day, it would hit me at night. The crash. The loss of my two best friends. The moment my life changed in innumerable and unimaginable ways.

He continued. "For a rock group. I did what I could with the first album, but you need someone else for this. You need James." He meant James Aaronson, who'd already produced one of my favourite songs I'd ever written, when Joe was unavailable.

"But you're our guy," I said.

"Yeah but you'll have a lot of guys."

Teddy was nodding. This didn't surprise him.

"I'll always be a fan," he assured me. "Me and Violet will be at every concert. I promise." His daughter loved my music.

There was no arguing. Teddy was looking at me. He smiled at me like it was all okay. "Okay," I said.

Then we were heading to James'. I'd called him after Joe had left and asked if he'd be willing to produce the whole album. He said, "I thought you'd never ask."

James had a very different energy than Joe. Joe was sweet and wise, a modern day Jesus with his long locks and beard. And James was frantic with a shaved head that was always dyed a different colour. When I first met him it was orange. This time it was blue.

We played him the first song we'd written, the same with Joe but he didn't just sit there listening. He was writing, he was thinking, he started adding things straight away, trying things with the lyrics and melody. We got right into the thick of it within the first ten minutes. He'd cut one bit from one song and added it to another.

I never imagined yelling at him, but I did. We all yelled at each other in the first week. Mostly it wasn't because we didn't like something, but because we hated the other person for thinking of it. We spent all day and night in that eclectic apartment surrounded by brightly coloured mismatched wallpaper, eating Chinese food, and screaming at each other and making music. We brought Lucy in much sooner than last time, and she thought we were all insane. But James loved her. She had such a mountain of instrumental knowledge and a mastery of guitar. She moved around his apartment, picking things up and playing. Things I had no idea were actually instruments.

Toward the end of the month, we were all practically living in his downtown studio apartment. One morning I woke up at 6am, draped over James in his too high bed. Lucy was on the other side of him, her rose inked leg slung over his. Teddy was on the lounge, his pale arm thrown over his face. My phone was ringing somewhere inside my discarded jeans. I reached down onto the floor and pulled them up, my phone falling oddly from one of the legs. It landed with a crash.

James shot up. "Who's there!"

"Sorry," I said, pointing to the phone. He just fell right back down and went back to sleep. It had to be Saffy. No one else called me at that kind of hour.

"Hi, best friend," I said, in a whisper.

"Hi back. Did I wake you?"

She never could wrap her head around the time difference between the US and our home in Australia. "It's okay," I said as I made an attempt to put on my jeans and then gave up.

"Have you heard it?" she asked, as I tip-toed across the apartment floor to the balcony.

"Heard what?" I lifted the window, which squeaked awfully.

"Talia!" my name, said with great agitation, came from both James and Teddy. Lucy was unmoving.

I climbed through the window and moved myself to the furthest edge of the balcony. The morning air was cold against my bare thighs. Saffy had said something I couldn't hear. "Sorry?" I asked for a repeat.

"His new song?"

"Whose new song?" Laurie, I thought. It had to be. Why else would she be telling me?

"Laurie. He's playing it at his concerts. I'll send you the link." An alert sounded on my phone and I opened up a YouTube link.

"Are you watching?" she asked. The video was called 'Laurie Siler – Stay'.

"Yeah," I said as the sound kicked in. A roaring audience. I turned the volume as low as possible. And there Laurie was, on stage, in an effortlessly cool blue suit. It was iPhone footage, a little shaky, but the person was seated close to the stage. Laurie was standing still in front of his band, behind a mic. His long hair was held back in a man bun. His green eyes sparkled from the spotlight. His skin on his chest shimmered from the slightest sheen of sweat where it peaked out of the white button down shirt tucked into blue floral patterned slacks. His jaw was closely shaved, it could cut glass. He was so good looking it sucked all the air out of my lungs. There was a long musical intro and then he started singing. I turned it up, just a little, fearful of my sleeping friends' ire. I couldn't make out all of the lyrics.

"What is he saying?" I asked. I could only get a few words. "Gone… Scared…"

"I woke up and you were gone." Oh god. "Got scared until I remembered everything I'd done."

"Shit," I said.

"There's more…"

"Wait," I said. I could make out some more lyrics.

I don't know how to say all the things I should say.

I could never say all the things I wanted to say.

Now you're gone. Away from me. Away from me. Away from me. Away from me. He kept repeating those words over and over. *Away from me. As you should be. Stay away from me.* And, that was the end.

. . .

His smooth voice was deeper and more powerful than I'd ever heard it. The screams almost drowned him out. I wanted to yell at them to shut up. Holy shit, I thought. It was about me. About the morning after I'd left. He couldn't say what he wanted to say? He'd said plenty when he ended things. He was telling me to stay away from him, which would've felt brutal if he didn't sound so sad... so broken.

"Talia?" Saffy asked. "What are you thinking?"

I couldn't say.

"It's a good song," she said.

"Yeah," I answered.

Lucy climbed through the window, a cigarette hanging loosely from her lips. "Hey," she said with a raspy morning voice.

"Hi," I answered.

"Should I let you go?" Saffy asked.

"I'll call you later," I said. "Thanks."

"Yeah," she answered. "Love you."

"You, too." I hung up. Lucy saddled up beside me. She offered the lit cigarette. I shook my head.

"You okay?" she asked. I nodded. We stood there in silence, as she smoked, and I thought. I couldn't stop myself thinking.

Even as we ate breakfast, my cereal melted into the milk, I didn't touch it. Even as we set ourselves up on the lounges ready to start again.

Lucy and Teddy were talking about a lyric. "It should be don't try and..." She sang it. "Don't try and make it more complicated. It doesn't have to be so complicated."

"No," Teddy argued. "Don't try and complicate it, baby. It doesn't have to be so complicated."

"Talia?" James asked, swinging around in his torn up leather office chair.

"Let's take a break," I said finally.

"What?" Teddy said. Last night I'd been full steam ahead. And, we had less than a week until we left for the rest of the tour. He was confused.

James nodded. "Yes. A break. Refuel the engines. Let's go to New York."

"What?" Teddy said again.

"I wanna visit my boyfriend," James answered.

"Oh my god. I could go to the American Open," Lucy said.

"I could go to New York," I said, shrugging, a little noise would do me good.

Teddy threw his hands up in defeat. "New York."

James' boyfriend, Fisher, picked us up from the airport in his little hatchback. Lucy, Teddy, James, and I squeezed illegally into the back. Leif got the front seat but still, he barely fit. Fisher drove like a maniac through the busy city streets. Teddy and I held on for dear life, but James and Lucy barely noticed. We were all staying at Fisher's apartment. He had a fourth floor walk-up in Brooklyn with a roof top garden.

"Carry me?" I asked Leif, as the stairs overwhelmed me.

"Do not," Teddy chided me.

"I was joking," I said.

"You were not," Lucy said through panting breaths.

"Y'all are unfit," Fisher made fun of us as we climbed.

We cooked dinner on a barbeque in the roof top garden and were joined by some of Fisher's friends including Sofie, a director I'd worked with on a music video, who'd moved to New York a few months before. The drinking led to dancing and we decided to go clubbing. Sofie took us to her new favourite place, *Dixie Disco*.

"It sounds like a kid's show," Lucy claimed, as we pulled up out front. The building was shuttered up like it was closed, but there was a door girl and a security guard and a little queue. There was barely a line, but the woman at the door came over to welcome us in ahead of everyone.

"They're all with me," I said, gesturing to the half dozen people waiting in line.

Her face froze. I didn't like jumping the line. "Just let us all in," Lucy said.

The woman's mouth tightened, but she nodded to the security guard, who moved out of the way of the small crowd. "Hey, thanks Talia Shaw," one of the guys wearing pink lycra short shorts said.

"You're welcome," I said, following behind them.

The music hit first. They were playing James' band, *Draino*. "Oh shit!" Fisher said, jumping on James. James ducked his head a little, modest.

Then I noticed the people, in bright colours, eighties wear. "Is this an eighties club?" I asked Sofia.

"Seventies, Eighties, Nineties, whatever you want it to be," she said. There were people hanging from the roof on wings and in cages. The floor was 70s disco style, all different coloured lights, red and yellow and pink and blue. A ginormous silver disco ball hung in the centre of the room sending sparkles of light over the crowd and the walls. The place was all throwback and barely half full.

"Holy shit," Lucy said, grabbing my elbow. "This place is sick."

"I'll get some drinks," Teddy said, never one to step foot on the dance floor. Leif took a post on the edge of the dancefloor as the rest of us found a spot to dance. We were going wild to the song, perfectly matched to the club itself. James danced half-heartedly to his own song while Fisher danced circles around him. Next came

Backstreet Boys remixed with Abba in a way that made me want to scream. It was all so good.

"Excuse me?" a voice called from behind me. Three drag queens dressed like factory girls were standing behind me holding up a phone. "Can we?"

"Of course," I said. "Everyone in," I called to my group. Leif took the phone and snapped a picture of us all.

"You're the sweetest," one of them said.

"You look fantastic," I said, admiring the white shift mini dress he wore.

"You too, baby girl," he said, returning the compliment. "Killing it." I hadn't dressed for dancing, just dinner. I wore a tan leather mini skirt and a black silk blouse with black ankle boots. My blonde curls were pinned back from my face and dangling long against my back. I'd given myself the slightest bit of makeup and wore one piece of jewellery, a chunky gold chain necklace with a black jewel in the centre.

They were the only ones to approach, no one else seemed to care who we were. Or so I thought til the DJ shouted me out. "This one is for Talia Shaw! Welcome to Dixie's, darling!" I was too into it to feel any modesty. They'd remixed *Sails* with *Around the World* and it was glorious.

We danced all night. My feet felt like they could fall off at any moment. We stumbled out of the club at 3am to a crowd of paparazzi. They followed us all the way back to the apartment.

They were still there in the morning. The apartment wasn't very secure. Leif insisted we move to a hotel, so I got everyone rooms at The Bowery.

We spent the day recovering by the pool but started drinking again early. When it got dark we moved our drinking to the lobby bar downstairs. Teddy wanted to eat to line his stomach, imagining the kind of night Fisher would bring about all over again, and we found ourselves eating at the restaurant, *Gemma*, where I'd eaten with Laurie and his friends. We were seated across the room from the table Laurie and I had the first time. I pictured us all sitting there, Laurie with his arm thrown around me. Before we went on our road trip. All aglow.

Someone must've told Bucky we were there because he came out of the kitchen and over to us.

"Talia," he said in greeting and kissed my cheek.

"Hi. Everyone this is Bucky. The Head Chef," I introduced him.

"Your food's amazing, mate," Teddy said. Our group hummed in agreement, their mouths full.

"Thank you," Bucky tipped his chin. He leaned down to me. "How are you?"

I shifted a little, uncomfortable. He must've known all about the breakup. "Really good," I said, hoping it was believable.

"I heard you were staying. I hoped you'd come for dinner." I smiled. "I'll send out something sweet when you're done."

"You don't have to do that," I assured him.

"My pleasure," he said. He squeezed my shoulder and walked back to the kitchen.

"How do you know him?" Teddy asked.

I shrugged. "Met him last time." Teddy didn't push. He knew I didn't want to discuss anything to do with Laurie. I left my meal half eaten, preferring to drink at that point, and ordered another couple of jugs of sangria for the table.

I was very sloshed by the time Bucky sent out the Tiramisu that I felt comfortable gorging myself. It was delectable.

We made our way from the hotel to Fisher's favourite club, a basement spot called *Sink*.

I barely remembered the evening's events when I woke up in the morning with a splitting headache.

Lucy brought me a fresh pastry and juice and surprised me with a facial treatment at the spa.

"What's going on?" I asked as we waited for our treatments.

"What? You got us our rooms. I can't do something nice for you?"

I eyed her.

"Okay. I have tickets to the tennis and I need someone to go with me."

"Seriously?" I asked. "I'm so hungover."

"You'll feel so much better after this treatment."

You wouldn't have thought she was a tennis fan to look at her. I definitely couldn't imagine her in all whites and a visor running around a tennis court.

"Come on," she pleaded.

"I don't like tennis."

"So what? They're box seats. We'll lay out and get drunk." I laughed. "There might be paps," she continued, with a tone that suggested it was a positive.

"That's not an incentive."

"You don't want Laurie to see how good you're looking?"

I didn't feel like I looked any different. In fact, *Dixie's* and *Sink* had left me a little worse for wear, but Lucy didn't seem to think so. I'd had my curls relaxed a little, it's why they were so long. And, thanks to Ari, the magazines that had always picked on my clothes and hair had started praising my style instead.

"Please?" she begged.

I relented. But no one else would go with us. Leif didn't want to go but tried to hide it. Teddy, James, and Fisher were going shopping. Or James and Fisher were dragging Teddy along like Lucy was dragging me. We texted each other our sympathies.

After our treatments, Lucy and I got ready and organised a car. I did feel better, fresher, after the facial, but then it took us an hour to get from the hotel to the Tennis Stadium in Queens and I lost my glow.

The box was nice. Great seats. But an hour into it, I gave up following the game. Leif brought a book to read. I wished I'd had the same idea. The game was simple enough to understand, but I was bored. Lucy got riled up every now and then, which was entertaining, but mostly our heads just went back and forth watching them hit the ball. And it was so quiet. I tried to read along with Leif, but it was a biography and it bored me even more than the game. I checked social media, sent some messages to some of the fans I'd been following. I even responded to a few of Manny's emails. Finally, I asked Lucy how much longer we had to go.

"At least another hour," Lucy said, quickly, not wanting to be speaking when something exciting happened.

"Are you serious?" I asked. She shushed me. "I'm getting alcohol," I said, standing. Leif started to rise, but I put a hand on his shoulder to keep him seated. The bar was on the same level as the private boxed seats. I didn't need him.

I waited at the bar as the bartender served the others waiting. I heard footsteps on the stairs and looked to see a man stumble on the last. He caught himself with the rail but mere feet from there he tripped again on a lump in the cement path. I couldn't help but laugh. He recovered quickly and acted like nothing had happened.

Then I recognised him. It was Jack O'Halloran. He was an actor. Late twenties maybe thirty, I thought. He had a short beard that I'd never seen in his movies, but I recognised him. He had striking blue eyes set in a boyish face. His jaw was strong, his lips thin, and his nose sharp. His short dark brown hair was dishevelled and pushed back. He was shorter than I thought. About the same height as me. He was dressed very casually. Jeans, a t-shirt hanging loosely from his strong frame, and vans. His chunky matte gold watch looked expensive.

I stopped laughing and was merely smiling when he looked at me. "Shit. I was hoping no one saw that," he said, lightly embarrassed.

I laughed a little. "I saw it. It was hilarious."

He smiled back. "I'm glad I could amuse you."

"Are you okay?" I asked, feeling a little badly.

"Nothing hurt but my pride."

"What can I get you?" asked the Bartender.

I looked to Jack. "Can I get you a drink?"

"Ah sure. Just a beer," he said, coming to stand beside me.

"Four please," I said to the bartender. He started pulling them.

"Four?" Jack asked.

"Not all for me," I explained.

"I wouldn't judge you," he shrugged. "Are you enjoying the match?" he asked as the bartender handed over the beers and I gave over the cash.

"Honestly," I started. "I'm not super into it."

"You don't like tennis?" he asked, as we started walking back to the stairs.

"Not really. My friend had the tickets and didn't want to go alone."

"That's good of you. It's not a short game," he advised.

23

"I'm starting to see that," I said. I elbowed him a little as we approached the bump. "Mind the bump."

He laughed a little and dramatically stepped over. "I'm Jack, by the way," he said, shuffling his beer to the other hand to shake mine. I nodded because I knew.

"Talia," I answered. He nodded like he knew.

"Nice to meet you, Talia."

We quickly reached the top and paused. "I'm this way," I said, pointing to the seats further down.

"I'm this way," he gestured to the right. "Thank you for the beer," he said with a chin tip.

"Anytime," I offered. We stood there awkwardly a moment longer until I took a step toward where I'd been sitting with Lucy. "See you round."

I didn't look back as I walked toward Lucy. She was still intensely watching the match. I shuffled in beside her and handed over the beer.

"Thanks," she said. I gave Leif his. He took it with an exasperated sigh. He wasn't supposed to drink on the job. He drank it anyway.

"Did I miss anything?" I asked him.

"Hillary has just been made Secretary of State," he answered, referring to his book. I nodded along.

I turned around and found Jack in his row, sitting with two other guys. One of them I didn't know but the other I recognised as an older actor. He'd been in a lot of action films but nothing lately. They were all looking at me. Jack ducked a little with a smile, caught. I smiled and turned back around.

Leif stood up. "Be right back." He left his book on the chair.

Moments later Jack was shuffling into the empty seat beside me.

"Hi," he said, leaning into me with his wide white movie star smile.

"Hi," I said back, my heart beating a little faster. I was glad to know it could still do that.

"You mind if I sit?" He already was, I thought.

He leaned across me holding out a hand to Lucy. "Jack," he offered.

"Hi," she said, her attention going quickly back to the court. Maybe she didn't recognise him. Or she was too distracted.

"I wanted to keep talking to you," he explained.

I was flattered. I hoped I wasn't blushing. "That's nice," I answered and then berated myself for the stupid response.

"Do you live in New York?" he asked.

"No, just visiting," I answered.

"You still living in Australia?"

"No, I live in LA."

He nodded. "I moved to LA a year or so ago. I miss New York though."

"I love this city," I agreed.

"What do you like about it?" he asked.

"Everything," I started. "The air, the noise, the people."

"The air isn't usually on people's lists."

"Maybe not the scent, but there is something in the air. Like a buzz. A liveliness that you can't find anywhere else."

He nodded. "I know what you mean."

"Are you here for the tennis?" I asked.

"I'm doing a stint on Broadway."

"Oh wow," I exclaimed. "What show?"

"*Barefoot in the Park.*"

"I've seen that movie. Jane Fonda, right?"

"Yeah. And, Robert Redford," he answered. I saw Leif return but he took an empty seat a couple of rows back.

"Is that why the beard?" I asked.

He laughed a little. "They thought I looked too young without it."

I nodded. "How old are you?"

"Almost thirty," he answered. I nodded. That's what I had guessed. "How old are you?" he asked, his brow furrowed like he had been trying to figure it out.

"How old do you think?" I asked.

He hissed through his teeth. "That's a trap."

"It's not," I assured him.

"I'm going to say… twenty-three." I shook my head. "No?"

"Close," I answered.

"Higher or lower?" he asked. "Please be higher."

I bit my lip a little in response.

"Shit. Really? Twenty-two?" I shook my head. "Twenty one?"

"I will be in February," I answered with an excited smile.

He threw his head back with a laugh. "You can't even drink yet."

"You've got strict laws but lax bartenders," I answered, taking another gulp of my beer. He laughed.

"Only twenty. Wow. You're doing pretty well for yourself."

"Thanks," I answered. "I didn't realise you knew who I was."

"Your face is up in Times Square," he answered.

"What?" I asked. I didn't know that. It must've been for Burberry.

"It's a good face," he said in response. "If there has to be a face up there…" He became a little red.

I laughed. "Thanks."

We talked for the next half an hour, driving Lucy crazy I was sure. Then the match started to heat up and he watched more carefully. The crowd was becoming louder then.

He got so much more into it than I thought. He started screaming when Lucy did. I was sandwiched between two zealous sports fans. And, the game did become more interesting.

Finally, one of the players won. I couldn't for the life of me tell you who, but Lucy and Jack were ecstatic. They both looked at me for my reaction and I gave a big fake open mouthed smile and thumbs up.

Jack laughed at me. "Incredible match," Lucy said, shaking her head in awe.

"Great one," Jack agreed.

"Jack," a voice called from behind us. Jack looked back and held up a hand. "Well, I better get back to them."

I nodded. He didn't move. I smiled, waiting.

"I'm supposed to go to a thing tonight," he said, like an excuse for not asking me what I was doing later. "But, what are you doing tomorrow?" he asked, a glint in his eye.

"I go back to LA tomorrow... to get back on tour" I answered a little sadly. I had almost forgotten.

He nodded, a little disappointed. "Well then," he said, shrugging. He started to stand up. I put a hand on his arm to stop him. He looked at me.

I took a breath, searching for a little confidence. "I'm back in October."

THREE

Getting back into touring life was easy. It felt like I never left it. We travelled, performed, drank a little, slept even less, and repeated. Teddy was a little different this time round. If I traced it back, he was a little different after his shopping trip with the boys in New York. When we all arrived back in the evening, I asked them how it went and they were cagey.

"We had a nice long lunch," Fisher said.

"A nice long chat," James continued.

"About what?" I asked.

"Nothing at all," Teddy had said, and quickly changed the subject.

We used up our writing days back in LA, perfecting a few songs but not writing anything new. I thought we'd continue writing on the tour, just Teddy and I, but he started going out with the crew most nights then all of them. In the second week, he started hooking up with one of the new dancers. She wasn't the nicest or the prettiest in the bunch, I thought, but good for him…

I wrote on my own, using James as my sounding board. We were emailing ideas back and forth, Skyping when the hours worked for us. We were in the middle of doing just that on the night of my last Melbourne show. I was replaying the rhythm section he'd just sent me, trying to improve it.

"This bit," I said, "I like the toughness here, but is there a way to make it prettier toward the end?"

"Uh, yeah. I'm sure we could that," he said.

"So, it starts out broody and becomes kind of…?"

"Dancey?"

"Exactly." We were on the same wavelength. I wasn't making the same mistake as the last album. Nearly all of the new songs were anthems but this one would be the most anthemic. The lyrics themselves were epic and unapologetic about love.

"I got a lush sound, right here," he said, about to play something for me on his keyboard. My phone started ringing. It was an American number. "Who is it?" he asked.

"I don't know," I answered. Someone back home. Even though I was back in Australia, I had started referring to LA as home. I wasn't sure when that happened.

"You can answer it," James said. "Give me time to remember this."

"Okay," I said before pressing answer. "Hello?"

"Hi. Is that Talia?" the voice on the other end was quiet but deep and American-accented.

"Yes, it is," I answered.

"Great. They gave me the wrong number at first. I worried that I was getting brushed off." I realised who the voice belonged to.

"Jack?" I asked. James was mouthing, 'who is it?'

"Yeah. I asked your manager for your number. I'm sorry if that's weird."

"It's fine. I'm glad." I mouthed 'Jack O'Halloran,' but James couldn't make it out.

"Where are you?" he asked.

"Melbourne."

"Australia? Is that where you're from?" he asked.

"I'm from Sydney," I answered, feeling all of the awkwardness.

"Oh."

"I'm actually on a Skype call with my producer. Can I maybe call you back?" I asked.

"Is this the brush off?" he asked. "You think I'm a stalker now?"

I laughed. "Not at all. We were just in the middle--"

"Okay. I believe you."

"I'll call you back."

I hung up and looked at James who was waiting for explanation. "Jack O'Halloran," I explained.

"Really? The actor?"

"Yes. We met a week or so ago. At the tennis."

"Shit. I should've gone. He is super attractive."

"I know, right." I looked back down at my phone.

"So, what are you doing talking to me? Call him back."

"It must be early morning over there," I thought then counted. Around 8:30am. Not that early.

"He called you. He's obviously up."

"I don't know," I answered, trying to find an excuse. "I'm not really looking to date right now."

"Why?" James asked. "Because you're still hung up on Laurie?"

I had told James everything when we started writing the album. Teddy didn't want to hear the whole thing over again, so he took a walk. Since that first day, we'd just referred to him as the boy. Not necessarily Laurie, but the boy that people would think of listening to the songs. The boy they fell for. The boy who broke their heart. Whoever he was.

"I'm not still hung up on Laurie," I insisted.

"Yeah, you are. Probably because we're not done writing your therapy album about it, but you know what might help? A new boy. Not even a boy. He's thirty, right? A man. You need a man."

"He's a lot older, isn't he? It seemed to bother him when I told him I was twenty, but then he's calling."

"Probably realised that age is just a number," James said. "I'm hanging up now and you're calling him back."

"Wait. The lush sound?"

"I was gonna make it up," James said. "Bye," he said quickly before hanging up.

I laughed and closed my laptop. I looked at my phone again. I googled the time in LA and I was right: 8:12am. I stood up and took myself over to the lounge in my suite. I got myself comfortable. My stomach was a little knotty. I dialled.

He took a long time to answer but when he did, he was a little breathless, like he'd been running. "You called back."

"I told you I would."

We found ourselves talking for over an hour, while he walked his dog and ate breakfast. I moved around the room, going from the desk to the lounge and eventually into bed. It was small talk, mostly. Learning the basics about each other. When I finally had to go to sleep, he asked if he could call me again. "Definitely," I said. And, he did. The next night. And, the next. All the way through my Australian tour spots and then through North America. It took time away from writing the album, but James only encouraged it. Jack made me laugh and he made me feel... wanted.

One night, after performing in New Orleans, Jack told me I had to go to Café Du Monde.

"Will it still be open?" I asked.

Megan and Vienna had packed their things and were heading for the door. 'Bye,' I mouthed as they waved.

"It's open 24 hours."

"What?" I exclaimed.

"Go on," he insisted. I was tired, but I knew I'd be talking to him for the next hour at least anyway.

"Okay. I'll go," I said, putting him on speaker as I got changed.

"Am I on speaker?" he asked.

"Now you are. I'm just changing."

"Is anyone listening?"

I looked around though I knew I was alone. "No."

He took a second. "What are you changing into?" he asked, his voice a little deeper.

"Jack," I said, teasingly. "Did you just ask me what I'm wearing?"

"Go on, describe it all for me." This was a step. Our conversations prior had been flirty but could easily be categorised as simply friendly.

"Okay," I started. "I'm taking off the dress I wear for my last song."

"Taking stuff off, now that's a whole different ball game. What kind of dress?"

"It's purple. Corsetted. Short."

"That sounds hot," he said. My eyebrows rose. Definitely not simply friendly. "What's underneath."

"Jack," I said, scandalised. No one had ever talked to me like this over the phone.

"What? Am I making you uncomfortable?" he asked.

"Yes," I answered automatically. "Not necessarily in a bad way," I clarified.

"Really?" he asked. "Can I tell you something? I can't stop thinking about you."

My breath hitched a little. "Since that day we met. I can't get your face, your eyes… your fucking legs out of my head."

I looked over to the mirror where I stood in my underwear. They'd rubbed off most of the makeup, but my eyes were still smoky, and my hair hung in loose waves over my shoulders. My legs were long and my stomach flat. And, hearing him talk about me that way. I felt sexy. I imagined him looking at me. And, I felt hot.

"What are you thinking?" he asked.

"I'm thinking… I wish you were here."

"Oh yeah?" he asked, his deep voice becoming breathy.

"What would you do if I were?" I asked as my hand found my breast and I massaged it gently.

"I'd help you out of your dress," he started. "Then I'd run my hands over the lines the corset left in your skin."

I ran my fingers over those lines. A loud thump outside my room, probably some equipment, brought me back to the moment.

"Let's stop," I said. I was not going to start masturbating in my dressing room. We'd met once, I had to remind myself.

"Too much?" he asked. "Too soon?"

"Maybe a little of both. But mostly, there are a few dozen people walking around outside my door right now."

"Ah. I see."

"I'm back in a week," I said, though I knew he knew.

"I can't wait," he said.

"Do you maybe want to come see my show one night? I could get you tickets."

"I don't know. This is new. Don't want to get the rumour mill going already."

"I get that," I said. Laurie had felt the same way.

"Café Du Monde?" he reminded me.

"Yes," I said, as I opened my door. Leif was there. "You hungry?" I asked him.

"I could eat," he answered, as always.

"Let me just see if anyone else wants to go," I said to both Leif and Jack. Leif knew not to respond. My phone against my ear had become a usual sight for him.

"No, cause then you won't talk to me," Jack argued.

"Yes, I will. I at least have to ask Teddy," I said. "He's the only one who would be pissed he didn't get to go." Leif nodded, agreeing.

I walked toward Teddy's dressing room. I tapped quickly and walked straight in. Teddy and Crystal, my dancer, were on his lounge making out. She was on his lap, grinding against him.

"Oh," I said, bringing their attention to me and backing out.

"Shit, Talia." Teddy shifted Crystal off him and stood up.

"My bad," I said and closed the door, quickly.

Leif was looking at me, concerned. "He's busy," I explained.

"What did you just walk in on?" Jack asked, a little amused. "Were they doing what I want to do to you?"

I hummed a yes and continued down the hall toward the exit.

Leif drove me to the café, which was more restaurant than café. The place was overflowing with people. Leif looked at me, adamant. "No way," he said.

"Leif doesn't think I should go in," I told Jack.

"Get it takeout. It tastes the same."

"Would you mind?" I asked Leif.

"I'll be right back," he answered and got out of the car. He rushed over to join the line.

"It's a long ass line," I said. "Better be worth it."

"I promise. It'll change your life," he assured me.

"How's Pepper?" I asked, referring to his beloved dog. Pepper, I'd been told, was an Irish Wolfhound. She was apparently ginormous, grey, fluffy, and sweet as can be. "She's good. She's right here beside me. Say hi, Pep."

Silence. I laughed a little. "She got her morning walk?"

"Of course. I got papped picking up her shit," he said. "So, look out for that one."

I laughed again. "My niece wants a dog. It's her birthday in a couple weeks so I've been thinking of buying her one."

"Would Lyndsay be okay with that?" I asked. Lyndsay was Jack's sister, also an actor, whose husband had left when her daughters were two and four to be with another woman. Jack had made it sound like the siblings were close.

"She'll survive," Jack said.

"What kind of dog?"

"George wants a yellow lab, but Daisy wants something small. Like a Chihuahua."

"Whose birthday is it?"

"George's." Georgina was her name, but I loved that they called her George.

"Yellow lab it is, then?"

He clicked. "We'll see."

"I watched one of her movies on the plane," I said.

"Which one?" he asked.

"I can't remember the name. It's about lobbying," I said, searching for the name.

"Oh, yeah. That was not a good movie," he said.

I laughed a little. "She was so good in it."

"She was. She always is, but she picks some awful films. Did you see that one about the pancake competition? So flat."

35

I cracked up laughing. "That was really bad," I said, when I could.

"But you laughed," he teased. "Seriously though. That was a terrible movie."

"Like all of yours have been hits," I argued.

"You're already on her side. This is a problem," he joked.

A couple passed by the car, their arms around each other. The girl looked back at me and stopped. Sitting in the front was becoming a problem. The front window had no tint. "Oh my god," she said. "It's Talia Shaw."

"Somebody can see me," I said to Jack.

Her boyfriend tried to make me out but shook his head, disbelieving. There weren't many people around.

"Who?" he asked.

"A couple on the street," I said. The girl waved at me. I waved back.

"I've got to say hi." I unbuckled my seat belt and opened the door. "I'll call you back."

"I'll wait," he said.

I stepped out. "Hi," I said.

"I told you," she said to her boyfriend. "Can I get a picture?" she asked.

"Of course." She looked for her phone while her boyfriend looked at me.

"How's your night?" I asked, as he looked me up and down. Ugh, I thought.

"Oh my god. My phone is dead," she said, turning to her boyfriend. "Give me yours."

He handed it over to his girlfriend. She came to stand beside me to take the picture. She was short and her arms were likewise short, she couldn't get the shot. I offered. "I can take it."

She handed it to me. I took the selfie, dropping my own phone in the process. Her boyfriend picked it up, luckily the screen was still intact.

"Jack O'Halloran?" he asked, reading the caller's name. "The actor?"

"Different guy," I said, holding my hand out for the phone. The guy held it to his ear.

"Is this Jack O'Halloran from The Guard?" I'd never heard of that movie. "Holy shit, man, I love that movie."

The girl was looking at me. "I'm so sorry about him."

"It's fine," I assured her. "What's your name?"

"Candice," she answered.

"It's nice to meet you, Candice." Leif was running over with a bag of donuts in hand and a look of concern on his face.

"Yeah, yeah. But when you guys are running out into the stadium and you look around at all the people there for you..." The guy was still gushing.

"Can I have my phone back, please?" I asked.

The guy held up a finger as he continued. "I cried. Swear to god."

Leif approached. The boyfriend took in his size. Leif held out his hand for the phone and the man immediately gave it over. Leif handed it back to me.

Candice was looking at her boyfriend with a similar level of disgust as I had when he was blatantly checking me out beside her.

"Nice to meet you both," I said.

Leif opened the back door for me and I got in with a dismayed expression. He handed me the donuts and walked around to the driver's side.

"I'm so glad you didn't hang up on me. That was hilarious," Jack said.

"That was awful," I said. "That guy was a dick."

"Did you get the beignets?"

"Yes," I said, as Leif took off. We passed the walking couple. Candice looked to be berating him. I was glad to see it.

"Are you eating them?" I took one out and gave the bag to Leif. He took out his own.

"Okay, I'm taking a bite." I did. "Oh my god."

"It's good, right?" he asked. It was melting in my mouth. Hot buttery pastry and sweet powdered sugar.

"Oh my god," I said again, with a bit of a moan. Leif laughed a little from the front seat.

"Okay. Now I'm turned on again," he said. I laughed and a puff of white powdered sugar flew from my mouth.

After New Orleans, we did Detroit, Louisville, Kentucky, and the rest of the southern states. Our last show was Los Angeles. Home.

The show was perfect. Not a single thing went wrong, and everyone was in their element. The crowd went wild for Teddy. His album had been blowing up. And, they went wild for me. It was the first time I'd been back at the Staples Centre since the Grammys. I didn't even think about the humiliation I'd endured there. The crowd was too beautiful.

When I started the tour, the first few nights I was filled with dread. Now, at the end of it, I didn't want to stop. I came off the stage and into Teddy's arms.

"Wow," he said. "What happened to you out there?"

I shook my head. "I don't know. But I'm not ready for it to be over."

I looked to the stage hand and she knew from my look what I was doing. I walked back on, the lights came back up and the crowd erupted. They rushed back to the stage, screaming. The band had furrowed brows.

"Can I?" I asked Vinny, reaching out for his guitar. He handed it over.

I walked down the platform, toward the centre of the crowd on the floor. The spotlight followed me.

"I didn't want to leave you guys," I shouted out. More screaming and then quiet as I started playing, just the smallest melody.

"*Red Light* was about heartbreak." I'd played it a few songs before. "This is another song from the new album. It's about what comes before the heart breaks. About the good stuff. It's called *Sunrise*."

They started screaming again. I played the intro over and over again until it quietened down. The crowd started shushing people as well. I wasn't waiting for silence. I was just trying to ready myself. It was the first time anyone, but Teddy, James and Lucy had heard the song. And, this was the acoustic version of it. I wanted them to know the song as it was supposed to be. There was no anger in this song. No pain. Just love. So that is how I had to sing it for them. I took a few breaths, letting my mind shake off the layers to get to that first feeling. The purity of those first few months with Laurie.

Finally, I was ready. I looked up to the crowd. They were watching me intently. Almost, encouragingly. Like the friends I thought they were. I smiled back at them and started singing the first few lines.

It's a tequila sunrise sky
I'm tucked into your side

Don't ever let me go
Don't ever let me go

I played on, sang on, remembering all of of that first love, new love feeling and letting it rush out of me. I finished the song and looked up. Hundreds of cameras were recording. The cameras came down as they started clapping. Clapping gave way to screaming and I waved goodbye. "I love you guys."

I walked back up the platform and off the stage.

"Talia," Lucy said, shaking her head in awe. "You killed that song." She crushed me in her arms.

Teddy was looking at me from behind her. "That was beautiful, Talia."

There were lots of hugs that night. Everyone hugging everyone. I took off the corset dress but kept all the glitter on. I wanted to shimmer all night. Vienna just added to my makeup with gold glitter on my eyes. "More, please," I kept saying, so she added more.

Megan undid my hair and got to work on it, breaking down and batting up my golden locks into 70s disco curls.

Ari had given me a dress specifically for the after party. A very short dress, skimming the tops of my thighs, with bell sleeves. The entire thing was covered in all different shades of gold sequins.

I looked like something out of a magazine. But I loved it. I was ready to drink and dance the night away.

Everyone had already left for the party by the time I was ready, so Leif and I were alone in the car.

"You look incredible," he said.

"Thanks Leif. You look pretty spiffy yourself," I returned. He always wore the same black suit, but he'd slicked up his short hair and shaved.

We'd hired a rooftop for the night, just minutes from the Staples Centre. I had no idea what they'd planned to do with the space, but I was blown away. The space was filled with lounges, bars on either side, a dance floor space in the middle, and Fenix, a world class DJ, was spinning. The sound of champagne bubbles mixed in with the music, the street sounds and the whole place was alive with chatter.

I walked in, all aglow, and Fenix looked right at me. "Welcome to your after party, girl! Talia Shaw everybody." The crowd looked to me and clapped. There were a few hoots here and there. I wandered through the crowd, shaking hands and hugging the crew, my dancers, my band. Eyes were widening at my look, none more than Lucy's, who nodded enthusiastically. I climbed up onto the DJ platform and greeted Fenix.

"Can I?" I asked. He handed over the mic.

"I just want to say that these last few months have been some of the greatest of my life. I need to thank you all for making this tour so fucking amazing. I love you all so much and I can't wait to work with you again. Have a great night, everyone."

They held up their champagne and Fenix put his in my hand. I saluted the crowd and drank. Finally, I saw the mop of dark shaggy red hair in the crowd. I ran over to Teddy. I jumped on him, hugging him tightly.

"It's all over," I said.

"Nah, kid," he started. "I keep telling you. It's just the beginning."

We grabbed two more champagnes from a passing tray and had our own private toast. I missed this closeness while he'd been spending so much time with Crystal, I realised. A Phera song came on and I had to dance. I tried to drag Teddy with me, but he refused. I went on my own. Lucy was there, as were almost all of my dancers. I let myself be carried away with the music, and the buzz. I felt the city breeze against the sweat on my neck and going down my back, but it didn't bother me. I just kept dancing. Until I saw him.

I wasn't sure he'd come but there he was. His beard was cut short. He was just scruffy then. His hair was shorn closely on both sides and longer on top. He was watching me with those blue eyes. He looked good. As I moved through the crowd, I got a better look at what he was wearing. Black jeans. Navy button down. Leather jacket. He looked really good.

"Hi," I said, as I arrived at his side.

"Hey," he said, his perfectly straight white teeth glistening through his smile. "You looked incredible out there."

"Thank you. Why didn't you come join me?"

"You don't want to see me dance. It would ruin your opinion of me completely."

"I doubt it."

He seemed to search the room. "Can I?" He took my hand and started leading me through the crowd.

"Where are we going?" I asked.

"Is there somewhere private?" he asked.

"I have no idea. I've never been here before."

We went down the stairs and rushed down the empty corridor. I didn't think there was anything down there. It was all dark. But there was a freight elevator. He pressed the button and it was already on the level. It opened up and he pulled me slowly inside.

"What are we doing?" I asked. Jack looked down at my lips, then quickly licked his own, then leaned in and gently kissed me. It was sweet and soft and when he pulled away I pulled him back in. I ran my hands over the shorn hair on each side of his head and tugged his neck to bring him closer, giving him permission to press his body against me.

He pushed as I pulled and then I was against the wall of the freight elevator. His hands roamed down behind me and started lifting my skirt, squeezing my ass, gently, before pressing it against the cold metal cage with his hardened crotch. He gripped my thighs and lifted them up, wrapping my legs around him. He was strong. The feel of him against me was undeniably good. But I couldn't stop my mind from thinking about how dirty it was in there. What was my bare ass touching?

I told myself to forget about it. Focus on him. He tasted good. Like Jack Daniels and Coke. I ran my hands over his scruffy jaw and pushed it back a little.

"Jack?" He started kissing and sucking softly on my neck. "Jack?" I said again. He pulled away, keeping a grip on my waist.

"Yeah?" he asked, breathing heavily.

"Can we find somewhere else to do this?" I asked. "Where is your place?"

"I'm in the Hills," he answered.

"Okay," I said. "Let's go there."

I wasn't sure I wanted to leave yet but I did want to be with Jack and not in a dirty elevator. He pushed the ground floor button and we started moving down.

Leif was still at the party, so Jack hailed a taxi. It was late enough that the trip was relatively short. I gave my address when the driver asked since Jack didn't readily offer up his. We arrived home within the half hour and before I had the front door open, his hands were back on me. I pushed the door closed behind me before he started pulling me up the stairs.

"God, this is finally happening," he said eagerly, as we reached the top of the stairs and he searched for the bedroom.

"This way," I said, leading him through my door, a little worked up from all the little touches and kisses, impatient to have the weight of his body on top of me.

I kicked off my heels as Jack ditched his shoes and his jacket. I expected him to come to me, but he stayed still. "You're into this, right?" he asked. His voice had gone back to the one I remembered on the phone. A little bit nervous and insecure. I remembered all those phone calls and how much I liked him.

I smiled a little and then lifted the gold sequin dress over my hair. A few of my curls got stuck but eventually it was off. I looked back at Jack, who was palming himself over his jeans. I walked over to him.

He ran his hands over my arms where most of the glowing glittery makeup remained.

"What is this stuff? Your skin looks delicious."

"Body makeup," I said. "You're gonna need a shower after this."

"Here's hoping," he said and brought his lips back to mine. I started unbuttoning his shirt and pulled it over his muscular shoulders. His skin was perfectly creamy. No ink at all. His chest was hairy, but not overly so, leading down in a trail to his belly button and further. I palmed the hard length of him before unbuckling his belt and bringing down his jeans.

His hand trailed down my stomach and dipped into my underwear, cupping me and using his middle finger to run circles around my clit. Lightly. Too lightly.

He wore light blue boxers and I brought them down next. He groaned a little as I took him in my hands, skin on skin.

I took a few steps back toward the bed and climbed on. I got a good look at him, perfectly adequate I told myself. Not too big, not too small. I quieted my mind, not wanting to compare him to anybody else.

He climbed onto the bed, between my legs. He ran his hands slowly up my thighs until he reached my core. "Can I touch you?" he asked. I wished he hadn't.

"Of course," I answered. His fingers found my sex and he ran his index and middle finger up and down laboriously, deliciously. I closed my eyes with the pleasure of it, internally pleading for him to speed up and press harder, to put his fingers inside me and stretch me out. I was never very patient. But I let him go slowly.

Finally, he did slip both fingers inside and I gasped a little at the surprise. His fingers stilled at the sound and I opened my eyes to reassure him. He moved further up my body, his eyes staring into mine as his fingers worked me. He brought his lips to mine and kissed me deeply. I reached down to touch the length of him. "I'm ready for this," I said, giving him a firm squeeze.

"Yeah?" he asked. I nodded. I pushed him off me a little and he stood waiting.

I reached over into my bedside drawer and found a condom. I handed it over to Jack who fumbled with opening the package and then sliding the latex onto himself. I lay back and spread my legs. He eyed me, hungrily. Then came closer and pushed into me, holding himself above me with straining muscles.

He let out a sharp grunt as I let myself adjust to him. I started moving my hips a little, ready for him. "Wait," he said. I stopped. He was savouring it.

"Okay?" I asked. He nodded and then started to move in me. I ran my hands down his back and gripped his arm to bring him closer. It felt good. It felt really good. It had been too long. I couldn't get him close enough.

I brought his mouth back and kissed him quickly. He grabbed

one of my legs and pulled it up. The move made me moan a little and I felt Jack getting bigger inside me.

Wait, I thought. "Touch me," I pleaded. Jack grabbed one of my breasts and squeezed. "Lower," I said. I ran my own hand down, but Jack was already there. He circled me again, lightly.

"Harder," I pleaded. "Please." He was too soft, too gentle.

Jack was pulsing in me. I moved my hips, I moved his hand away and pressed down on my bundle of nerves trying desperately to come with him.

I felt him still over me, and then he came. Quickly, loudly and dropped hard on top of me.

I wrenched my hand out from between us.

"Talia," he said, breathily. "Welcome home."

"Thank you," I answered. His weight, which I had been so desperate for, seeming to be crushing me a little. "Jack, can you--?"

He shifted off me and lay down beside me, his arm still over me, holding my tightly. I gently moved his arm and stood up.

"Are you okay?" he sat up a little. "Was it good?"

"Yeah, of course. I'll be right back," I said, moving to my drawers and taking out an old t-shirt. I looked back at him. His eyes were closed. He looked so boyish with them closed, even with his scruff. I moved to the bathroom and threw the shirt on before sitting down on the toilet.

I couldn't help but remember the first time I'd slept with Laurie. This was the more likely version of the first time with a new guy. I couldn't blame him. It didn't mean anything. And, it was nice. Next time would be better, I was sure.

FOUR

I woke up the next morning and Jack was gone home. He'd left a note.

Had to walk Pepper.

I thought about the night before. How I'd almost forgotten how gorgeous he was. How strong he was. The fact that I barely got to party at my end of tour party. The good but not great sex. I told myself that I had high standards now. Laurie had been special. I couldn't hold Jack to the standard he'd set. And, just because things didn't start perfectly doesn't mean they couldn't become even better than things with Laurie and me. But they definitely couldn't if I kept thinking of Laurie, kept comparing the two. So, I had to strip him from my mind. I had to finish the album and forget about him.

I spent the morning going through all the emails I didn't have a chance to check while I was touring and working with James. I had my next in-person session with James two days later, so I needed to get some things done. I went to see Ari to refill my wardrobe with new looks. I went for a facial to cleanse my skin of the thousands of different types of air it had been exposed to in the last several months. I ordered some groceries because my bungalow was sorely lacking food. And, I worked with Sabra to schedule the next few months of my life.

Daniel, my business manager, wanted a meeting. His three emails made it seem urgent. So, I set a meeting up for that same afternoon. We met at his office and had a quick coffee before getting into it. He sat me down and started discussing investments. "Your best option is diversifying into a large number of low risk and a small number of high risk investments."

"Why do I need to invest at all?" I asked. "I bought the house." I figured it was something to do with taxes.

"You can't let that amount of money sit there. You'll get killed in taxes."

"What amount?" I asked. I didn't think I had more than a few million.

"Well, the tour netted you a little over $100 million so altogether--."

I couldn't move. "Are you being serious right now?"

"Didn't Manny tell you your earnings?"

"It was probably written down somewhere. I don't pay a lot of attention."

"You really need to start paying attention. And, you need to do something with this money. It can't just sit there."

"Of course," I said, and my mind started going. "I want to give to charity. The right charities, where the actual majority of the money goes to the people in need."

"We can organise that," he assured me.

"And, I want to buy my parents a house. And, my friend Saffy."

"Okay. Slow down. I know it's a lot of money, but you can't just throw it at your friends and family. You've got to think about how it will affect their lives and your relationship with them. Just think long and hard about any huge gifts first, okay?"

"Okay," I answered. Seemed reasonable. But I couldn't not take care of my friends and family, with that kind of money. I couldn't live with myself knowing that people were struggling to pay their bills while I had nine figures in my bank account.

Manny had never gotten back to me about the families of the pilots or the fiancé of the flight attendant who had died in the plane crash. I started putting together a list of what I wanted to do with the money. I wanted to set up trusts for the families. I wanted to set up a trust for my family, Kelly's brother, Steven, and Ashley's mother, Nadine. I wanted to become a patron to Saffy so she could make the art I'd always believed in. If she wouldn't accept that then I'd fund a business for her. I needed to know she'd be taken care of. And, I knew I'd be able to take care of my parents. That gave me a mountain of relief.

And, finally, I wanted to do something good. I had to do something good. I told Daniel as much. I wanted to give at least $50 million to charities.

"Listen," he started. I worried that he couldn't possibly understand it or support it. "I understand you want to help, but the problems of the world can't be solved by only giving."

"What do you suggest then?

"Impact investing," he said. "Investing in businesses that will benefit communities." It made sense to me. I wanted to have a social impact. And, if at all possible, an environmental impact. I explained this to Daniel and he said it could easily be done. There was an initiative that specifically invested that way and I could be part of it.

I told Manny I wanted to be available for any and all charitable events. He argued that this wouldn't always be possible, but I pleaded he make it possible.

The next day I had nothing scheduled so I spent it laying by the pool, napping, listening to new music. I wanted to be refreshed before getting back into the new album. I called Mom and Dad and spoke to them both for a long time. I had an even longer call with Saffy and tried to test the waters on buying some of her art for the house. She said she'd give it to me for free, but I insisted on paying. She finally agreed. I fell into bed intending to get online and connect with my fans, but I went straight to sleep at about 5pm. My exhaustion was catching up.

James and I started at 10am the next day. Lucy had gone to Denver to see her family and Teddy had gone back to the UK for a week, so it was just James and I writing. I woke up at 8am and couldn't wait. I packed a little overnight bag, imagining the way it would be and got Leif to take me to a café to pick up all the different breakfast options. The café was dead and the two employees working there were fans. I took selfies with them and danced around singing when they played my songs from their iPhones. They pumped me up even more for the writing.

I arrived at the door with both hands full and Leif behind me the same way. James opened the door wearing a jester's hat on his head. "Listen to this." He shook his head right and left, the bells tinkled. "I have the perfect moment for this sound." We were already going.

Leif ate breakfast with us and then left us to work. We had the same energy as always between us. Even without Teddy and Lucy, we were bouncing around, off the walls, and then it was midnight before I knew it. We fell into that same pattern and I slept there for three nights. On the fourth night James kicked me out because he had a birthday party to go to.

"What time tomorrow?" I asked, as I searched my phone to call Leif.

James furrowed his brows. "I won't be here."

"Oh."

"It's Thanksgiving on Thursday. I'm flying to New York tomorrow." Oh… I had forgotten.

"Of course."

"I'm back Sunday night. Start back up Monday?"

I nodded. "Yeah. Sounds good."

I found my phone and there were missed calls from Jack. We hadn't been having our nightly chats.

I called him and told him I was done writing for a few days and he asked to drive me home. I said of course and told Leif I had a ride.

Jack came to the door to get me like he was picking me up for a date or something. I kissed James goodbye and went to grab it.

"Hi," I said quickly, as he grabbed my cheeks and kissed me. James hooted in the background. I could barely hear it. Jack let me go and I took a breath. "Hi," I repeated.

"How you doing, man?" Jack waved at James. James rushed over and held out a hand. They shook.

"Nice to meet you," James offered.

Jack pulled my hand and we rushed down the many flights of stairs. It reminded me of that first night together, rushing out of the after party. After a couple of floors, Jack turned around and kissed me again. I was a few steps higher and I had to bend my head down to kiss him. I ran my fingers through his hair, languishing in the taste of him. He moved away a little.

"What are you doing for Thanksgiving?"

I tried to recover. "Um… we don't really celebrate it."

"So, nothing?" I shrugged. "Do you maybe want to come with me?"

Was he inviting me to spend Thanksgiving with him? Wasn't that a bit of a big deal? "Where are you going?"

"Back home. Upstate New York."

"With your family?" We've never even been on a date, I thought.

He nodded. His expression became all nervous again. It got me. And, I had nothing else to do. "Okay."

He smiled wide. With his face fully shaved, I noticed his jaw and his smile were a little bit lopsided. It was charming.

We ran down the rest of the stairs and rushed out to his car, a black Escalade. He took off, driving towards my house.

"You're taking me home?" I asked.

"Did you want to go somewhere else? Are you hungry?" I shook my head. "You gotta pack."

"When do we leave?" I asked.

"Tomorrow morning." I took in a breath. Things happened quickly in this world, but I wasn't sure I wanted things to go this quickly with Jack. He was so sweet and so handsome, but I was unsure. I kept making excuses. I shook them out of my head. What could be wrong with a trip to upstate New York with a gorgeous guy and his probably lovely family?

I told Manny and he was fine with it. Of course, it was good publicity.

The flight was relaxed. I don't think Jack thought about my accident, though I'm sure he knew. It was convenient that he was a talker. He told me about his upcoming project, a film which he was going off to shoot right after Thanksgiving. And I was glad that we'd at least have these few days to spend together. I wanted to know what he was like, in person and for an extended period of time.

We got a hired car to drive us the two hour distance from the airport to the Hudson Valley. The drive was so picturesque. The trees and leaves were the perfect autumn colours and I'd never seen that before.

I told Jack about how I'd felt the first time I came to New York. Apparently, he'd seen Laurie's and my performance on Jimmy Fallon. He didn't ask me about Laurie other than that. But then again, I hadn't asked him about the exes that I knew of. He'd dated one certain blonde actress for about five years and according to the media, broken her heart when he'd refused to marry her. According to the media, I'd been crazy jealous of Laurie's other women and he had ghosted me. They were full of shit.

We arrived at his mother's house in the early afternoon. Jack carried my bag and his up to the front door and I rang the bell. A series of light but urgent footsteps came toward us. A cherubic face peeked through the window low by the front door and then it came swinging open. The little girl smiled up at us both. A woman came soon after from around the corner.

"You're here," she said, her expression a mixture of delight and curiosity.

"Oh my god," the little girl said.

"This is my sister, Lyndsay and my niece, Daisy."

I held a hand out and shook Lyndsay's hand. "So, nice to meet you, Lyndsay. And you, Daisy. Such a beautiful name," I said to the little girl with auburn curls. She grabbed onto her mother's leg and hid her face.

Another pair of rushing feet brought another cherub. Almost a twin to her sister though they were two years apart. "And, this wild cat is Georgia also known as George."

"Nice to meet you." George smiled brightly at me and then looked at her sister. "Sorry about her. She's a big fan."

Lyndsay rolled her eyes. "Like you aren't. We all went to see your show," Lyndsay remarked.

"Oh really? Thank you."

"You were fantastic," Lyndsay added.

"Can we come inside?" Jack said, acting as though the light bags were straining him.

Lyndsay shifted Daisy a little and welcomed us in. The house was just as homey as I'd imagined. Like the family home in a Christmas movie. Lived in and comfortable, and with a fire going in the living room, it was toasty warm.

Lyndsay set us up with tea and told us that Sonia, Jack's mother, was working on a play in New York and wouldn't be home until late that night. We drank tea and chatted for a little while. Daisy found her way onto my lap and played with my curls as Jack caught up with his sister, who intermittently asked me questions. She was very friendly, but there was something between them that they weren't saying out loud. I think she knew how soon it was in our relationship to be taking a step like this. I hoped she didn't think it was my idea.

Jack showed me his old room, where we'd be staying. I was disappointed to see it had obviously been updated since his days of being a sullen teenager. I could just imagine him reading classic American novels with independent movie posters on his walls. He still had a bookshelf, but it had only a few books beside a baseball and a few sporting medals. "Swimming, huh?" I asked.

"How do you think I got this body?" he answered. I laughed.

"Your sister is lovely," I said, taking a seat on his bed. He dropped our bags in the walk-in wardrobe.

"She's great, isn't she? I'm sorry about the girls. I was told they were fans, but I didn't think--"

"They're sweet," I insisted.

Jack came over and pushed a piece of my hair behind my ear. "I'm glad you're here."

I took his hand in mine and pulled it down until he came closer to my mouth. I kissed him, gently.

Lyndsay knocked on the door with a smile. "You ready to go?"

Jack nodded. "Meet you downstairs."

"Where are we going?" I asked, as he took off his shoes and put on some sneakers.

"We're going apple picking." My eyebrows rose.

"Apple picking? That's a real activity?" I questioned.

"It is when you've got small children to entertain." He looked at my boots. "Are those comfortable?"

"It depends." He grabbed my bag back out of the cupboard and sat it on the bed beside me. "You bring anything else?"

I opened the bag and took out the pair of vans I'd packed, showing them to Jack.

"Perfect."

I started putting them on. "You don't want to just relax with your family?" I asked.

"We've got one day before the paparazzi know where we are. We need to take advantage of it." I hadn't thought of it that way. I got the last one on and Jack pulled me up. We rushed downstairs to find Lyndsay and the girls, in matching plum coloured coats, waiting at the door.

"Let's do this thing," Lyndsay said. She drove us in her small silver Range Rover to an apple orchard. The girls were given big red wicker baskets and Jack got one for me too.

The orchard was beautiful. Row upon row of yellow green

leaves and bright red apples. There were dozens of other families there doing the same thing. We picked the apples up from the ground and reached up to pull them from the branches. Jack just started eating one on the spot.

"You don't want to wash that or anything?"

"A little dirt never hurt anybody," he said, apple juice running down his chin. I wiped it with my thumb and then kissed him, tasting the sweet juice.

The other kids there were too excited to notice either of us at first or maybe we were too much in our own world. But George threw an apple at her uncle and Jack chased his nieces around, screaming after them like some kind of monster and our anonymity was over. The mothers eyed him, knew him, and spread the message. My arm looped through his brought their attention to me and the daughters recognised me.

After an hour or two of doing our own thing, we were approached. Sometimes for him and sometimes for me. I could tell he didn't like it, but he was friendly, at least. George definitely didn't like it.

"Why won't they leave us alone?" she asked her mother. She was an actress too but a little less recognisable. No one approached her.

"Because your uncle and his girlfriend are superstars," Lyndsay answered.

Girlfriend? I thought. We definitely hadn't had that conversation. But, it was a reasonable thing to assume when he's brought me to their family home. Would we ever have that conversation or was it simply decided?

"They're not even apple picking anymore," George complained. I took as many photos as I could and then excused myself from the girls who had gathered around me. I rushed over to George and took her hand.

"You wanna look for the prettiest red apple on the farm?"

"Okay," George agreed. Jack extricated himself and we moved to the furthest reaches of the property. Eyes still followed us, but there was some acknowledgement that we deserved a little alone time.

We stayed until the earliest moments of the sunset. When we made our way back to the carpark, a much larger crowd had gathered. Daisy had fallen asleep in Jack's arms. He handed her back to Lyndsay and Lyndsay took the girls to the car while we met some more folks and took some more photos.

"I didn't know you guys were dating," was one of the more common things I heard that afternoon. They tried to get photos of us together, but Jack brushed it off easily.

Finally, we got back into the car and took off. Daisy had the cutest little snore in the world. George was annoyed again that she had to wait for us, so Lyndsay took us through a drive through for dinner.

George demanded Lyndsay play my CD that happened to be in their CD player and then demanded I sing along.

"You don't have to do that," Jack said, an apologetic look on his face. I shrugged, happy to, and sang along with the little girl. George only knew half the lyrics, but she sang them with all the enthusiasm of a real fan.

She wanted to stay up, but she was too exhausted, and Lyndsay insisted on bed. I hugged her tightly before she ran off upstairs with her mother.

"You're great with her," Jack started putting his arms around me. "With both of them."

"Me?" I scoff. "You're amazing with them."

"I love 'em," he shrugged.

I rubbed his arms, feeling the peaks and valleys of his muscles, wrapped tightly around me. "It was a turn on."

Jack's head turned a little to the side, his eyes squinting just a little.

"How thin are these walls?" I asked, as I broke out of his arms and started pulling him toward the stairs.

"I'll hold a pillow over your head," he said.

I laughed. "That's terrifying."

We made our way to the bedroom and started stripping off each other's clothes. I ran my hands over his chest and noticed my hands, the dirt and dust from the day's activity. "What?" he asked.

"Shower?"

He nodded enthusiastically and moved toward the ensuite. It was a shower over bath. I immediately imagined us in there, soaking in some bubbles, maybe drinking some bubbles, lit by candles with a little music playing. "Or what about a bath?" I asked.

Jack turned on the shower, making the decision, getting in there without me as I pulled off my jeans and underwear. I stepped in behind him and he turned. I put my hands on his slick skin. He had that thing. That V thing where rock hard abs meet hip.

He was looking at me the way I was looking at him. Taking in every inch of me, every mark, every scar. "These are from the accident?" he asked, touching the pale patchwork scars on my arms.

I nodded. It was the first time he'd mentioned it. He had scars, too. There was a long gash just over his ribs. "What's this from?" I asked.

He took a breath, his eyes rolling back a little as he remembered, "I was riding a dirt bike and it spun out of control. I got nicked on a barb wire fence."

"Ouch," I said, touching it gently.

"Not as cool as your story," he finished. Before I could tell him that my story wasn't 'cool', he was kissing me. I let myself relax into it.

He turned us around and pressed me up against the wall. My back pressed against the hot and cold taps, painfully. I tried to push away but Jack pressed harder, rubbing the length of himself against my stomach. "Wait," I said. He kissed down my neck as his hands travelling to squeeze my ass. "Jack," I said.

He looked at me. "What?"

"This isn't comfortable," I answered, finally able to step away from the wall.

I moved around to the other side of him and he turned to face me. He kissed me deeply, probing me with his tongue, as he pressed me against that wall. But, the tile was cold against my back, too far away from the steaming water. The air was colder, still.

He looked at me with a smile as I felt him hard against me. He moved himself lower. His expression was seeking permission.

"Let's just get out," I said.

"What?" he asked, exasperated, dropping his arms.

"It's too cold," I said, as I climbed over the rim of the bath. I threw on one of two white fluffy robes and warmed myself. Jack turned off the shower and climbed over behind me. I stepped into the bedroom and took a seat on the bed as Jack towelled himself dry.

He stood in the doorway, completely naked, still hard. "Comfortable?" he asked. I smiled and nodded. I expected him to walk closer to me, but he stayed still. "Open up your robe," he demanded.

I looked to the door, nervous about sound travelling. "Do it," he said, insistent.

"Alright, Mr Grey. Do I get a safe word?" I joked, though I was definitely getting turned on. I opened up my robe and watched as Jack started to breathe a little heavier. He grabbed himself and stroked laboriously.

His voice hitched a little as he spoke again. "Spread your legs."

Any coolness I felt from the open air disappeared as he spoke. I felt my cheeks flush. I spread my legs slowly. Jack lowered himself a little, getting on the right level to really look at me. My legs wanted to close but I forced them open, forced myself to push away any embarrassment I was feeling. I liked him looking at me. I felt all the anticipation of what was coming.

He rubbed himself harder. He spoke through hard breaths. "Touch yourself."

I trailed my fingers lightly over my stomach, bringing them up to stroke my breasts, teasing my nipples.

"Lower," he demanded, seemingly hurried.

I did as he asked, bringing my hand down to where I was pulsing with the moment. I rubbed myself, spreading the wetness and teasing my clit.

"Shit, Talia," Jack choked out. He stood up taller and moved toward me.

"Condom," I said, quickly.

"Fuck," he huffed. "Aren't you on anything?"

"I am. I still want you to wear one," I said. He rolled his eyes but started searching the room. He found his bag and walked to it, grabbing what he needed and fixing it on. He came back to me, still gripping himself, and eyeing where my hand was still working away. I opened my arms and legs to him as he met me on the bed. He lifted me and pulled us both backwards to lay down. He pushed my legs wide apart and pushed into me with a groan. He moved hard and fast. The sheets were too soft. I was moving around. I had to grip the headrest. He licked and sucked at my chest and neck as he worked in and out of me. After a while I knew I wasn't getting there this way. I wanted him to keep talking to me, but he didn't seem to have anything else to say.

"Let me get on top," I said, grabbing at his arm to turn us. He turned us quickly.

"Come on, Talia," Jack said. I kept a grip on the headrest as I rode him, until I needed my hand to take me the rest of the way. Jack came just before me with a tight grip on my hips and an expletive-laden exhale.

The night was cold, but we were both sweaty. I climbed off him with some difficulty and fell beside him, my back still half on his big arm. I was too exhausted to move any more. He didn't seem to mind it. We fell asleep like that.

I woke up a little past midnight. My stomach was growling. I hadn't eaten the fast food dinner planning to get something from home but never did. Jack was quiet, sleeping beside me. I slid myself across the bed and out from under the duvet. I pulled on my robe and tiptoed to the door. I looked back as Jack shifted a little, turning over. I opened the door, trying to keep the squeak to a minimum. I shut the door behind me, just an inch from closing fully. The house was too dark. I wished I brought my phone for a guiding light. I followed the wall and found the stairs, taking my time moving down them. It was a little lighter there. The porch light had been left on.

I moved toward the dark kitchen and opened the fridge. A yellow glow lit up the space. I hoped they wouldn't mind me raiding its contents. My stomach groaned again as I took out cheese and ham and other midnight snack trappings. I left the door open for the light and found the bread in a box on the bench.

I sang as I made my sandwich, just quietly. I picked up the butter to return it to the fridge, but it was taken from my hand. Jack was there. He put it back on the bench and spun me around.

"What are you doing?" I asked. He brought my close, one arm on my back and the other in my hand.

"I'm dancing," he swayed us, to the same beat of the Van Morrison song I'd been singing.

He turned me in his arms, more adept than he had led me to believe. "You said you were a bad dancer."

"I lied," he admitted.

I shook my head, I couldn't be mad. "How'd you learn to dance like this?"

"I've had training." I gave him a disbelieving look. "For a movie."

I stumbled into the dining room chair. "Ouch."

"What happened?"

"I stubbed my toe," I explained. He laughed a little at me.

"Keep singing," he requested. So, I did. Still quietly. Suddenly the strange moment felt wildly romantic. The kitchen floor was cold on my bare feet, but I felt warm in his arms. I couldn't imagine him ever pulling the rug out from under me. In that way, I felt safe. And, that was exactly what I needed.

"When it's not always raining, there'll be days like this," I sang. He pulled me closer, bringing our arms in and to his chest. He touched his cheek to mine.

"Now, this is a sight to see."

I looked up to see his mother standing there, leaning against the bannister, lit by the same refrigerator light. She had a smile on her face. Jack let me go to wrap his mother in a hug. She kissed him loudly on the cheek and they turned back to me.

"My mother, Sonia," Jack introduced her.

I waved, keeping my arm low and tight against me, fearing the opening of my robe. "A pleasure to meet you, Mrs O'Halloran."

"Absolutely not. You'll call me Sonny. And, I am so glad to meet you. I heard you were young, but good lord, you are pretty."

"Me? No. I see where Jack's good looks come from," I argued. Even in the dim light, she was extraordinarily pretty.

"You're very flattering." She tapped Jack on the shoulder. "I'm exhausted so I'm going to head up. I'll see you two in the morning?"

"Night, Mom," Jack said.

"Goodnight," I said. She smiled at us both and headed up.

I bit my lip. Jack looked at me with an easy smile. "Can I have this?" he asked, picking up my sandwich and taking a gigantic bite.

"Hey!" I complained. He smiled wide, his mouth full of my sandwich. I laughed at him. "Rude," I joked, as I took the butter back out of the fridge.

The paps had learned where we were. We went out for coffee the next morning and they followed. We spent the rest of the day inside with Jack's mother, Sonia. She looked so much like her son. She was a very opinionated woman. She was also in the industry as a writer and director.

After breakfast she busted out the family albums and showed me Jack's baby pictures. He was handsome, even as a little boy. The same striking blue eyes. A movie star smile.

"Okay, that's enough," Jack said, as we landed on one of him naked. I laughed. He was embarrassed.

The next page had a picture of sullen teen Jack, just as I'd suspected, with an emo band t-shirt and acne covered cheeks. "So angsty," I said, referring to his expression.

Sonia kept going turning the pages, but Jack slammed the photo album closed. "Jack," Sonia berated.

"Relax," I said as Jack tossed the album aside. "We all had our awkward phase."

"You'd know," he said, "Yours was only a couple years ago."

A dig at my age? "You're the one dating me," I answered. Sonia stood up and backed out of the room, giving us some space.

"I was joking," Jack said, as if I were overreacting.

"Hilarious," I answered, standing up to follow Sonia to the kitchen. Jack grabbed my hand as I passed and pulled me onto his lap. I tried to get back up, but Jack held me down.

"It's not exactly fun for me," Jack said, in explanation. I didn't get what the big deal was, but it obviously bothered him.

"Well, we're done now," I answered, still annoyed at his reaction.

"I bet you were cute," he continued, gripping my chin and dipping it down a little to kiss. "I want to see your pictures." I let myself kiss him back, sliding my lips against his until George came in holding the board game, *Risk,* above her head.

We spent the day playing board games and I watched as Jack and Lyndsay bickered like siblings do, arguing over the rules of *Uno* and who got to be the banker in *Monopoly*.

Sonia and Lyndsay decided to make dinner and since they refused my help, Jack and I took a drive. He showed me his old high school and the game shop where he and his friends used to hang out. Two big black SUVs followed our every move, so we stayed in the car, but it was sweet, just seeing the little places that made him who he is.

We came home to a ready Thanksgiving meal. We held hands as Sonia gave her thanks that we could join her, welcoming me specifically to their house. I thanked them all again for having me before we dug in to the turkey and roasted vegetables, drenched with cranberry sauce.

After we had stuffed ourselves silly, all votes were for a movie. "Something the kids can watch," Lyndsay said as Jack searched the channels. I sat on the other side of him. Daisy sat with her grandmother and George found herself a bean bag and sat right in the centre of the room.

Jack landed on *X-Men* and George screamed out, "This!"

"No way," Jack argued and kept scrolling.

"Jack," Lyndsay berated. "Put it back."

Jack landed on *Pan's Labyrinth*. "This is a good kid's movie."

"Isn't that supposed to be scary?" Sonia questioned.

Lyndsay grabbed the remote from Jack's hand and switched it to *X-Men*. I laughed a little as Jack tried to steal it back. Lyndsay put it down her dress.

"What are you doing?" he argued. George watched the movie as it began, engrossed. Daisy seemed confused.

Jack got up and changed the channel at the base. "Are you serious?" Lyndsay asked. She took the remote from her dress to change it back, but Jack blocked the base with his arm. I cracked up. "Seriously?" Lyndsay asked.

"Uncle Jack!" George said, kicking at him with her legs.

"Ow," Jack said, as she got him in the shin. "That's it."

He gently crash-tackled her into her bean bag, tickling her furiously until she screamed through her laughter for him to stop.

Finally, he did and gave in to watching *X-Men*. He came to sit back beside me. "What are you, five?" I asked, as he nestled into my side.

"You were no help," he said. We watched the whole thing before dragging ourselves and our still full stomachs up the stairs.

We left early the next morning. Lyndsay had gotten the girls up or they had wanted to get up, and they came out the front to say goodbye, still half-asleep.

Jack and Lyndsay hugged before Lyndsay pinched his cheek. "Later little brother."

Jack went to kiss his mother as I hugged Lyndsay goodbye.

"You two are so sweet together," I said. "I'm a little jealous." I had always been a little jealous of Kelly and her brother, Steven, too.

"You don't have siblings?" she asked.

"No," I answered. "Though sometimes it feels like I do. One of my best friends, Teddy, he's like a brother." I wondered how he'd feel about that descriptor.

"I'm glad my girls have each other," she said, looking back at her daughters.

I crouched down to hug them both goodbye. "I was so glad to meet you two and spend Thanksgiving with you." Daisy looked like she would cry. "I promise that at the next concert, you can come backstage and watch from right up front."

Daisy and George both smiled at that. I hugged them again and stood up to see Sonia waiting for me. She brought me in for a hug and squeezed tightly. "Nice to meet you, Talia."

"You, too," I said. Jack guided me to the car and opened the door for me. With one last wave, I got in. He ran around to the other side and then we were driving away.

I couldn't help but think that his mother had been standoffish. Not in an obvious way. It had been so subtle I barely realised it.

Maybe she was simply a refined woman, not prone to too much affection. Or was there some other reason she'd kept me at a bit of a distance?

I started to imagine the other girls that I knew Jack had dated. The long-term girlfriend who Sonia had probably imagined he would marry. And the array of women who followed. That was probably what I was to her. Some random twenty-year old. Nothing she should take seriously. I couldn't blame her for that.

Jack picked up my hand and kissed it. I smiled at him. I hadn't taken this relationship so seriously at first, but it had been a good weekend. Not perfect but who said it needed to be? Should his mother's reaction to me hinder that at all? No, I decided.

I let myself feel the happiness that the weekend had given me.

Back in LA, a driver took us to my house. Jack carried my bags to the door and handed them over.

"You're not coming in?" I asked.

He shook his head, "I've got to go home and pack. I fly out again early tomorrow."

"You should've just flown straight there."

"I wanted to bring you home."

I smiled at him as I rose up onto my toes and pressed a kiss to his lips in thanks.

"Thank you for coming. I know it was soon to do that to you."

"You didn't do anything to me. I had a great time," I said honestly.

"My family loves you."

"I'm glad. I liked them to."

He pressed his forehead into mine. "I don't want to go," he said.

"Yes, you do," I argued.

"I don't want to leave you. Why don't you come down to New Mexico? You could finish the album there."

"I really couldn't," I said, apologetically. "But, we'll talk. I miss our calls."

He nodded. "Okay."

I kissed him, sliding my lips over his, sucking gently at his lower before pressing another to his cheek. He held my waist tightly. "Bye," I said.

"Bye." He was nodding and not turning. He came in and kissed me again, surprising me, probing my mouth with his tongue. I kissed him back before breaking away. I laughed a little and waved as he finally started walking away.

It suddenly occurred to me that I had this movie star idea of him. The charisma and humour and sex appeal of his characters where just that. His characters. The real Jack was... nerdy, a little awkward... sweet but also kind of pretentious... and really into me. I felt lucky to be the girl who got to kiss him goodbye. And, I couldn't wait to welcome him back.

FIVE

We had barely written a thing since all of us got back to LA. James and I had written one song. A really good song. But we didn't have lyrics. The opening was light. It felt like something new. But it got dark in the middle and then a little twisted, a little angry. It almost sounded like the way it all unfolded with Jack. First meeting him and thinking he was one thing and finding out he might be something else and comparing him to Laurie... trying to stop myself from comparing him to Laurie. Wanting desperately to be over it already.

Lucy was playing on the drum set and James, Teddy, and I were hunched over notebooks.

Teddy tossed his notebook on the table. "I got jack shit."

"You were back home for ages... you got no inspiration there?" I whined.

"What do you have?" he asked, defensive.

I ground my teeth. "James?" I asked, hoping he'd have something. He tipped his notepad to me. He had a dozen lines, I smiled hopefully.

"Nothing good," he insisted. "Maybe we should eat."

"We literally just ate. It still smells like bacon in here," I argued.

"What do you have?" James said, sliding over in his wheelie chair to look at my book. I held it up to my stomach.

"I don't know," I started, ready to blow it off. But maybe it was something. "Play the intro for me."

Lucy stopped with the drums. Teddy looked curious. James looked excited. He cued it up and played. "From here?"

"Yeah," I said, and he re-cued it. I cleared my throat and waited for it.

Yesterday, I met someone new.
   He's been helping me forget you.
   I've been trying to forget you.
   Maybe I can't forget you.

Teddy laughed a little darkly. I furrowed my brows at him, questioning. I wasn't sure what his attitude was about lately. Lucy was biting her lip, looking at James. James was quietly nodding, his eyes unfocused, thinking. He swung around in his chair and put the notebook against his desk, writing.

My phone vibrated on arm of Teddy's chair. He looked at it quickly. "Speak of the devil."

My heart stopped. I waited for his clarification. "Laurie or Jack?" Lucy asked unsubtly.

"The latter," Teddy answered. He tossed me the phone. I looked at it for a second and ignored it.

"What's that about?" Lucy asked.

"Did you hear the lyrics?" Teddy questioned her.

"They aren't about him," I argued, half-heartedly. Lucy snorted. Even Teddy minutely shook his head.

"Has he told you about Rayne Porter?" Lucy asked. That was Jack's co-star in the movie he was away shooting. She was beautiful with short blonde hair and dark brown eyes. She had just been divorced despite only being 27. There were pictures of them on the internet, flirting on set. Not that I had searched for them. Katie, my publicist, had a habit of sending me anything that remote related to my life.

"She's nice, apparently," I answered.

"She seems kind of into herself," Lucy commented.

"Who gives a shit," Teddy snapped. Lucy held up her hands in surrender.

"What is wrong, Teddy?" I asked, exasperated.

"Okay, I've got something," James said, bringing us back to the song.

James played the intro.

Could be that you broke my heart
Knew you would right from the start

That was good, I thought. And, I had something to add. I sang the first two lines and added my own.

Could be that you broke my heart
Or that his face looks like art

A better thing has come along
Saying things to prove you wrong
A better man has come along
Made it easy to write this song
It's the easiest thing I'll ever do
Falling out of love with you

Once James gave me those first two lines, I couldn't stop. People would think it was about Jack. Lucy definitely did. And, maybe Teddy, too. I knew James didn't care. But I wasn't writing about Jack. Not completely.

Teddy seemed to snap into gear, the possibilities of a good song overcoming whatever issues he was having. And the ball was rolling again. We didn't stop for a month. Jack and I had barely spoken during this time, despite the assertion that we'd keep up our calls. His work hours were insane and mine were worse. He usually called early in the morning when I'd just gotten to sleep.

"Hello?" I asked. My throat was dry with sleep or the cold air of the morning.

"I'm back." Jack sounded excited. His voice was smooth and warm.

"Welcome home," I said, quietly, not wanting to wake up the others. I looked at the clock. 7am. At least I'd had five hours sleep this time, I thought.

"Welcome me in person," he requested, his voice becoming husky.

I sighed. "I can't leave. We're so close to finishing."

"I'd like to be close to finishing." I laughed a little. Teddy shifted beside me. "Finish tomorrow. Come see me," Jack pleaded.

"I can't. But the second we're done..."

"Okay. Fine. Go back to sleep." He hung up. I let go of the phone and drifted back to the sleep. Lucy mumbled something. I opened an eye and saw she was still asleep.

"Mama," she said loudly, dreaming. Teddy and I chuckled. I shifted closer to him, my nose almost pressed to his back for warmth. He turned over and looked at me.

"Morning," I said.

"Morning," he answered closing his eyes. He opened them back up. "You okay?"

I nodded. "Just cold."

He brought the duvet up higher around us. "Better?" he asked. I nodded even though it had done nothing. I wanted to snuggle into his chest and take advantage of all that man heat. He knew it because he smiled and opened his arms up. "Come on then." I snuggled in, pressing my cold nose against his grey shirt. It wasn't fair that men were always warm. He put an arm around me and we drifted back to sleep.

One more week and one last song and the album was finished. And I was prouder than I'd ever been about anything. And, grateful to my friends, my collaborators.

Teddy could make you feel a song in your blood. He'd send it from his guitar, from his loop, through the floor, up through your feet, through your veins until it reached your heart and made the beat of it match the song. It felt like it was inside you and you wanted to be inside it. And, he brought a deep romance to the writing, which I loved him for.

James had the wild ideas. The new textures and sounds I'd never heard in my life but as soon as I heard them I knew they belonged with the songs. He made them surprising and exciting and weird and perfect.

Lucy added a mastery to the guitar and bass playing, even a little drums, and a level of cool to the sound that none of us possessed.

I was pulling my weight, though. I poured myself into the writing, into the singing. I pushed my voice. I pushed it further than I ever had before. I hadn't been brave with my voice in writing the first album. I wanted to make this album incredible for my fans, but I also felt these songs in my bones, and I wanted to sing the hell out of them.

The album, now titled *Two* was loaded with love songs, heartbreak songs, desperate, hopeful, ragey, sad, and above all, fun. Teddy and James and I made each of them into anthems. Songs that belonged in soundtracks of cult classic teen romantic comedies. Songs that I knew would get people up and dancing and singing and crying all at the same time. I hoped.

We delivered it to the label and I had no fears that they would be disappointed. None at all. Within days they released the first single. *Under the Stars* was the title. I wanted to go out and celebrate, but again, Jack just wanted to relax. I understood that it had been a long and hard shoot. Lots of stunts and hard physical work. It was a war movie. But, how hard could it be for him to come out for a few hours, have some drinks, maybe dance a little? If I even attempted to argue the point, Jack would just tell me to go without him. And, maybe I should have, but I convinced myself that I was tired, too, and just snuggled into his big warm arms.

It turned out he was happy to go out when it was what he wanted to do. We went to see the Lakers play. We sat in the very front row, eating popcorn and drinking beer. One of my legs was on top of the other. Jack pushed it off and took the leg closest to him, bringing it over his own leg and squeezing. This was PDA. Pure and simple. He'd quickly gotten over any wariness of the press.

This relationship was completely foreign to me. There was no fear of getting close to me. He was basically living in my house for the next three weeks. And, mostly, we just lazed around in plaid. Laurie always wanted to go out and do things and see people, even if it were secretly.

The morning before he was leaving again, I woke up in pain. Pepper was crushing my legs with her weight. She always slept on the bed, even in my house despite my protestations to Jack. The whole room smelled like dog.

Jack took her for a walk and brought back hot breakfast.

We ate on the back deck. Jack brought out a script and tossed it to me. "Read lines with me?"

"I'm really not much of an actress," I contended.

He shrugged. "That's okay. I just need the prompts."

He sat back with his coffee, stretching his head back to feel the sun. I started reading. In the middle of one of the lines was the word 'beat' in brackets. I was unsure, so I said it.

Jack laughed at me. "It means a break. Like a pause."

I became distracted and accidentally read Jack's line. "Are you paying attention?" he chided me.

"Sorry, maybe you should do this with someone else."

"It's just reading. It shouldn't be this fucking hard." Jerk, I thought. I threw the script at him and stormed off.

He found me reading a book on my bed and nuzzled his head into my stomach with apologies. "I'm just stressed about this shoot. We have such a limited amount of time on set and I barely have half the script memorised."

I forgave him. Maybe, too easily.

That night we set ourselves up in front of the TV. Jack went to make some microwavable popcorn while I scrolled Netflix. "What have we got?" he asked when I returned. I was in the rom com section. "Please no," he said, as he plonked down beside me.

"What?" I asked.

"Let's watch a thriller or something. No rom coms."

"What happened to ladies choice? We're always watching what you want."

He huffed. "Fine."

I kept scrolling. I landed on a movie with Jack's face. "What's this?" I asked teasingly.

"Nothing," Jack said, trying to take the remote.

"A romantic comedy starting the Jack O'Halloran? We have to watch this," I continued, laughing as he tried harder to take the remote that I held far over my head.

"Give it to me," he continued.

"I want to watch it," I stayed firm. Suddenly he backed off, his expression angry. I thought we were just kidding around.

"Why are you throwing this in my face?" he asked. I started to apologise, I hadn't realised he was really bothered, but he cut me off. "I don't throw your music in yours."

I half coughed. "What the hell does that mean? That I should be embarrassed by my music?" He only listens to male indie records, I thought. Pop was probably a hideous word to him.

"Hey, you said it, not me." I looked at him with distaste. Had he always been such a ass? No, I thought. He hadn't. Was this him becoming comfortable? "What?" he asked, exasperated.

"I'm just trying to figure out what's going on."

He rolled his eyes. "You're too sensitive." I didn't think I was. He was just more of a jerk than I thought. "Watch whatever you want." He got up and walked to the bedroom. I turned off the TV.

. . .

He didn't ask me to go home with him for Christmas. The answer would have been no and maybe he knew that. Saffy and I were inseparable during that week except for Christmas Day spent with our parents. We hadn't seen each other since the Sydney shows of my tour and I had spent most of that time with my parents. She begged me to stay for New Year's, but I went back to LA a couple nights before. Laurie and I had spent last New Year's together in Sydney. A change felt warranted. Teddy was going to Mexico and Lucy was going to a hot shot entertainment lawyer, Ryan Beecham's, New Year's Party. I wanted to go with Teddy, but it seemed to be understood that Jack and I would be spending the night together.

"Marco's having a party," he told me. Marco was another actor. Last year's Academy Award winning Best Actor in a leading role.

"Okay," I said. "Sounds good to me."

But the night finally arrived and after I'd spent three hours doing my hair and makeup, he was still just lying on the couch. He paused the TV show he was watching, something dark and moody. "Woah," he said, looking over the black bodycon dress I was wearing. "You look unbelievable."

"Thank you," I said, fixing the back of my earring. I looked down at his grey hoodie and jeans. "You're not ready?"

"I know." His expression looked apologetic.

"What? Are you sick?" He shook his head. I guessed. "You don't want to go?"

"I just can't be bothered," he answered.

"Are you serious?" I questioned. "It's New Year's Eve." He'd suggested the party in the first place. I'd said no to Teddy. And, Lucy. And, Saffy.

"I know. I'm sorry. You can still go out if you want to." I didn't want to go crawling to my friends to tag along after I'd rejected them.

Jack lifted himself up a little and grabbed onto my thighs bringing me closer to him. "Come here." He pulled me down on top of him. My dress was too tight to spread my legs around him. I lay there awkwardly, stiff, as he squeezed me.

"Can't we just do this?"

He looked at me a while before I nodded. It was useless to argue. He brought my head back down to lay on his chest before planting a kiss there. I left to get changed into my sweats and he snuggled me back into him again.

The show was boring. It was about two men with tormented pasts and a mysterious mystery to solve. It was something unoriginal, masquerading as something special. We fell asleep before the ball dropped.

Jack went away to do press all over the world for a big budget movie he had shot the year before. It was fine by me because I had my own promotion to do. It was the same as last time, but everything was bigger. The budgets, the shoots, the amount of interviews. Sabra and I had been working non-stop.

I was trying to work when she distracted me. She huffed loudly and tossed her phone.

"What's wrong?" I asked.

She shifted a little, surprised I'd been paying attention. "Nothing."

"Are you sure?" I asked.

She nodded. I went back to my work. I could sense her looking at me. I tried to be patient figuring she'd say whatever it was she needed to say but I couldn't focus. "Spit it out," I suggested.

"What?" she asked. "It's nothing."

"Sabra! What is it?" I repeated.

"Okay," she began, leaning forward a little. "All my girlfriends have tickets to Laurie Siler tonight."

"You don't have a ticket?"

"They didn't get me one cause we were supposed to be at the shoot."

"Oh," I answered. That was my fault. I cancelled the shoot. "You want me to try and get you a ticket?"

"I didn't want to ask," she started.

I stopped her. "It's okay. I'll get you a ticket."

"Really?" she asked, her eyes lighting up. I nodded. She reached for her phone and started texting. I took a breath and reached for my own phone. I found the last messages we'd last texted. About Lucy and Lolla. Nothing since. Why would there be? I started typing:

Talia: Hey. This might be a crazy request, but my assistant missed out on a ticket for your show tonight. Any chance you've got a spare?

I set the phone down. Sabra was looking at me hopefully. "I'm sure it will be fine," I assured her.

"You're the best," she said.

"Did you get the looks for the *Island in the Sun* shoot?" I asked. I couldn't find them in my own emails. She started looking in hers. Laurie's message came in.

. . .

Laurie: Look whose got herself an assistant! It's no problem. I'll get them emailed to you.

Talia: Thank you.

That's two interactions that sounded stilted and professional. It still made me feel uneasy that this was how we communicated now. The email came in from Jeremy, his assistant. I didn't read it, just forwarded it to Sabra. She screamed.

"VIP Tickets!"

"Oh," I said. Would she not get to be with her friends?

"Two of them!" she cried out. Maybe I should have asked for more for all of her friends.

"Did you need more?" I asked.

"No. I only needed one for myself, the others already have tickets. But you have to come now," she pleaded. I shook my head. There was no way. "Why not? You're obviously friends."

"We're really not," I answered.

"Have you ever seen him live?" she asked.

"No," I answered. "Only when we sang together."

"Oh my god. I almost forgot about that," she said.

Another text came through.

Laurie: You get them?

Talia: Yes. She's very grateful.

Laurie: Are you coming?

Talia: I've got a night shoot. Have a good show.

The lie came too easily.

. . .

Laurie: Next time.

"You're not doing anything, right? He's supposed to be incredible," Sabra continued. "Seriously, please come with us."

She was right. I had no plans. I was going to see if Teddy wanted to watch a movie or something. I had already told Laurie I was busy. But, he didn't have to know I was there.

"Okay," I shrugged. "Why not?"

I was so casual while agreeing to it but the second I actually had to get ready I started to sweat.

Sabra was going to go home to get ready, but I needed her help. I told her she could wear anything in my wardrobe if she helped choose something for me. Apparently, it was a good deal. She picked out four outfits and laid them out for me while she went to shower.

There was a silver dress, sparkly and dainty and showing way too much skin and some strappy silver heels. A pair of leather pants with white button down shirt and leopard print pumps. A body con knee length green dress with a black bomber jacket and black stilettos. Or, a red tartan mini with a shearling leather jacket and black combat boots. Such a variety of looks. I sent them to Ari. She responded asking where I was going. I said a concert and she was quick to respond.

Ariel: The leather pants or the tartan skirt.

I tried on the pants, but they wouldn't get over my thighs. Had I put on weight? Or was I emitting so much heat that I'd shrunk them? Tartan mini it was.

Sabra came back in a towel and asked if she could wear the sparkly dress. "Be my guest," I answered.

Leif argued that I shouldn't be going without him, but I assured him I'd be in the VIP section where there would likely be security. He gave it up and insisted on waiting outside the arena the whole night.

"You don't need to do this," I said, as we were getting out of the car.

"You have your phone? It's all charged?" he asked.

"Yes, Dad," I said, rolling my eyes.

He smiled at me. "Have fun."

"Thank you," Sabra said and pulled me toward the VIP entrance. We were a little bit late. Everyone else was already inside.

"Welcome, Miss Shaw," the attendant at the VIP entrance said. He escorted us up to a balcony level.

"Talia!" Adelaide Mills, a singer I'd met at the Grammy's, came running over. "How are you?"

She kissed both my cheeks. "Adelaide. I'm great, how are you?"

"Really good. This is impressive. You two are still friends?" she asked, referring to me and Laurie.

I nodded. "This is my assistant, Sabra. She really wanted to come."

"Good excuse," Adelaide laughed. "Nice to meet you." They shook hands.

The opening band had finished, and the stage was being reset for Laurie. "How's your brother?" I asked.

"Ugh, a pain in my ass," she answered with a laugh. "I better get back to my girls. Have a good night."

She walked away and Sabra widened her eyes at me. "You dated her brother, right? Michael Mills?"

"Barely," I answered. We'd been on one date in the months before my tour. He was my second attempt at dating after Laurie. The first was a basketballer who called me Tania. Twice.

"Her skin is incredible," Sabra continued.

"You want a drink?" I asked.

"Oh, I'll get it," Sabra said, looking for the bar. "What can I get you?"

"Sab, you're not working right now. Beer?" I asked. She smiled and nodded. I moved to the bar and ordered.

"Two beers, please."

The bartender was tall with long light brown hair. He smiled flirtily at me and handed them over. "How much?" I asked.

"Not a thing," he answered. "But, I'll take your number."

I laughed at the line. "I'm seeing someone."

"So am I," he answered. "I still want your number."

I put away my wallet and grabbed the beers. "Thanks for these."

"Gavin," he said.

"Thanks, Gavin," I walked away.

He called out to me. "You're welcome, Talia."

I handed the beer over to Sabra. "Were you just flirting with the bartender?" she asked me.

I didn't have time to answer her as the screaming began. The first notes of his first song started. The lights shot up from the stage. Vinny looked incredible. At ease, of course, and stylish in a red silk suit. Laurie came out, finally, with a huge note. He was in silk too, but a black and red floral patterned suit instead. He looked good.

Sabra and I turned our full attention on him. We couldn't help ourselves. He was magnetic.

His on-stage persona was immediately obvious. It wasn't like our duet on the Jimmy Fallon stage. His music was nothing like that, so I shouldn't have been surprised. He moved around the stage with wild moves and sizzling energy like Jagger or the lead singer of Coldplay. He sang like he loved his songs and he loved every second of being up there. There were beats where the crowd would sing his song back to him and he just lapped it up, so happy to be living his dreams. It made me want to appreciate my own blessings more.

The song finished and the crowd erupted. The screaming gave me flashbacks of my own tour. Laurie started talking to the crowd. "Los Angeles!! You look so good. You're so attractive all of you."

The crowd screamed. Even Adelaide let out a wild scream. I laughed a little.

"This is my last show on this tour." A booing followed.

"No booing," he demanded. "I want to thank you so much. I'm so overwhelmed by your love and support. Thank you for coming."

After more screams, he continued. "My job tonight is to entertain you. I am going to do my darnedest. You have a job, too. I want you to have a really really really really good time."

He smiled that gorgeous smile. That knee shaking smile. The one I used to get all the time. I'd missed it. My senses were going into overload.

"Let me introduce you to my friends." He introduced his drummer, Jean, his bassist, Leo, and Vinny on guitar. The girls went wild for Vinny. I laughed, I'd had to tease him about that the next time I saw him.

"How you doing in the back? The sides? How about down here at the front? I love your jacket. Let me see that jacket. That is a nice jacket!"

So much confidence and charm. He was effortless up there.

Another song started. A slow one. He stood by a mic and something was wrong. The guitar was too loud. As soon as I thought it I saw him gesture to the soundies. It was the smallest smoothest gesture. He pointed to Vinny's guitar and then used his fingers to signal down. He pointed his mic and signalled up. So suave.

The songs were incredible, but I had already known that. His performance was an experience I was so happy to have had. And, the way he talked, he was so loving and grateful to his fans. I was so inspired. I must have looked starry-eyed. Sabra looked and me every now and then.

As the concert was coming to an end, I was tapped on the shoulder. "Excuse me?"

I turned around to see a short stagehand looking up at me. "Hi?"

"Miss Shaw, Mr Siler has asked if you'd like to join him backstage." Shit, I thought. He knew I was here then. Word travelled quick. He also knew I was a liar. Seeing him in person was one thing. Seeing him up close. Within arm's reach. I wasn't ready for that. Not if I had a choice.

"Oh my god," Sabra said in my ear.

"I'm fine," I said.

"What?" Sabra yelled. The stage hand was confused, not used to invitations like this being turned down.

"Can my friend go?" I asked, for Sabra.

"Um," the stage hand said. "I guess."

"Have fun," I said, giving Sabra a little push.

"Really?" I nodded. "I'll wait with Leif."

"I was going to go out with the girls," she said. The stagehand looked down at her watch, nervous.

"All good. Have fun."

She hugged me tightly. "Thank you for tonight."

"You're welcome. See you tomorrow."

She ran off with the stagehand. The bartender was looking over at me. He smiled, wide. I smiled back. He was trouble. I didn't want to stand there by myself or chance anyone else coming to get me. I walked to the stairs and rushed down, hoping to beat the crowds leaving as the show ended.

"You're leaving early?" Leif asked as I climbed into the front beside him.

"I got hungry," I answered, though food was the last thing on my mind.

"Pizza or burgers?" he asked.

"Gentlemen's choice," I answered. I lay my head against the seat belt.

I had almost forgotten my birthday when Saffy called on my way back from the *Island in the Sun* video shoot.

"Happy birthday, best friend," she screamed into the phone.

"Thank you," I answered, rubbing my ear.

"What are you doing? What are your plans?" she asked.

"Nothing," I answered. "I had a video shoot and now I'm going home."

"No party or anything? What about Jack?"

"He's on a press tour," I explained.

She huffed. "That sucks. Your first birthday together."

I laughed a little. "It's really fine."

"Why is it fine?" she questioned.

I looked to Sabra, sitting in the front seat beside Leif. Leif saw me in the rear view mirror. He smiled and put up the partition. I smiled back. It wasn't that I didn't trust Sabra, but things had been leaking to the press. About the album and about me and Jack. Even about Laurie's show. Maybe she'd just been talking to her own friends but either way, Katie and Manny had been on me about being more careful.

"It's fizzling out. Just the way it is."

"No," she argued. "It's just the distance."

"I don't think so," I answered.

"I thought you were really into him?"

"I thought I was, too," I said.

"It's probably just the distance. I'm sure when you see each other again things will be good."

I was suspicious. "Why are you so on his side?" I asked.

She clicked a little. She was keeping something from me. "I'm not. I just thought you really liked him," she argued. "I gotta go."

"Wait," I demanded. There was a voice in the background. A few voices.

"Love you. Talk soon," she said and hung up. The car stopped as we waited for the gate to open.

Sabra and Leif stayed back, clearly some business to discuss, as I headed to my front door.

I turned on the light and almost fell over. About a hundred people jumped up from there hiding spots and screamed, "Surprise!"

"Oh my god," I said as I scanned the room. Mom and Dad were there, Saffy, Lucy, Megan, the crew and the dancers from my tour. And, Jack. Jack came toward me with a smile. That charming wide white movie star smile. His eyes looked at me like they had in the beginning. Like he adored me.

"Happy Birthday, beautiful," he said. It seemed like he was going to kiss me on the cheek, but I put a hand on his jaw and kissed his lips.

"Thank you," I said quietly to him before turning to the group and shouting out my thanks to them. Music started to play then, I wasn't sure from where. Mom and Dad descended upon me next, hugging and kissing my cheek.

"My baby girl is 21," Mom said, shaking her head like she couldn't believe it.

"What are you doing here?" I asked her.

"Jack flew us out. He organised everything." I looked to Jack who gave a small shrug and reached out for his hand.

"This house. Wow," Dad commented. "Though I don't know any of these people. Except this one."

Saffy hugged me tightly. "Surprise," she said, her expression wary.

"Incredible surprise," I said, genuinely. Saffy's worry faded. "Can I have one of those?" I pointed to the beer in her hand. Saffy reached behind her to where a waiter was carrying a tray of champagne, wine, and beer and handed one over.

I left Jack with my parents and made rounds, accepting birthday wishes and thanking everyone for coming. I discovered the music was coming from a DJ set up in my backyard and a makeshift dancefloor already had half a dozen dancing there including Lucy. Lucy and I danced with Saffy and Peter, and even Mom and Dad did a little dancing. I called Jack over to dance, but he shook his head, too busy talking to some actors I recognised but had never met.

At around eleven, the music was lowered, and another waiter brought out a birthday cake. The thing was huge and dark chocolate with white icing spelling 'Happy Birthday Talia'. There were 21 lit candles and I had to make my wish. All the birthdays I could remember before this one, that moment came so quickly that I had never had time to think of a good wish. I would just think of happiness. I looked around at my family and my best friends. I looked for Jack thinking that would be my wish, that we would work out. But I couldn't find him. I couldn't wait any longer and blew out the candles without a wish as cheers came up around me. When they started handing out pieces I took two and went in search of him.

He wasn't outside, he wasn't downstairs. I went upstairs and found him on the bed, petting the dog he brought with him. "What are you doing up here?" I said, as I took a seat beside him.

"Just needed a little quiet."

"You have a headache?" I asked.

"Yeah. I'm tired," he said, throwing a hand over his eyes.

I ran a hand over his hair. "Well, I brought cake," I said as I sat it on the bedside table.

"I'm good," he answered. I was starting to feel like he was mad.

"Hey," I said, waiting for him to take the hand off his eyes and look at me. It took a while, but he did. "Are you mad at me?"

He huffed a little. "No. It's just getting late. How long do you think they'll be here?"

I laughed a little. "Jack, it's not even midnight."

"What a pain," he said.

I furrowed my brows, confused. I stood up and walked out with my cake. I expected he would come back down but he never did. People started leaving around 2am. I went to bed at four, beside a snoring Jack and his snoring dog.

I woke up the next day to find him already gone, walking Pepper. I showered and dressed and moved through the house quietly so as not to wake up my parents or Saffy and Peter who were in my spare rooms. I made coffee and went outside to wait for him to arrive home. He arrived, looking much fresher than I felt, smiling. "Aw, you waiting for me?"

"Yeah," I said, in a tone that let him know I wasn't happy.

"What's up?"

"I want to talk about last night."

"What about it?" he asked, confused.

Was I overreacting? "I thought the gesture was so sweet. I was so surprised and happy, but then you became kind of grumpy. You went to sleep at like 11:30."

"I was tired. I flew like 12 hours to get back to LA in time," he argued.

"I know that," I said.

"I didn't realise I was expected to entertain everyone. And, it's not like you wanted to spend your night with me. You barely talked to me."

"I was saying hi to everyone you invited. I didn't want to be rude." He was nodding but obviously unconvinced. He was turning this on me. Like he had gone to all this effort and I was ungrateful. Maybe I was. I didn't feel like I had any leg to stand on. "Let's forget about it."

"Fine," Jack said. He was the oldest guy I'd ever dated but sometimes he seemed more like a teenager.

Jack and I showed the visitors around LA, and on and off, he would become grumpy, even rude. If they noticed his behaviour, they didn't say anything. Saffy gave me a look now and then but we never got a chance to talk it through. The two days went too fast and then I was driving them to the airport.

Jack was leaving the next day for set. I used the drive home to think about what I could say to him.

He was already packing his things when I got back. "When is your flight?" I asked.

"Tomorrow afternoon," he answered without looking at me.

I stood by the balcony door, watching, waiting for him to speak before I remembered he wasn't the type to start anything, just seethe until I did. "I don't get you."

He was quick to comeback. "What don't you get?"

"You bring over my friends and family to surprise me, but then you act like an asshole. What am I supposed to do with that?"

He stopped packing and looked me. "I don't know, Talia. Do what you want."

"You don't care what happens?" I asked.

He took a breath and closed his bag. "I really don't."

I wasn't upset, I was mad. I opened the balcony door an inch to let in some cool fresh air. Was this the end? Another failed relationship. What would the media say this time?

"Why don't we just take some time," Jack spoke. The edge to his voice had dropped off. "We're too worked up."

"Okay," I answered, it sounded reasonable. He approached me and kissed my cheek. I closed my eyes at the feel of his lips on my skin. I watched as he picked up his jacket and suitcase and walked out my bedroom door. I listened as he walked down the stairs and out the front door. I pushed the balcony door wider and stepped out into the sun. I sat on my lounge chair and tried to think of anything else.

He was on set for a few more weeks. The time would be useful. To figure out what the hell I was feeling and if I wanted to keep it.

The second single *Island in the Sun*, an ode to its namesake, came out the next morning. I had a few radio interviews to introduce it. As soon as I was done, I headed out to the pool to relax.

I had just closed my eyes when Sabra called out to me. I got up and walked back to the living room door.

Sabra was carrying a huge bouquet of white roses in a rectangular box from the front door. "What is this?" I asked.

"A gift."

"From who?" I questioned.

She seemed nervous to say. I waited. "Easton Vane."

I took in a shocked breath. "Are you serious?" Easton was the rapper who had humiliated me in front of everyone at my first ever Grammy Awards.

"See the card," she offered, holding the roses closer to me to grab the small white card.

There it was, a messy scrawl; *I've never been so sorry for anything in my life. I regret what I did to you. I hope you'll forgive me. Congratulations on the new album. Easton.*

SIX

I was going to ignore it. I had thought about it and it seemed like ignoring it was the best option. But the impoliteness of it was gnawing at me. "What should I do?" I asked Sabra and Ari as they unpacked the clothes Ari had brought for me. I was supposed to go to New York Fashion Week for the publicity while I was promoting the album. According to Ari, though I was regularly being provided with new and fashionable clothing, I needed a whole new wardrobe.

"What about just an email?" Sabra suggested.

"That's too cold," Ari argued. "What do you think of these?" She held up a pair of gold sparkly ankle boots. I clicked a little like probably no. She put them in the yes pile. I laughed.

"What about a note?" Sabra continued.

"What do you mean?" I asked.

"Well, like the way he sent flowers and a note. You could just send a note."

"That feels weird," I answered and let out a breath. "Maybe I should just call him."

"I could get you tickets to his show," Ari suggested.

"A concert?" I asked.

"No, he's performing his new album at Bradford's show," Ari explained. Bradford was a young Malaysian designer.

"Oh. Probably not."

She held up a deep maroon silk dress over the gold boots. "Yes?" she asked.

I shrugged, she did what she wanted anyway. "I'm just going to call him. Sab, can you get me his number?"

"Yeah," she answered and rushed from the room.

"I didn't mean now," I said, to the door she walked through.

"She's an eager beaver that one," Ari said as she handed me a pile of denim. "Try these on."

I did as she said and modelled the jeans for her approval. Sab came back within minutes with a yellow post-it in hand.

"That was quick," I said as she handed it over. "Thank you."

"What are you going to say?" she asked.

I groaned. They laughed. "These don't fit," I said, pulling up the black jeans mid-thigh.

Ari sucked in a hissing breath. "You might wanna schedule some time with Per."

Per, my trainer, had been leaving passive aggressive voicemails on my phone. I didn't believe any of the people who said they enjoyed working out. I longed for a time when I didn't have to care at all about gaining a few pounds after eating half a chocolate cake.

After the fitting, I went to the gym and let Per torture me.

"What are you thinking about?" he asked me, as he stretched me out.

"Nothing," I said, automatically.

"Come on, how long have we known each other now?" There was something about this relationship. Per had seen me red faced, soaked with sweat, and making expressions that would horrify me to see in the mirror. He knew my weight and all of my measurements, not to mention my daily diet and steps. We rarely talked about anything unrelated to health and fitness, yet he knew what I was feeling at any given moment. "You're trying to figure something out."

"Yeah," I answered.

"Let me help. Other leg." I gave him the other. I hissed as he leaned his weight against it, pushing it back. "What's the problem?"

"It's not really a problem," I started. "I'm guessing you saw the Grammys."

The way his expression changed I knew he had. "Yeah."

"Well, Easton sent me flowers for the new album," I continued. "With an apology."

"Wow. Better late than never."

"I have his number. I feel like I should call and thank him. But..."

"You're scared?" he asked.

"Not scared," I said even though, yes, I was scared. "I just don't want to do it," I admitted.

Per nodded, thinking. He stood up and held his hands out to help me up. He picked up my water and towel and handed them over. We walked toward the door. "I'm not a huge Easton fan. But, it seems pretty obvious to me that he has some problems. There is a lot of grace in forgiving and befriending someone who has wronged you."

"Grace, huh?" I asked. He had some wisdom. It felt like what Laurie would say, too.

He shrugged a little. "I'll see you tomorrow."

I laughed loudly and obnoxiously, that wasn't happening, and waved goodbye. He laughed back and I walked out the door.

I heard the clicking and felt a few flashes as the paparazzi got me. That was one of the worst parts of going to the gym. The sweaty red-faced pictures in the magazines. I was becoming more and more vain.

I got home, showered, and sat on my bed, playing with my phone and the yellow post-it. The numbers were so harmless. I unlocked my phone and slowly typed them in. I shifted a little to make myself more comfortable and waited. It rang a while. I started to feel relieved like I could hang up and feel content that I had reached back. I had pulled the phone from my ear just a little when the voice came through, soft and low. "Hello?"

"Hi," I said, my voice a little dry.

"Who's this?" he asked.

I swallowed. "It's Talia… Shaw."

"Oh shit. Talia. How you doing?" he sounded pleasantly surprised.

"I'm really good. I was just calling to—"

"You got the flowers?" he asked.

"I did," I answered.

"You like em? It was hard to pick. Flowers are hard, man. But my girl helped me out."

"They were lovely," I answered. "Thank you."

"Good. Good. You're welcome. We all good now?" he asked.

"Ah…" I didn't know how to answer that. Was he trying to end our call? Or the 'beef'? "Yeah."

"Good. Good. I'm glad. You know it's not good for me. For my soul. Creatively. It was hanging over me, man. I felt like the worst piece of shit."

He spoke so confidently, it wasn't a humble tone, but the words themselves were humble. "I don't think that."

"Yeah?" he asked.

"No. I'm actually a big fan," I finally got to say, having missed out on the first opportunity.

"Oh nah. You are?" he shouted to whoever was there with him. "Talia Shaw likes my shit."

I laughed. He seemed to be moving away from the noise. "It sounds like you're busy—"

"No," he stopped me. "I'm just getting away from these assholes. I gotta tell you, Talia, I'm grateful to you. I've been depressed. I've been drinking. That night I was drinking. I'm in AA now. That's why I reached out."

"I'm glad to hear it," I said.

"You know we should work on something. I got a few tracks we could collab on," he suggested.

"Wow," I definitely didn't know what to say to that. That might be too far, I thought.

"I dig your stuff," he continued. "These two new ones. Fire."

"Thank you," I said.

"You're coming in. Sophomore album. I'm excited for it."

"Thanks," I repeated.

"Okay. Okay. I'll let you go. Let's talk soon though," he said.

"Okay," I answered.

"Later," he said and hung up. I let out a breath and dropped my phone.

Two weeks later, I arrived at Bradford's show and found myself with Easton's arm wrapped around me as photographers shouted our names from various different directions. "You look stunning," Easton whispered into my ear.

According to Ari, Bradford's brand was all about contemporary versions of classic couture silhouettes. She'd styled me in one of his earliest designs, a pale pink long sleeve bone corseted mini dress with a whole section from the throat to mid-stomach cut out and laced with string. She put me in chunky black runners and insisted I wear a pair of classic black wayfarer Raybans. I felt a little ridiculous, but she assured me it was the way to go. Easton seemed impressed. People always talked about him having great style. I looked over his outfit, an all leather ensemble with two heavy gold chains around his neck. "You, too," I assured him.

"Are you guys friends now?" One of the photographers yelled.

"We all good, man," Easton replied. I smiled and nodded.

Easton had to go get ready for his performance and I had to find my seat. I was led to my spot by one of the show's staff and found myself seated next to Adelaide Mills, again.

"Oh my god," I said.

"Hey!" she said, equally shocked. She stood up and hugged me. "Long time no see!" I joked.

Another photographer found us. "Ms Mills, Ms Shaw, can we get a photo?"

"How are you?" I asked as we turned together to face the man. He snapped his pictures and moved along. We sat back down.

"I'm good. Just working on the new album. I know yours is out soon."

"It is, a week or so to go," I answered. "How is your brother?" I don't know why I still asked her that. It felt impolite to ignore his existence when we'd dated.

She laughed a little. "He's fine. He goes on about you, though."

"He does?" I asked.

She nodded emphatically. "Really proud of himself."

I laughed. "I don't know how to feel about that."

The lights dimmed as the show started and Adelaide and I sat in awe of Bradford's designs. They were colourful and modern but with hints of edge like a little leather and chain in just the right spot. Easton walked down the runway as he sang and rapped, and the models moved around him. His music was the perfect accompaniment to the show. He gave me a wink as he passed me by. Adelaide looked over to me. "What's that about?" she asked.

"He's apologised," I answered. She pursed her lips a little. "What?" I asked.

"You gotta be careful with that one," she answered.

I saw Adelaide at another show and even sat with Easton at the last show of the week. He told me all about his new girlfriend who had inspired his sobriety as well as his apology to me. He took out his phone and showed me pictures and I was shocked to discover that it was an actress that I'd met at before at one of the events Manny insisted I attend. Easton and I made plans for us all to get together for dinner when we were back in LA.

I returned to LA next day for more interviews and shoots and another performance, this time on Jimmy Kimmel. I was glad of all my concert practice that I didn't have to beg someone to come up on stage with me.

The questions last time were all about Kelly and Ashley. They were still brought up sometimes. What would Kelly and Ashley think of the new direction of this album? Are any of the songs about Kelly or Ashley? But the number one question, which I was stupid not to expect, was about my love life. About Laurie and Jack. Everyone asked the question a different way but my simple answer, that it was all in the music, seemed to move them along to other subjects.

Only one journalist was less moveable. She kept asking me the same thing, just in different ways. "Your fans have analysed the lyrics, using paparazzi photos, and other stories from your time with Laurie Siler and have guessed that at least two of your songs are about the rumoured relationship with Laurie Siler."

They're all about him, I thought. But I'm wasn't telling her that. The journalist looked at me like she already knew. "Your relationship with Jack O'Halloran is thought to have started after your album but did it start earlier?

"I'd really rather talk about the music itself," I urged, looking to Katie whose arms were tightly crossed. She seemed ready to jump in. I gave her a little smile. I could handle it.

"Surely what inspired the album is talking about the music," she pressed. I just smiled. "You've got to give our readers something."

"I gave them an album. Isn't that enough?" I joked.

"That's about time," Katie said, stepping between us.

Two goes to number one! Manny was emailing me every five seconds with a new article, review, or blog post about the album. It dropped the night before and any fears I had about it failing to live up to the first seemed to be unfounded. Sabra hovered around me trying to ensure I stayed off social media. "Trolls are always going to be trolls. You don't want anything to ruin today," she insisted.

Once she had left for the day I jumped straight on. I found my hashtags and started reading.

This is just a total step up. Every song is incredible. Talia Shaw is EVERYTHING!

OMGGGGG I AM DYING I CANNOT STOP LISTNENIN

This is everything I never knew I needed!

IT'S ABOUT LAURIE!

A mountain of positive comments, a lot of comments about Laurie, as always. And, then, the unavoidable.

Why'd she go all pop? I thought she was unqiue1

TALIA SHAW is T.R.A.S.H

What a rip of Roon Child's last album! One hit wonder 4 sure!

I didn't even know who *Roon Child* was. I tried to avoid those comments. I wanted to reply to the fans, to tell them how much I appreciated their support, but I started to notice people arguing about the album. The fans were fighting back against the trolls and both sides were saying horrific things to each other.

I posted a message about not rising to hate, and spreading love, but then the trolls jumped on that too.

I suddenly realised it was dark and I'd been consumed by this social media ridiculousness for well over four hours. I slammed the computer shut and went downstairs to make myself dinner. As I was straining pasta, my mobile rang. I spilt hot water on my hand as I leaned to see who was calling. "Shit."

Jack, it said. I dropped the pasta and picked up. "Hello?"

"Hi," he said, his voice quiet.

"How's it going?" I asked, because he didn't.

"Good. It's our last day."

"That's great."

"How are you?" he asked.

"Good. Cooking dinner," I answered.

"What are you cooking?"

I looked at the sad looking pasta in my sink. "Pasta."

"Sounds good." It had been weeks and I hadn't really missed him at all. Sure, I had been pretty busy with work, but I'd also had plenty of time alone. Lucy was doing a short North American touring with an alternative band and Teddy had been writing his own album. It had just been Leif and I, getting In and Out and watching action comedies. And, I didn't miss him.

"I miss you," he said, finally, the words sounding hard for him to say. I didn't know how to respond. I couldn't just say, well I haven't. "I want to see you when I'm back. Can I take you to dinner?"

"I don't know, Jack."

He spoke quickly. "I'm going to be better. I know I've been tough. I—"

"I don't know," I repeated. "I really... I have to get back to my dinner. Can I call you later?"

"Yeah," he said. "Take your time."

We hung up then.

After an early morning shoot in Malibu, Leif and I walked along the beach back to the car. "What do you think of the new album?" I asked. Leif's eyebrows jumped a little. "Be honest."

"I like it," he said. "I was never a big fan of pop—"

"But, do you like it cause it's me? Or do you actually like it?" I pressed.

"I guess I can't really know," he answered. "Why?" he asked.

"I've just been reading the bad reviews," I answered, thinking of one particular phrase. 'Her lyrics are as unsophisticated as children's pop can be, and her voice is immature and unpolished.'

"I thought the reaction was really positive?" he questioned. "Didn't it go to number one like straight away?"

"Yeah," I answered.

"Then what are you talking about?" he pushed.

"Nothing," I answered. I wondered if there had been just as

many bad reviews for the first album and I just hadn't known where to look.

"I don't think you need to worry about a few critics," Leif said, his eyes looking toward the car park. A group of fans had gathered before the sand and stood waiting with their iPhones at the ready.

I put on my brightest smile for them.

As we drove home I got a call. Saffy. "Hey," I said.

"Hey."

"What's going on?"

"Um," she started. "This is a little bit weird."

"What?"

"Jack called me."

"What?" I repeated, louder. Saffy and I talked through the so-called 'break' that Jack and I decided to have after the birthday incident. She thought it was best, too, being surprised by his mood swings.

"He wanted advice," she continued. "He misses you."

"So, I've heard. He called you?" I asked, needing confirmation. Why would he do that? I thought.

"Yeah. He sounded really upset."

"It's a little creepy," I said.

"I thought it was kind of sweet," she offered.

"You think we should get back together?" I asked. Leif looked over to me, concerned.

"Not if it isn't what you want," she answered.

I got home and washed the sand off in the pool. I sat out by the sun, willing myself to stay put and not go find the laptop to further torture myself.

He called again, around the same time that I heated up the sad leftover pasta from the night before.

"I heard you spoke to Saffy," I started.

"I did," he answered. "I wanted to find out if I had a chance."

"What did she tell you?" I asked.

"Just that you've been really busy. Haven't had much time to think."

"It's true," I confirmed, though it really hadn't.

He spoke firmly. "I have had plenty of time. I know what I want."

I didn't know. And, that should've been enough to end it for good. "I think we probably—"

He wouldn't let me say it. "Talia. I really think I was falling in love with you. Don't tell me I screwed it up."

There was a time I thought I could fall in love with him, too. I wasn't naïve enough to think people could change as easily as that. Him or me. But, I was low enough that I wanted to try and get a little of that good feeling back.

So, we got back together. And, all we did was fight. He picked them and I ended up screaming and then we'd give each other the silent treatment until he needled away at me to forgive him. And, I would. Because I couldn't be bothered with the alternative.

His film was finished but it missed the cut off for the Oscars. Even so people were talking about him getting nominated the next year. He was invited to the Vanity Fair Oscar Party. He came over with the invitation in his hand.

"You'll have fun, I'm sure," I said, kissing his cheek in hello.

"Talia, you're invited," he said, looking at me like I was daft. "Jack O'Halloran and Talia Shaw."

I looked at it. He was right. My name was written on the invitation beside his.

"Do you want to go?" he asked.

"Sure," I said, without thinking. Jack was unpredictable at parties. Then there were all the other things. Dress. Hair. Makeup. I shot Ari a text and she assured me she was already on it. Manny had sent me an email with Katie's new talking points for the album if any journalists want an interview, so he already knew as well.

Ari had another whole clothes rack of event dresses for me to try on. I was immediately drawn to a sheer floral gown, with a pattern of pink flowers and green leaves. Then I realised it was sheer sheer. As in completely see-through.

"Who is this?" I asked.

"Ayperi," she said. "An Egyptian designer."

"How does it work?" I asked Ari, lifting it up in the light, figuring it was missing a slip.

Ari looked at the dress and then searched through some lingerie boxes she brought alone. She pulled out a tan bodysuit. It wasn't even a full bikini. It was a Brazilian cut. I put the dress back. Ari laughed. "I'll get you to take a chance eventually."

Sabra laughed and tried to cover it up with a cough. There were plenty of the same kind of thing I would usually wear. Lots of lace and simple silk figure hugging gowns.

"You keep looking at it," Ari said.

"What?" I asked.

"The Ayperi," she said with a smirk.

"I do not," I protested.

"Sab?" Ari asked.

"It is gorgeous, Talia," Sab agreed.

I looked at it again. No harm in trying it on, I thought. No harm at all. "Give me the bodysuit."

Ari smiled wide and handed it over. Sab and Ari stepped out of the room and closed the door. I got undressed and slipped into the bodysuit. Definitely Brazilian, I thought. But at least Per's workouts had made my bum less of a pancake. I stepped into the gown and pulled it up carefully.

"Ready," I called, and they came back in.

Ari got to work immediately, lacing it tightly in the back. Sab just looked at me, her hands clasped over her chest.

"You like it?" I asked. She nodded. I looked at myself in the mirror. It was gorgeous. More interesting than anything I'd worn before. "My parents would kill me."

"Sorry, how old are you?" Ari asked, sarcastically.

"Ok. I'll do it," I said before I could change my mind. Sabra let out a squeal and Ari covered her ears.

"Jesus."

"Sorry," Sab offered.

"We're going to have to do something about this hair," Ari said, as she lifted my curly locks away from the laces.

"What do you mean?"

"If you're wearing a dress this interesting then you can't have the same boring hair," she insisted as she pulled the gown down.

Sab and Ari stepped out again as I changed back into my jeans and t-shirt.

"I can't believe you just said my hair is boring," I whined.

I opened the door back up for them. "It's nice, Talia, but it's old. You need something fresh."

It had been long and a classic blonde colour for a long time. My whole life, basically.

"What do you want to do with it?" I asked.

Ari's lips pursed. "I was thinking caramel. Maybe a fringe."

I scoffed. "A fringe? I can't pull off a fringe."

Ari rolled her eyes. "Honey, you can pull off anything."

Maybe when your personal life was boring, you became amenable to suggestions like wear this dress that shows most of your ass or let's totally makeover your hair. I found myself agreeing and Ari set the appointment for the morning of the event. "We don't want the paps spoiling it. You have to debut it on the red carpet."

The hairdresser, a friend of Megan's, came to my house at 6am. God knows why it needed to be so early when the event didn't start until 4pm. He and Ari talked about the colours and then came for my approval. I saw the caramel and was kind of excited. He put on the colour, foiled me up and then sat down with me and asked for all the gossip about my love life. I refused to give him anything really juicy, so he told me I was boring. I told him I absolutely was boring and that is why I was dying my hair, so I could distract people from my vanilla personality. It made him laugh.

I washed out the colour and it was very dark. Scarily dark.

"Don't stress, young blood," the hairdresser advised me. "It's much lighter than that."

He turned on a hair dryer and got blasting. And, he was right. Much lighter than it looked wet. But still, it was caramel. Quite a change from yellow blonde. I thought it made my eyes bluer and maybe made my skin look more tan.

"What do you think?" Ari said though she was smiling like she knew. I was smiling too.

"I love it," I said.

"Yaaas" said the hairdresser and then started on the styling. "How are we doing this hair?"

"Ari?" I asked her.

"It's got to be out to show off that colour. And, straight."

"You will be unrecognisable, young blood," the hairdresser said as he plugged in the straightener.

Vienna came shortly after to do my makeup. She was shocked and delighted to see my hair and even more excited when the dress came out. Sabra had steamed it and hung it on a mannequin and the excitement kept building.

Vienna bronzed me up and put gave me a very fresh makeup look with light pink eye shadows and blush and a red lip. Ari gave me a pair of chunky retro looking gold earrings. I put them on, as well as a chunky gold ring with a huge emerald in the centre. I tried not to think about the cost of it.

And then I was finished. All but the dress. They stepped out to let me change.

As Ari finished my laces, Jack arrived in his suit. He rushed up the stairs to see me walk out my bedroom door.

I tensed for a bad reaction.

"Wow. You look stunning," Jack said. He brushed my fringe back a little.

"You like it?" I asked, shocked.

"Love it," he said. "The dress, too."

"Show him the back," Sabra spoke up. I tensed again as I turned. Jack's mouth made an 'o' and he let out a breath.

I bit my lip as I waited for him to say something. "That's your ass."

"Yeah," I said.

"It's out," he said again but I couldn't get a handle on the tone. He wasn't the type to tell me the skirt I was wearing was too short. He laughed a little and then shrugged.

It was all very covert. Ari had Leif use an umbrella to walk me from the house to the car. Jack held my hand on the way, rubbing his thumb across the skin on the top of my hand. "Are you nervous?" I asked.

"There are some people here who we're trying to get funding from," he admitted.

"I'm sure you'll do it. You can be very charming."

We stepped out onto the red carpet and it was almost as if people didn't recognise me. Usually there'd be shouts of my name, but it was all, "Jack! Jack!" That was until we stepped directly in front of the cameras. I smiled and it was like a lightbulb went off. The photographers pulled away from the viewfinder and looked at me. "That's Talia Shaw!"

"Talia! Talia! Why the new hair?"

We were pulled by Jack's publicist toward a few interviewers and they asked nothing about the album, only about Jack's movie and my hair. I understood that I had new hair, but I also had a new album. Maybe the hair had been a bad decision. But I liked it. I felt good. I felt great actually, walking into that party on Jack's arm.

At the Grammys, I had walked into a room of my favourite musicians. But I also loved movies. And, that party was filled with the people who acted in them and made them. I was more than a little star-struck all over again.

Groups of actors and filmmakers came up to talk to Jack. He introduced them to me and we made some small talk. "Shall we get a drink?"

I nodded and he led me toward the bar. We each got a few fingers of whiskey. Mostly because he didn't ask me what I wanted.

"I'll be right back," Jack said and walked toward the bathrooms, leaving me alone. I didn't have time to think about that because all too suddenly I was approached by a very tall brunette. I recognised her immediately. Rita Victor. She had been in many 90s romantic comedies that I could recite by heart throughout high school.

"Oh my god, Talia Shaw," she said, gripping my arm. "I love your music. My daughter and I are such big fans."

I gushed. "Thank you. I am such a fan of your films."

"Can I get a picture?" She was asking me?

"Of course," I said. She came beside me for a selfie, taking out her phone and turning it on to flash.

The flash brought some attention to us and suddenly three other actresses who I'd grown up watching in some of my favourite movies had come to say hi. It was a love fest for the ages and we found ourselves drinking and dancing and singing along to Rihanna songs together. I realised I had been away from Jack for a while and remembering my birthday party, I went off to find him.

He was in the outside area, with a few guys smoking cigars. He introduced me to everyone, but I quickly forgot their names.

One of the guys, a director or a producer, was tall with dark slicked back hair and bad breath, he put his arm around me for a picture and it stayed there as we talked. I tried to take a step away, but he laughed at a joke which gave him an excuse to pull me in tighter. I didn't worry about it, thinking he was just a touchy feely friendly guy. Until his hand started to slide a little lower. It was so slow. Almost unnoticeable. Until it wasn't just a low-slung hand but a full palm clutching one of my ass cheeks. And, then squeezing. "Get off," I said, pushing him away.

"Woah," he said, his hands up in surrender. "What's the problem?"

Jack looked between us, confused.

"Just keep your hands to yourself," I said.

"I'm sorry. I throw my arm around people. I wasn't trying to be a creep." Jack just stood there.

"We good?" the creep asked.

"No."

"Talia, come on. It's a party," Jack said. He grabbed onto my wrist and tried to pull me toward him. I shook it off.

"Excuse me," I said and walked away.

"Talia!" Jack called out.

I walked out of the party with Jack on my tail. I texted Leif. Jack didn't say anything to me as we passed the photographers. He shook a few hands and I waved goodbye to some of the girls.

On the street, we tried to be quiet, but he wanted to have it out.

"I don't get why I'm the bad guy."

"You're not the bad guy. You're the guy who sees the bad guy do something bad and says nothing."

"What was I supposed to say?" he argued. "It seemed like he just accidentally touched your ass and you freaked out."

I had to work hard to keep my voice low. "It wasn't an accident. He grabbed my ass cheek."

"Well, that's fucked up," Jack said and pulled a little at his head. "In his defence... I mean the dress..."

I took a step back. "You did not just say that."

Jack winced a little and stepped towards me. "I didn't mean that. You weren't asking for it."

I seethed.

"Well, what did you want me to do? Punch the guy?" he asked.

"I didn't need your protection I just wanted you to believe me, support me. You left me alone."

"When did I leave you alone?"

He didn't get it. He wasn't going to. "That's it. I'm breaking up with you."

He shook his head like I had just told a stupid joke. "Talia!"

"I'm sorry, but it's time. You know it is." He was shaking his head as he realised I was serious.

"I don't know that. I don't want it to be over."

"I'm sorry. I need it to be."

"Just like that? Because of this?" he asked.

"No," I argued. "Not just like that. Not because of this. It's just over."

"Let's just go home," Jack said, rubbing my arms. He was not getting it.

I pushed him away. "I texted Leif. He's pulling up the car."

"Great."

"Not for us. For me. You're not coming," I said as firmly as I could.

Jack didn't say anything. So, I didn't either. Jack waited with me, silently, as Leif pulled the car around. "I'll call you later," he said, and kissed me on the cheek. I didn't bother telling him not to. But I wasn't answering. At least not for a while. We weren't getting back together.

I got home and changed and showered. I got into bed and just breathed.

It was done. And, I was relieved. But a little dread started to rise. The media had gone wild after three boys. I didn't want to keep adding to their list. I needed a lift of spirits and, if I did, then probably some of my fans did too. God knows there were definitely people struggling more than me. I jumped on social media to chat with some of my girls and maybe see if anyone needed a little helping hand.

I loved to see them realise that I was online and freak out. I loved to answer their questions and just say hi. I started to realise that this community had memes and jokes of its own and they made me laugh out loud.

I was scrolling, as I usually did, jumping over the pictures of Laurie that came up in my hashtag when I saw a video I'd never seen. He'd shaved his head. Why would he do that? It occurred to me that we'd both undergone a pretty hefty hair transformation at about the same time.

It was an interview. The poster wrote in all caps; 'THIS IS SO

CUTE. THE INTERVIEWER ASKS ABOUT TALIA AND HE IS SO SWEET AND FUNNY OMG #TAURIE'.

I clicked on it. Of course. The interviewer was a young woman. She was pretty and he smiled at her and she giggled, and I hated her.

"I saw you perform in San Francisco and you were incredible."

"Thank you. Thanks for coming," he said, gratefully.

"I wanted to ask you about your band. It seems like you guys are all really good friends, the way you interact with them on stage."

"I love 'em," he said, tapping his chest where his heart is. "They're really the best. I'm not just saying that. Touring with this band, the whole crew really, has been the time of my life. And, to be able to see all the fans all over the world. I'm so lucky."

"A couple nights after the San Francisco show, you had a Seattle show and someone threw a bra at you," she continued. He laughed a little.

"I'm not sure what that was about. Maybe I had a spider on me," he joked. She cracked up.

"Do you get a lot of bras thrown at you?"

"I get all sorts of things thrown at me. I appreciate a gift, but it can get a little dangerous. I do try to encourage people not to throw things at me."

She laughed again and then became a little serious. "I've got to ask about Talia Shaw." Laurie's smile got smaller, but it was still there. "Her new album is out. Have you heard it?"

He nodded. "I have."

"A lot of people are saying that you were the inspiration behind a few of those songs. Do you have anything to say about that?"

He laughed a little. "You know... I don't know who they're about. But I do think she is a phenomenal writer. Truly one of the best song writers out there. I'd be honoured to know she wrote a song about me."

"Wow," the interviewer said.

"Yeah. Honoured," Laurie repeated.

"But, no confirmation?" she asked.

"Of what?" he asked very innocently before laughing a little.

"Laurie, such a pleasure to meet you and speak with you."

"Likewise, Donna. You have a great day."

The clip ended.

SEVEN

Twelve Missed Calls. Three Voicemails. I almost felt guilty for ignoring him. I remembered all the times I saw his name flash across my phone and felt giddy. Then I remembered our last conversation and saved my guilt.

The magazines had pictures of my dress and there were plenty of comments about the sheerness of it but most of the conversation was about Jack and me. They had pictures of the fight as well. Manny wanted to talk it through. I assured him we didn't need to do that and I didn't want to make any kind of statement, with or without Jack.

Teddy called me, for the first time in a while. He wanted me to listen to his album and help tweak some things. So, I invited him to come with me to Jimmy Kimmel's show. There was usually a little waiting around, and I thought we could kill two birds with one stone.

Leif drove us in. Teddy wasn't forcing me to talk about Jack, but I knew he was curious.

"It had been a long time coming," I started.

"Feels weird that you had this long term boyfriend and I only met him a few times," Teddy considered. "What went on?"

"He was just all over the place… Sometimes he was great and sweet and other times he was awful."

"Moody," Teddy offered.

"Really moody," I agreed.

"You met his whole family, didn't you?"

"Yeah," I nodded. "They were great. Honestly. I'm a little sad to never see them again."

"What was the deciding factor?" he asked.

"It should have been my birthday," I said.

"Sorry, I couldn't make it to the party," he cut in.

"Hey, it's okay. I know what it's like when you're in the middle of writing." He had wanted to do it on his own, with no other writers or producers or musicians and see what he could do.

"It didn't go well?" he asked. I told him about the argument we had and then the calls to get back together and then about the Vanity Fair Party. Teddy got angry.

"Who was the guy?"

"I don't even remember his name, honestly."

"What an asshole," Teddy continued. "Jack, too. I'm glad you dumped him."

"I'm glad you're coming with me."

"Of course," Teddy said, giving me one of his smiles. A smile like that, from one of your best friends in the world, is better than any cheesy movie star smile.

"What's going on with your love life?"

He hummed a little with half a smile.

"What does that mean?" I asked.

"There might be someone," he continued. I eyed him, impatiently. "It's Crystal."

"Crystal?" I repeated. I knew Teddy had been hooking up with Crystal on the tour. I never thought it was anything serious. "I thought that was very casual?"

"It's become... less casual."

"You like her?" I asked.

"Yeah. A lot. She's a little crazy..." he said, hesitantly.

"Crazy how?" I asked.

"She gets a little jealous," he started. "Argues with fans online."

"She does?" I asked. I had no idea he was even seeing her seriously, much less she was having twitter wars with his fans. "I tell her not to pay any attention. It's all bullshit. I don't know why she lets herself get sucked into it."

"Are they saying awful things to her?" I asked, remembering getting sucked into that whirlpool myself.

"Honestly?" I nodded for him to continue. "I don't know if you know this but there is kind of a big contingent of people who want... You and me..."

"The shippers?" I asked. His eyes lit up, realising I knew. "What's the name? Taleddy?"

He laughed. "Why didn't you tell me about this?"

"I don't know," I shrugged. "I didn't think you'd care."

"Well, Crystal cares," Teddy explained.

"But, she actually knows us," I questioned. How could she let that bother her when she could clearly see that we were only friends?

"I know. She just thinks it gets thrown in her face," Teddy shrugged. "Have you been seeing anyone? Since Jack?"

I shook my head. "I need a break for a while," I said with a huff.

A long while, I thought. Teddy nodded, but his expression seemed to say he didn't believe me. "I'm serious."

"Okay," his tone expressing the same disbelief.

"What is that?" I asked, offended.

"Nothing," he said, throwing his hands up.

"How many guys have I dated since I've known you? Seriously?"

Teddy thought for a second. "I see your point," he admitted. I threw my pillow at him. He laughed and held on to it. I grabbed it back and shoved it behind my back.

The paparazzi outside the studio seemed to make Crystal's point. "Are you sleeping with Teddy?" and "Did you break Jack O'Halloran's heart?" they shouted to me. And, "Did you break up Talia and Jack?" to Teddy. Teddy and I looked at each other knowingly.

There were fans there, too, and we stopped for pictures. It made me so happy to see Teddy getting red-faced and humble and being sweet to them. That was the way it should always have been. His singles had shot up the charts and his fan base was already huge. People were dying to hear the new album. I was dying to hear the rest of it.

He took out his phone once we were inside, I assumed to text Crystal.

Teddy played his album while I got ready. He hooked it up to the speaker system and jumped onto my lounge to lay down. A manicurist came first, followed by a makeup artist that Vienna had recommended because she was busy, who also did my hair. Teddy asked if they minded listening to his album and both admitted that they were fans. We all listened in rapture as the first half of the album played.

Some of the songs I had heard on the tour, but they'd been

tweaked and perfected. Others were brand new. The songs were pop, anthemic but also very Teddy. There were rap elements and RnB elements and folk elements. It was such a mixture of things, it surprised and delighted me. I wanted to hear the rest, but it was time for me to go on. "I love it so much," I told Teddy, hugging him tightly.

He laughed a little and coughed. "Too tight," he said, but he held me tightly too.

We broke apart as the stage hand knocked on the door.

Jimmy Kimmel wasn't as over-the-top friendly as Jimmy Fallon but perfectly nice. He assured me that his wife and their daughter were big fans of my music and he had heard some of Teddy's stuff, too and really liked it. I had started to get a feeling, and maybe it was all in my head, but it seemed to me that some men were unwilling to listen to my stuff or if they did they wouldn't admit to liking it because it had at some point been labelled as 'teenage girl music'. Then there were the men who didn't see those labels and or didn't care about them and liked the music on its merits.

The performance went smoothly, and the audience seemed to love it, but then there was the interview.

"Your first album did extremely well but this album just exploded," he explained, holding up the vinyl version of the album for the crowd.

"Thank you," I said, unsure how to respond to a statement like that.

"And, you wrote all of the songs?" he asked.

I nodded, "Not alone. I had a lot of incredible help. My cowriters were Teddy Murray, Lucy Castillo, and James Aaronson." The crowd cheered.

"And, I know you have a very passionate fan base. You actually interact quite a lot with your fans online?"

"I do," I answered, surprised he knew. "They are so sweet and so supportive and actually so hilarious, I can't help but talk to them."

"We've found a few conversations," he started, and held up some cardboard pieces with screenshots of some of my interactions with fans. "Here's one. 'Talia is such a lurker.'"

He started reading. It was a post on Tumblr from when people started noticing that I was talking to fans and commenting on things and liking things. There were a bunch of responses in the form of memes and gifs of different characters lurking. I had commented in the form of a gif I had found of myself that someone had taken from me standing just off stage singing and dancing while Teddy was performing. The screenshot had been taken while my hands were so high in the air that they covered my ears and my expression was ridiculous. The crowd cracked up. He showed a few other very funny posts and then set them aside.

"What do you think of the album?" I asked.

"Oh," he said, caught off guard. "I think it's great."

I eyed him for a second and he started to laugh. "Okay, so I haven't heard the whole thing, but I've heard some of the songs and you're very good."

"Thank you. Which songs have you heard?"

He laughed again, "Uh oh." The crowd laughed. "Honestly, it's hard to get me to listen to anything other than podcasts."

I smiled. "You should try some other things. Give things a chance. Listen with an open mind. You might find something special." I wasn't talking specifically about my album and I hoped it didn't come off as arrogant.

He nodded. "You know what, you're right. I'm going to listen to it." He held my album up again. "*Two* is out now. Stick around."

The audience clapped and we went into break. "Sorry to put you on the spot," I said.

He smiled, "No, please. You're right. I'm pretty bad about music. I listen to the same old stuff over and over."

I laughed. "Well, thanks for having me," I said, shaking his hand.

"Thanks for coming. I hope you come back," he said. I walked off stage to find Teddy waiting there.

He smiled at me. "You were great."

"Was I?" I asked. "It wasn't too much?"

"No, you were great," he repeated, and I was glad to know he didn't think I seemed arrogant.

Teddy and I went back to my house, ordered some food, and listened to the rest of the album and then I forced him to play it all over again. I had barely any notes, but we still worked away on it for the rest of the night, finally falling asleep around two. It was just like the first days of our friendship. I realised how much I'd missed him.

Teddy and I had just woken up and were pottering around making ourselves breakfast when I got a call from Manny.

"I have some exciting news."

"Okay?"

"Ayperi has invited you to be her guest and wear her gown to the Met Ball." My mouth dropped.

"Wait, the designer I wore to the Vanity Fair Oscar Party?"

"That's the one!"

"Wow. That's so lovely."

Manny huffed a little. "More than lovely, Talia. It's very hard to get invited to the Met Ball. You have to be approved by Anna Wintour."

"That name is familiar," I said, I couldn't place it.

"She's the editor of Vogue!"

Manny was getting impatient with me. "Sorry," I offered.

"I've already informed Ari. I'm not sure if Ayperi has a dress in mind or if they want to work with you and Ari to design one especially. The theme of this year is Icons – Old Hollywood Glamour."

I had heard of the Met Ball, but I had very little understanding of it other than it being just another fancy event for fancy people. But, if Ayperi wanted me to go in one of her dresses, I was more than happy to do so. Even if it meant flying to New York within the next week. I spent a week at home, working out with Per, hiking with Lucy, and sunning myself by the pool and then headed back to New York with Sabra.

Ayperi had a dress ready to go. "As soon as I saw the pictures from the Oscar party, I knew you had to wear this dress."

"That's so kind of you," I said. Ayperi was a small Egyptian woman in a black silk shirt and slacks with great big red eyeglasses and a scarf wrapping up her hair to match.

"It was inspired by Elizabeth Taylor's dress in *A Place in the Sun*." I had never seen that movie, nor any movie starring Elizabeth Taylor, but of course, I knew of her. She was definitely an Icon of Old Hollywood, I thought.

It took four people to carry it out from the storage room of the studio.

It was a shockingly deep purple. The bodice was tightly fitted with just the bust covered in clusters of tiny fabric deep purple violets, the rest was bare, down to the full skirt which had more violets sewn in at random all over. The skirt was huge. It looked like a wedding dress. It was doubtless beautiful, but certainly an attention grabber. Although, at this point, there was no pretending that I didn't enjoy some attention.

I tried it on, Ari and Ayperi helping me carefully. Ayperi pulled at the corset strings so aggressively, I thought she might pop one of my organs. It cinched in my waist so tightly. It looked half its usual size. But I liked it so much. I almost wanted to dye my hair Elizabeth Taylor's darker colour. But the deep purple went well with my new caramel hair.

"This is the best part," Ayperi said as she began to undo the waist of the dress. "Step out."

I stepped out to discover there was a hidden skirt underneath. The same deep purple, the same style skirt but made of feathers and sequins and much, much shorter. "For dancing," Ayperi said. I laughed.

"I love it," I offered.

Once the dress was finished, I had a day in New York to get my hair colour refreshed, that same deep caramel. I had let my fringe grow out and brushed it off to the sides. I got a very thorough facial to prep for the heavy layer of makeup I'd be wearing. And then it was Gala day. Sabra was filled with jealousy that she couldn't come with me. I had asked Manny if there was any way she could go and was informed it was impossible. Sabra tried to explain the calibre of people who would be there but no reaction I gave her was good enough.

Megan styled my hair with thick shiny finger waves that fell just below my shoulders. Lindsey gave me light eyes and red lips. Ari completed the look with simple tear drop earrings and an enormous diamond cuff on my wrist. Ayperi wore a three piece tux with her signature glasses and scarf.

No other red carpets I'd ever walked before compared to this one. It was huge, lined with photographers and interviewers, and packed with men and women dressed to the nines and even higher. There were Marilyns and Audreys and Jane Mansfields. The dresses were extravagant and beautiful. I wanted to just look at everyone, but the photographers demanded my attention, this way and that way.

I felt a hand on my waist and turned. It was Meredith Laitham. One of those 90s supermodels you used to see in all of the ads and music videos. "I'm so sorry. I just have to say, you look so beautiful. I am such a fan."

"Oh my god, thank you. You look amazing." She did, she had a white silk gown hugging every curve with a long silk train in the back. Her hair was styled in 20s curls pinned close to her head.

"Can we get one of you two together?" Meredith kept her arm around me and turned to the photographers. We took a few shots and then she went to stand on her own a few metres behind me in on the carpet.

"Are you a big fan?" One of the photographers asked me. I made a fan with my hands and waved furiously.

"I adore her," I answered.

In my very high heels, the stairs seemed endless, but finally I was inside. We were directed to the exhibition, but it was so filled with people that they told us it might be better to try back later when it was quieter.

The actual room where we'd be dining was like something out a Disney Princess movie. Or Harry Potter. There were fairy lights and candelabras and humongous bouquets of fragrant and beautiful flowers all over the place.

I was looking up at the clear glass window roof top when Easton called my name. "Talia!"

I found him coming quickly toward me. He wore suit with tails, but the jacket was entirely covered in black pearls. "Easton," I responded. "You look amazing."

"So, do you. Fucking iconic," he said, looking over me. He kissed my cheek and I noticed the drink in his hand. He seemed to notice me noticing but neither of us said anything. Of course, it wasn't my place.

"I didn't know you'd be here," I said.

"I'm performing," he answered, gesturing to a small stage to the right of the room.

"Oh, awesome," I said, becoming ridiculously excited. He smiled, appreciating my enthusiasm. "This is my girl, Joan," he said, as a drop dead gorgeous tall black supermodel came over to his side.

"It's lovely to meet you," I said, holding my hand out to shake hers.

"You, too," Joan said, her voice thick with a Russian accent.

Ayperi was behind Easton and waved me over. "Will you both excuse me?" I asked, gesturing to Ayperi.

Easton looked and let me go with a "See you later."

Ayperi introduced me to a Vogue Editor named Edith who insisted that I had to be in an upcoming spread. I assured her I was not a model, but she wouldn't take no for an answer.

Ayperi took me around the room, introducing me to others from the fashion industry as well as other celebrities who came over to greet her. Keelin, Laurie's friend, was also there and came up to say hi. We chatted for a little bit before dinner was served and we had to find our places.

The first course was covered in cilantro and since I hated the herb with a passion, I used the opportunity.

"I'm going to check out the exhibit," I said to Ayperi and excused myself.

I walked in just as two others were walking out. I found myself alone, moving around mannequin after mannequin of costumes. There were costumes from *Gone with the Wind* and *Casablanca* and other old Hollywood classic films. Then there were suits and dresses from premieres and events. They had images from the films and explanations of the histories of the designs on plaques beside them. I could've spent hours in there.

I wandered into the next room and froze.

Laurie. He was looking at a costume, sipping on a beer.

I tried to sneak back out, but my dress was too big, one of my flowers scratched against the wall and alerted him. He turned around quickly and looked at me.

"Talia?"

"Hi, Laurie," I responded.

He looked so good. He was in a simple black suit with a white shirt, a bow-tie, and simple black reading glasses. His recently shaved hair had grown just enough on top to be slicked back. He looked like James Dean. Maybe that was what he was going for.

He was checking me out the same way. I felt like a big purple cake. "You look… fucking incredible."

I didn't expect that. "So, do you." I responded. "Look good. I mean… you look like James Dean."

Laurie smiled. "That was the goal." I nodded. I guessed that James Dean was one of Laurie's acting idols. Laurie swayed a little on his feet.

"Are you drunk?"

He smiled at me. "Maybe a little." I shook my head and raised my hand to wave goodbye. I started to move out of the room, but he came closer. "How's Jack?"

I stood still. "We broke up," I answered.

"Oh," Laurie said and started to smile. I shook my head, but he just smiled wider.

"Don't look at me like that," I said. I didn't imagine I'd be flirting with him like this again, I thought. But he got me so easily.

"Sorry," he shrugged. "How do you like the exhibit?"

I took a breath and moved deeper into the room, deciding to look at the costumes. "It's very cool. I'm sure you're loving it."

"I am," he nodded. "I've never been that interested in this thing, but I wanted to come to this one."

"The Met Ball?" I asked.

"Yeah," he answered. "I didn't know you were coming. It's a nice bonus."

I shook my head, deciding not to respond to that. "So… what have you been up to?" I asked, he hadn't put out any new music in a while.

"I've been auditioning a little." He was still so shy talking about acting. I didn't get it.

"How's that going?" I asked.

"Not great," he admitted. Maybe that was the reason for the heavy drinking.

"You'll get something, Laurie. I know you will. You have that quality," I said, thinking I'd maybe said it before. He looked at me, gaging how serious I was. I tried to express it in my look. But then it was too much.

I moved to look at other costumes and he moved with me, sidling up beside me.

"You know, you've been killing it, Shaw," he said,

"Thank you," I said, hoping he wouldn't mention the fact that I wrote all those songs about him.

"I'm really proud of you."

I swallowed. "Thank you."

There was a bench to the side. Laurie found it and sat. He patted the space beside him. "Come sit."

I touched my skirt, out at my sides. "I don't think it's possible."

"Well, just come here then," he said, gesturing with his head to the space directly in front of him.

I should've said no. I should've walked right out of that room. But instead I took three steps and stood in front of him. His fingers played with the fabric of my skirt. "You look like a princess."

"I should get back," I said.

He looked up at me, his eyes a little red-rimmed and glassy. "I think I made a mistake, Talia."

"What?" I asked. What could he have done? I thought. I'd never seen him like this.

"With me and you," he finished and looked back down at the floor.

Oh. I was glad he wasn't looking at me because I wouldn't have wanted him to see the look on my face as I swallowed that. I knew he didn't mean it. He was playing with me. Probably not intentionally. I didn't think he wanted to hurt me. But, it did.

"You're wasted," I said, stepping back. His fingers still reached for the dress though it was out of reach.

"I haven't had that many," he said and looked up at me again. I turned around and walked out. I told myself he was drunk. Over and over and over until I got back to the party.

I walked straight to the bar and ordered a triple vodka. The bartender looked at me with wide eyes. I smiled. "Please." Getting drunk was probably not the best reaction to a drunk Laurie, but it was the first thing I thought to do.

Ayperi found me at the bar and brought me back to a table to meet the folks seated there. I brought another triple vodka with me and paid more attention to it than my tablemates. They were definitely less interesting than the man looking at me from three tables away.

I recognised him, but I couldn't remember his name. Thomas

or Robert or something like that. I knew he was British. Another actor. He had just done a spy movie.

Dinner came and I inhaled the steak they served before going back to my drinking. I took champagne from a passing waiter's tray and drank it quickly.

Then he was there, his hand on the back of my chair, introducing himself to everyone at the table. I looked up at him. He was very tall. His short curly blonde hair was gelled back. He smelled amazing. Manly, and woody, and fruity.

He looked down and smiled at me. It crinkled the corners of his eyes. I smiled back.

"Jasper," he offered his hand and his name.

"Talia," I gave mine. He didn't shake my hand but kissed it. I laughed a little, as did Ayperi.

His British accent was different to Laurie's and Teddy's. More posh. He was a taller, younger, blonder Hugh Grant. Polite and slightly bumbling yet confident. And, good looking. Though much older than me. Probably older than Jack, too, I thought.

"Would you like to dance?" he asked.

I saw Laurie across the room, standing, leaning on the back of a chair at a table, watching. I looked back at Jasper and nodded.

He gave me his hand and pulled me up, leading me to the dancefloor. A DJ was playing 60s jazz music and I had only just realised it. It didn't faze Jasper at all as he put a hand on my waist and started leading me like he was from the 60s himself. He swung me around and dipped me and I was just holding on for life and laughing like crazy. I was drunk and totally pliable, and it was the most fun I'd had in way too long.

Finally, Easton came on stage, the lights came down, and he started performing. I watched, leaning against Jasper. We danced a little to the rapping, slow and a little dirty. He turned me around at some point and we were practically grinding together. I felt hot. I felt wanted and I wanted him back.

Midway through Easton's set I looked up at Jasper and he looked down at me. He looked at my lips and I looked at his. His hands tightened on my waist.

"Do you want to get out of here?" he asked me. I wasn't thinking when I nodded. I wasn't thinking when I held his hand and he pulled me from the room, down the stairs and outside.

Within seconds we were running across the wide New York city streets, chased by paparazzi. Fans behind barricades were screaming my name and his. Jasper grabbed a taxi and opened the door for me. I threw myself in and he came in behind me, closing the door and screaming at the taxi driver to drive. The driver sped through the lights just a second before they turned red.

Jasper and I were both breathing hard, recovering from the run. He smiled at me. I smiled back and then I was reaching for him and he was reaching for me. We started making out like animals, thoughtlessly, a little awkwardly, and rough.

"Where are you staying?" he asked me.

"Bowery," I answered.

There were photographers there, too. Jasper pulled my hand, helping me out of the taxi and through the throngs of paparazzi, into the hotel. We ran for the elevator and he pressed the button. We stayed steady, untouching except for our hands, as the elevator came down to us. It opened with a ding and we stepped in, not even waiting for the closed doors to start making out again. I thought I heard a hoot from one of the guests in the lobby.

EIGHT

Jasper picked me up by the thighs and pushed me back against the elevator wall. There was the littlest bit of pain, but it mixed so well with the pleasure and I let out a moan.

"Are you alright?" he asked. That posh accent just turned me on even more. I nodded and pulled him by the neck back to my lips. He pressed his crotch against me, rubbing his hard length where I was already wet for him. His tongue probed my mouth and his fingers kneaded my thighs as we worked together to gain some friction.

The elevator dinged again as it opened on my level. I was relieved to see the hall was empty because we were actually dry humping in the elevator. He carried me out for a few steps before dropping me back down to my feet and I immediately missed the feel of him. He asked which room. I pulled him to the third door down, almost running. He pressed against my back, kissing my neck while I struggled to find my key in my clutch. I got the door open and pulled him in. He slammed the door closed behind us.

We kissed roughly, moving through the room, kicking off our shoes, until we found the bed. We clumsily took our own clothes off, as if we were racing, and fell down onto the tightly made bed. We immediately grabbed for each other, bringing our bodies and our lips back together. I reached for his cock, he was long and hard and pressing into my belly. He rolled a little onto his back as I took him in my grip and rubbed him gently, tugging, squeezing just enough, feeling the soft skin and the wetness at the tip. He groaned a little. I thought I felt a shiver run through him. I wanted him to touch me, but he wasn't even thinking about it.

I climbed on top of him, using his length to rub myself, guiding the head along my folds. I fell forward a little as I moaned with pleasure but suddenly I was struck with a dizzy spell. I realised how drunk I was. "You okay?"

I shook my head. He flipped us over, slowly, so I was underneath him. "You okay?" he asked again. I nodded. Laying down helped the fog clear.

"I'm good," I said. "Fuck me."

I woke up stark naked with a blistering headache and a ringing phone. I was shocked to see Jasper beside me, equally naked and passed out. I began to remember moments from the night, before I started drinking, including Laurie looking like James Dean. My mouth was dry with the foulest taste and my eyes felt tight and swollen. I reached for the hotel phone with a groan.

"Hello?" I answered as I pulled the bed sheet up and over me.

"Talia, we need to talk." Manny sounded the same as he usually did, which was concerned.

"I'm still asleep," I claimed, ready to hang up.

"Katie and I have both talked to you about this," Manny started.

"You cannot just go out and about with whoever you want." Why did every part of my life have to go through him and Katie?

I didn't care enough about what Jasper would hear to get up and out of bed. "I'm twenty-one. I'm having fun."

"You're not just a twenty-one year old girl. You're one of the most famous people in the world. And, damage to your reputation cannot be undone."

"You're overreacting," I said.

"You have no idea," Manny scoffed. "Have you had a look outside your hotel? Had a look online? It's been less than a month since you and Jack ended things. People have already started saying that this is a PR relationship."

A publicity stunt? I was offended. "I would never do that. The people who know me, know that. I have to be able to live my life." I couldn't believe the conversation I was having when I had only been awake for a minute. "I'll talk to you later," I said, and hung up. I knew I'd pay for that but all I wanted to do was go back to sleep.

Of course, as soon as I closed my eyes, all I could see was Laurie. Laurie drunk. Laurie looking at me with those eyes. Telling me he made a mistake. And, all the drinks I had to have to try and forget about it. Not to mention the very wrong-for-me guy lying beside me. I didn't really know him. It was only a feeling – that he was wrong for me – but I don't think I'd ever have gone for him were it not for all of those factors. Anyway, it was done. Now I only had to deal with the awkwardness of the morning.

It didn't seem like Jasper was waking up naturally any time soon. I was aching all over. I wanted a shower and breakfast and to brush my teeth. But I didn't want to wake him up with all that sound. So, I just lay there and willed the image of Laurie from my mind. I willed those words out of my head. He didn't mean them. He never would. It was a waste of time and energy to think on it.

And, yet I couldn't stop myself. So, I found the same distraction I'd found the night before. I casually rolled over and into the big spoon that was Jasper.

I pretended to be asleep as I felt his body wake up. His body was well built, as seemed to be par for the course for a Hollywood actor, but he was taller and thinner than Jack. And, nowhere near as hairy. He had just wisps of hair on the middle of his chest and a snail trail leading down to where the sheets covered him. His arms came around me, pulling me in to hold. His hands held me around the ribs. His nose made a trail from the back of my head to the top of my neck. I hoped he wouldn't sniff, imagining that I had never smelled worse.

"Morning," he whispered.

I swallowed. "Morning."

Jasper shifted his body and I felt his crotch against my backside. A thought shot to my head. Did we wear a condom last night? I couldn't even remember if we'd had sex in the end. The state of our undress would indicate we did. But I couldn't remember. I hated myself for that. How stupid of me to get so drunk that I couldn't remember full chunks of the evening. How dangerous that was. But I had to know. I turned over toward him. He opened his pale blue eyes and smiled at me.

"Hi," he said. He looked at my lips.

"Were we safe last night?" I just blurted it out.

Jasper opened his mouth in shock. "You don't remember?" Did I offend him? I thought. "We did. Of course, we did." I felt a rush of relief as he turned over to his back and looked up at the ceiling.

"I'm sorry. I just drank way too much last night," I said, looking at him with concern.

"God, don't apologise. I'm the one who should apologise." He turned back over to look at me, his expression guilty, the gentleman in him ashamed. "I'm so sorry, Talia."

"What for?" I asked, feeling strange about the intensity of the moment.

"I feel like such a creep. I feel like I took advantage...."

I cut him off. "You didn't. You were drunk, too. And, I wanted it."

His blue eyes were still furrowed, tensely wrinkling the skin at his brow. I raised my hand to his forehead and rubbed, to get the lines to disappear. They did, and then his expression was blank. Except his eyes. There was something about the very clear blue of his eyes. They were the kind of beautiful that you could stare at for hours on end.

He ducked down and little and kissed my lips. He didn't taste amazing. We both needed to brush our teeth. But the kiss was gentle and sweet. The sheet fell away a little and my bare chest brushed against his. His hand ran down my thigh to hitch it up. I felt him bare and hardening against me.

A knock on the door broke us apart. Good, I thought. That was going too far, again. "That's probably my assistant," I said, bringing my leg back down.

"You probably have work?" Jasper questioned. I nodded. "I'll get out of your hair."

I pulled the sheet up to cover myself as Jasper pulled on a pair of white boxers from the floor. "You can shower here, if you want?" I offered. I felt bad about the idea of him doing the walk of shame. Especially if the hotel was surrounded by paparazzi as Manny had described.

"Actually, that would be great," he answered. I smiled and gestured to the bathroom. He picked up the rest of his clothes and moved to the bathroom. "Do you want someone to pick you up some clothes? I've been told there are lots of paparazzi..."

"Oh," Jasper said, that furrow returning to his eyebrow. "I'll get someone on it." He took his mobile out of his trousers and then closed the bathroom door behind him. I used the sheet as a dress and moved into the living room to grab the robe I wore for hair and makeup. I wrapped myself up in it as another knock sounded. I looked through the peep hole and found Sabra standing by. I opened the door and she rushed in.

"Oh my god," she said, in what seemed to be her loudest voice.

I shushed her. "He's still here."

"He is?" The shower started and Sabra smiled wildly. "I can't believe you hooked up with Jasper Middlebrook." That was his name!

"What are you doing here?" I asked, realising she must have wanted something.

"Manny wants to talk to you," she said.

"I already spoke to him," I assured her.

"He called two minutes ago and said you had to call him when he" she gestured to the bathroom, "was gone."

"Okay. Is that it?" I asked.

"No, we have to gather everything for collection," she said, looking at my kicked off shoes earrings still on my ears.

"Right, okay," I said, realising she wasn't leaving any time soon.

I found my clutch on the floor, my phone half fallen out of it. I picked it up and pressed the home button to find it dead. I looked for my charger, but Sabra yanked it from my hand. The charger was at the table with her laptop. She set it up to charge.

I emptied my clutch of everything else and set it up with the other clutches that Ari had arranged. I went into my bedroom and gathered up my dress and the jewels and placed them back with everything else. Sabra went to work putting things in tissue paper and in their correct boxes while I put together an outfit for my day.

I sat down on the bed to wait but stood right back up as the shower stopped. Jasper stepped out moments later, the bathroom steaming behind him and a towel slung loosely around his hips. "Thanks for that."

"No problem."

His hair was longer, wet out and out of its gel. Blonder, too. I stepped around him to take my turn. "My assistant is bringing some clothes. He should be here any second," he said.

"No worries," I assured him. I closed the door behind me.

The bathroom smelled like the hotel's free body wash. The free tooth brush and tooth paste had been broken into as well and set beside my own electric tooth brush and tooth paste.

I took off my robe and turned on the shower, relishing in the heat. I washed my hair and my face and then gave myself ten minutes to just soak before forcing myself back out.

I towelled myself dry, put my robe back on and wiped the condensation from the mirror.

I brushed my teeth and tied up my hair in a messy bun. I looked at my flushed face in the mirror, feeling the shame that wouldn't so easily wash away. I took a breath and stepped back out into the bedroom.

Jasper was dressed, in dark jeans, dress boots, and a light blue button down, and waiting for me on the bed.

"He came," Jasper said, by way of explanation. "I was just waiting to say bye."

I stepped towards him, unsure of the proper goodbye in such a scenario. I raised my arms for a hug and he wrapped his arms around my waist. He squeezed tightly and let me go. "Thank you. For last night."

"Thank you," I said, and bit my lip as a childish giggle strained to come out.

We let go and I waited for him to step away. He just kept looking at me.

"I don't know what your situation is…" he started. "But, I want to take you to dinner. Will you let me to do that?"

"Um. When?" I asked, I was supposed to fly home the day after.

"What about tonight?"

"Tonight?" He nodded. I tried to think up an excuse but decided against it. "I'm not doing anything."

He smiled. "7?"

I nodded.

"I'll see you tonight then". I nodded. He gave me a quick kiss and moved to the door. I followed him into the living room. "Bye," he said to Sabra. She waved. They must have talked when his assistant, or whoever, dropped his things.

"Bye," I said as he stepped out the front door. I turned around to see Sabra looking at me with a strange expression. "What?" I asked.

"Your phone is ringing," Sabra said.

"Who is it?" I asked, walking toward her.

"Jack." Sabra held my vibrating phone up for me. "He's been calling kind of non-stop."

I stopped walking. "Just ignore it," I said. Sabra nodded and set the phone back down. She opened up emails and started reading. We worked through the morning, confirming a meeting with the label for contracts and another possible tour as well as a photoshoot for Ayperi's vogue editor friend for when I returned to LA. We went for lunch at a nearby bistro and made an impromptu trip to the Met to see the parts of the exhibition I had missed the day before. Sabra insisted on organising security as well as a tour, so I didn't get to wander as I would've liked, and there were surprisingly a lot of fans there seeking selfies so we could only stay around an hour. I couldn't help but snap a few pictures when something stopped me in my tracks. I wished I could've stayed longer. I promised myself that next time I was invited to the Met Ball, I'd take advantage of the access.

At six, I got ready for my date. Ari had set me up with several evening dinner looks. I chose a sheer singlet, high waisted trousers, and a sleek long coat paired with simple pointed stilettos and no bag at all. I did my own hair, straightened it, and my own simple makeup. Sabra watched on impressed. "How did you learn to do that?"

"I've picked it up from Megan and Vienna," I said.

Sabra handed me my phone, in a case that held my ID and credit cards. The expression on her face was a little pitying.

"What?" I asked her. I turned over the phone to see the screen flash with another voicemail. Jack. He'd seen what the rest of the world had about me and Jasper.

"I suppose I should give him a call…" I thought aloud.

Sabra shrugged. "I don't know."

"Why are you still here, Sab?" I asked. She furrowed her brows. "Go out. Have fun."

"Okay," she said, grabbing her things. "I'll see you in the morning?"

I nodded. She headed out and I dialled.

Jack picked up straight away. "Finally."

"Hi Jack," I said, and took a seat on the lounge in the living room.

"How could you do this to me, Talia?" he said. I wasn't expecting an attack. Maybe I should've.

"I'm sorry. I didn't mean to be so public," I started.

"You obviously didn't care at all how I'd feel about it," he disagreed.

"Honestly, I drank more than I should have—"

He cut me off. "I knew you were too young for a serious relationship. I don't know why I let myself get sucked into it."

"Excuse me?" I asked, losing my patience.

"Why Jasper Middlebrook, huh? He's a narcissistic jackass."

"And, what are you?" I asked. "I have to go."

"Wait," he yelled quickly. "I'm sorry."

I didn't have anything to say to that. I kept waiting.

"I just miss you. All the time. And, I don't know how to deal with it." This is how it always was with him. Something sweet and something sour.

"I think it's better if you stop calling," I said, not wanting to hurt him, but feeling like he needed to hear it.

"I want to work this out," he argued.

I didn't know how he could possibly want to go back to arguing with me all the time. The good didn't outweigh the bad. Not even close. "I don't."

He laughed bitterly. "Fine. Maybe just learn some discretion." He hung up. My mouth was dry. I wanted to change my number. I stood up and reapplied gloss to my lips, trying to calm down. Our relationship hadn't been that strong. We hadn't even said we loved each other. Why couldn't I see someone new? It had been weeks since Jack and I broke up. Why should I be shamed for that? I refused to be. I told myself that when Jasper came, I wouldn't let anything get in the way of having a nice time.

He arrived at a quarter to seven. "Traffic was better than I thought," he gave as an explanation. "You look amazing."

"Thank you," I said, brushing the hair back from my face. I looked him over. He wore dress pants and black dress shoes with a white button down and a navy pea coat over the top. He looked good. He opened the door and held it for me.

"After you," I thanked him, and we headed to the elevator. "I've got to tell you, there is still a bit of a crowd outside."

"Still?" I asked. He nodded. They'd followed us to the Bistro and the Met through the day, but I assumed they would've cleared by then.

"Yeah," Jasper nodded. "There is a car waiting for us at the curb."

"Okay," I said. Jasper led us out of the elevator and through the lobby. The eyes on us were double what there usually were. The cameras started flashing before we were anywhere close to the doors. Jasper looked at me, as if to gage my readiness and then moved for the door. Hotel security opened it for me and huddled either side of us as we moved through the small but loud crowd.

"Talia! Can I get a selfie?"

"Talia, I love you!"

"Jasper!"

"Excuse me. I'm sorry," Jasper was saying to those calling to him.

"Are you two dating? Did Jasper stay the night with you?"

Somebody grabbed my elbow and pulled me hard, I nearly fell. Jasper saw it happen. He pulled me back and wrapped an arm around me, creating another barrier. He moved us quicker to the car and we jumped in.

"Are you okay?"

I nodded. "Thank you."

I was a little shaken. There was a difference in being yelled at and photographed and someone grabbing you. They didn't do it too often but when it happened, it shook me up. You never knew what people were capable of. Jasper reached out and grabbed my hand as the driver started moving. I let his touch calm me. He seemed to know innately that I needed it.

I was feeling fine by the time we got to the restaurant though a small group were there as well. Jasper kept me in his arms from the car to the Bistro as well and I was glad of it.

"Welcome. Mr. Middlebrook. Ms. Shaw. Can I take your coats?"

I opted to keep mine, remembering the sheerness of my shirt underneath, but Jasper handed his over. He wore a button down well, the thin material fitting loosely to his lean muscle. He put a hand on my lower back as the server showed us to our table at the edge of the room.

"Allow me," Jasper said, as the server moved to bring my seat out. Jasper took her place and pushed my chair in.

"Thank you," I said. The bistro was warm, lit with candles and quietly romantic. We looked at our menus and both chose pasta.

"Wine?" Jasper asked me. I nodded. "Do you prefer red or white?"

"Um… whichever."

"Can we please get a bottle of the merlot. Thank you." The server took our menus and moved back to the kitchen.

"A bottle? That might be dangerous," I joked.

He laughed a little, a touch of red appearing on his cheeks.

"I don't know what has me more embarrassed. The dancing or… the latter half of the evening."

I laughed. "Your dancing was amazing."

"Oh dear," he said, ducking his head at my perceived meaning.

"No," I protested. "The latter half was great..." The sentence dithered on my lips.

"You still don't remember it, do you?" he asked.

I shook my head, embarrassed. He laughed a little. "I'm almost glad," Jasper said. "Gives me the opportunity to redeem myself."

I must've made a face because he started babbling. "Not that there will be another... I'm not expecting... I mean..."

"I get it," I said, with a smile.

"Right," he said with an expression that made me sure he was berating himself inside his head. It made me laugh. The wine came and Jasper tasted it like he knew what he was doing. "This is great. Thank you."

We drank our wine as Jasper asked me about growing up in Sydney and my friends and family back home. I learned about his family in London and his years studying drama at the Royal Academy of Dramatic Art, followed by years of theatre work. He spoke eloquently and listened empathetically. I was thoroughly taken by him. We had entrees, mains, dessert, and coffee, and four hours had passed before I knew it. The restaurant was emptying.

When we finished, he insisted on paying and left a very generous tip. The crowd had dwindled somewhat, but there were still a few fans and paparazzi. Jasper asked if I minded him signing a few autographs before we left and, of course, I didn't. Ignoring the paparazzi, we stepped out and took selfies and signed autographs. I could feel Jasper keeping a watchful eye on me, in case things got a little crazier.

The drive to the hotel was too quick and then we were at my door.

"I should get home," he claimed, instead of coming in. He was trying to be polite. Ever the gentlemen. The night before notwithstanding, he didn't want to take advantage.

"When do you leave?" he asked.

"Tomorrow," I said, a little disappointed.

"Back to LA?" He asked. I nodded. "For work? Cause if you're not working, you could come with me to Cannes."

I furrowed my brows.

"That's crazy, isn't it? Forget I said that." He turned as if to leave.

"Okay..."

He turned back round. "Unless of course, you might want to go? It's beautiful this time of year. Have you ever been?"

I shook my head.

"Beautiful weather and beaches and great parties. You know about the film festival?"

Cannes Film Festival. I knew about it in the same way I knew about the Met Ball. It seemed very glamourous. Movie premieres and charity events and yacht parties.

Of course, I couldn't possibly go away with him to the South of France. We'd met just forty eight hours before, I thought. "I don't—"

"Of course," he cut me off. "Stupid idea. I just..." He shook his head, cutting himself off.

"That's where you're headed?" I asked.

"In a few days," he answered. "But, I'm back in LA just a few weeks after that."

"Well, we should get together again," I said, still not sure how I really felt about him.

"That would be lovely," he assured me. His eyes flicked to my lips. I let my mouth open just slightly. An invitation. He moved in slowly and kissed me. Softly, just a few long seconds. And, then pulled away.

"I gave your assistant my number," he said with a smile as he pulled away. "So, you can give me a call if you change your mind. Do you think you'll change your mind?"

I smiled. I kind of wanted to. But there were too many reasons not to.

So, I said no. And I said goodbye. And I got on a plane and went home. I spent three days in that house on my own but for Leif and Sabra. I didn't have anywhere to go. I didn't have any work commitments. I spent half the time eating and half the time laying by the pool. It was so quiet. I called Lucy but she was still touring. Teddy was busy with Crystal. When Leif and Sabra left for the day, the house was silent. When I went to sleep in my big empty bed, I thought about Jasper.

I had been pretty sure that he wasn't the right guy for me. But, why was I sure of that? I wondered. Simply because of his age? Or because he was a little more put together and mannerly than anyone else I'd dated? I'd written him off before I'd given him any sort of a chance. As soon as I gave him that chance, he proved himself to be charming. I liked him. And, I'd never been to Cannes.

I found myself dialling his number. He answered on the third ring with the remnants of a laugh in his voice.

"Hello?"

"Jasper?"

"Who's this?"

"It's Talia."

"Oh," he said, surprised. It sounded as if he were moving to a quieter place. "How are you?"

"I'm bored," I came right out and said it.

"I'm sorry to hear it," he said, a little eagerness in his voice. "You know I have the perfect remedy for that?"

NINE

Jasper met me at the airport in the early hours of the morning. The sun was already shining, and the day was already warm. He kissed my hand as we were driven from the small Cannes airport to the Hotel du Cap-Eden Roc. The hotel was a palatial house surrounded on three other sides by thick pine tree forest and another building built right into the azure coast. We walked down the long and wide stone pathway that connected the two and I recognised the view looking back up at the main house from Instagrams and Tumblrs of famous actors and models.

"This is so familiar," I said to Jasper.

"Everyone stays here," Jasper explained. "It's the most private. It's where the amFAR Gala takes place."

Another gala, I thought.

"It was just yesterday. It was quite a night," he explained.

We arrived at his seaside suite. A simple but elegantly decorated space with a king bed, a small living area and a balcony.

Jasper looked a little embarrassed. "I didn't think to get a different room. This is probably a bit modest for you."

I was embarrassed then. "This is incredible. Are you kidding me?"

The bellman arrived with my luggage and I unpacked a few things as Jasper took a phone call on the balcony.

"I've been invited to have lunch with Declan Sokolov. He's a shipping magnate whose invested in one of my recent films. Would you like to go?"

"Am I allowed to go?" I asked, not wanting to show up uninvited.

"I don't think he'll mind," Jasper laughed. I changed from my comfortable flying clothes into a summery floral button down dress with a tan belt and tan sandals. I hadn't told Ari where I was going so I had to pack for myself and hope she would approve of the outfits I chose.

We were driven from the hotel to a nearby port, Antibes, where Declan's yacht was moored. A deckhand met us at the gate and walked us to the furthest point of the rounded port where the biggest yachts were moored. I had never seen such ginormous yachts. They all looked to be around 500 feet long. They looked like they belonged to Russian oligarchs or members of Monaco's royal family. Declan's yacht, a sleek dark grey ship, was called *Poshlost*. There were already many people on board. The deckhand helped Jasper on first and Jasper helped me.

The inside was pristine and modern and far more spacious than I could've imagined from the outside. Jasper led me by the hand through the ship and to the top deck where we were greeted by the group of a dozen or so, including a short blonde man who introduced himself as 'Dec'.

I was seated beside a redhead who asked inane questions like, "is it just a nightmare being followed everywhere you go?" and even asked me about Jack and Laurie while Jasper was seated right beside me.

Midway through lunch, I broke away from the redhead to ask Dec, "What does your yacht's name mean?"

He laughed. "Take a guess."

I took a shot. "A posh person getting lost?"

He shook his head, raised his glass and answered. "It means to be godless, drinking, whoring... living life for pleasure rather than purpose." Classy, I thought.

"I'll drink to that," one of his friends spoke up. The entire group raised their glasses, Jasper included.

They group spent the afternoon celebrating the sale of their scotch company for $1 billion by drinking their weight in whiskey.

Some of the girls went swimming but I hadn't brought anything to wear. The day was warm, and I had sweat gathering at the base of my spine. I did desperately want to go into the water, even if I didn't want to spend any more time being asked about ex-boyfriends. One of the girls living on the yacht, I assumed she was Declan's girlfriend, invited me to her room to try on one of her bikinis.

Jasper encouraged me to go as he discussed a project for which one of his producer friends was seeking funding.

Her bedroom was grand with blush colouring and clothes scattered all over the place. She offered me a teeny tiny red string bikini and I bit my lip. "Do you have anything else?"

"Um," she continued searching and found another bikini, a shiny metallic colour and even smaller than the last.

"I'll take the red," I said. She left me to change. I put the red bikini on and looked at myself in the mirror. I was worried about the cellulite on my butt that would be left uncovered by the

Brazilian style bikini, but I was shocked to find my arse perfectly dimple-free. I guessed Per's training had been paying off. Still, I had never worn anything so tiny in my life. I kept my dress on over the top as I found my way to the deck at the back of the yacht.

The girls were splashing around, riding giant floating pelicans and drinking champagne from plastic flutes. "Talia! Come in," the redhead called.

I looked around at the other yachts floating nearby. I was worried about paparazzi, but it seemed all clear. I dropped the dress and walked to the edge of the small deck. The girls in the water cheered as did a couple of the men watching from the top deck. I jumped in quickly to avoid their gaze and got another cheer.

I swam over to the girls who were discussing the evening's dinner plans. I lay back and floated, letting the sun warm the skin peeking out from the water. Floating in the sea was always preferable to floating in a pool. The natural swell and sounds and the smell of salt. It was heavenly.

That was the way we spent the rest of the week. In restaurants and bars and yachts, but mostly in the water. I got myself a more reasonable size bikini and Jasper hired us a motorboat for a few days to take us to some of the prettiest and most private parts of the coast. We asked our driver to bury his head in a book and went skinny dipping off the coast of a nearby island.

One afternoon, as Jasper played tennis with another friend, I set up my laptop to skype with Saffy. I went onto the internet to check out the news while it loaded and found a story about myself near the top of the page. *'Jack O'Halloran pines for Talia Shaw as the singer moves on with Jasper Middlebrook.'*

I skimmed the article with distaste until I found a passage that made me pause. 'A source close to the singer said, "Talia wasn't going to go but Jack O'Halloran was practically stalking her, and she needed to get away."'

Sabra was the only person who knew Jack was calling me non-stop. Was I being paranoid? I called her.

"Hey! How's it going?" she asked.

"Not good," I answered.

"What's wrong?" Sab asked.

"Somebody is leaking things," I said, emailing her the article. "Look at your emails."

She did. "Oh wow. But, are you sure it's a leak. Don't they just make this stuff up?" she asked, confused.

"What are they, clairvoyant?" I said, she seemed to realise I had guessed it was her.

"Talia, it is not me," she said, emphatically. "I swear."

"Okay," I said. "Have you told anyone else about Jack's calls? One of your friends?"

"No. I don't talk about you with them," she assured me. "I wouldn't do that to you," she said, sincerely.

I believed her. "Okay."

"Now that I have you..." she started going through the other emails, work that I didn't think I had but apparently was missing.

When our week was coming to an end, Jasper asked me if I wanted to go to Paris. It was too close not to. I'd been there on tour, but I hadn't actually seen much of the city. And, Jasper and I were getting on so well. He didn't make me laugh too often, but he didn't make me cry either.

We visited the Louvre and Versailles and the wineries in the countryside. We knew the crowd would be intense visiting the Eiffel Tower, but we both wanted to go anyway.

They tried to give us an elevator to ourselves and I felt guilty and gross and insisted they let everyone else in. The whole ride, people were getting photos of us and asking us questions. They asked about touring my current album and I assured them it was in the works. They asked about Jasper and I and we told them it was just new.

When we got to the very top, they were just as taken with the view as we were, and we were given some alone time. We looked out over the city in awe.

We found ourselves a quiet spot looking over the Seine. Jasper touched my cheek. I looked over to him.

"Let me kiss you?" he asked.

I looked around at the people nearby, their eyes often flickering to us. "Here? In front of everyone?"

"Here on top of the Eiffel Tower." He wasn't thinking about the crowd. Just about the romance of a moment like that.

I smiled and wrapped my arms around him. He wrapped his arms around my waist and lifted me to his lips. We kissed passionately, touching our tongues and sliding our lips over each other, letting the moment wash over us. I didn't even care about the flashes of the camera phone lights.

I was supposed to go home after Paris, but Jasper was going to London to visit his family. "Why don't you come? I can show you my London," he pleaded the night before my flight.

"I've seen London," I answered.

"But, you haven't seen my London. And, I wouldn't mind introducing you to my parents. I know it's soon, but I'd love them to meet you."

Way too soon, I thought. Even with Jack it was at least three months. This was three weeks. But was that my fear of what everyone would say? That fear I told myself I'd forget about? So, I said yes.

We took his parents to dinner at a very fancy London restaurant. They were an older couple who had Jasper late in life, but they were lovely to me and seemed awfully happy to see their son.

Manny couldn't deal with my absence any longer and the tour details that needed to be hammered down, so he sent Sabra to London to do some work while I was there. She arrived the day after we did, and I let Jasper spend some time with his family on his own while Sab and I worked.

"How did it go yesterday?" Sab asked as we looked over designs for costumes.

"It was good. Fine."

"Good fine?"

I laughed. "I guess it still feels weird to have met his parents already."

"It is pretty soon," Sab agreed. "He'll be asking you to marry him soon."

I suddenly got an idea. That if I lied to her and that information showed up in the tabloids or on the internet, then it was a sure-fire way to know if the leak was her. It was deceitful and made me feel awful, but it terrified me to think she was sharing my secrets with the world.

"He's talked about it."

Her eyes widened. "What?"

"He's talked about marriage." Jasper came back to the hotel at that second and ended all talk of it. We left soon after to see a play in the West End.

Two days after that conversation, I went online. There were pictures from the whole trip. They'd even got me in the little red bikini from my first day in Cannes. And, then there were the articles. And, the quotes from a 'source'.

"His parents love her. He's been talking about marrying her.

She thinks it is too soon, but she does see herself marrying him one day."

It's Sab, I thought. I told Jasper, not that I'd said those things to her, just that I knew she was leaking things to the press, and he said she had to be let go. I called Manny to ask his advice. Sabra had come to be my assistant because of her connection to the label. Manny said I was allowed to fire her, and it was best for all involved. It made me nervous, but I needed to talk to her. I called her into my room and sat her down and asked straight out if she was selling stories to the tabloids.

"Of course not," she said, feigning offense.

"They're publishing things that only you and I know."

"They're just guessing or assuming or making things up that happen to be true," Sabra argued. "I would never sell you out like that."

Her explanations were certainly plausible, but her reaction to the accusation cemented the truth in my mind. I insisted that I knew it was her and she finally admitted it. It was only for the money. "I'm so sorry, Talia."

She started crying and I wanted to simply forgive and forget but I couldn't get over the feeling of betrayal. I thought she was my friend. And, it was not as if she wasn't well paid. "I'm sorry, too," I said, firmly so she understood, there was no second chance.

Sabra, quietly, still crying, packed her things and left. Manny got her flown home and Leif helped get her things out of the house.

Days later, Manny called to update me.

"I just wanted to let you know what has been going on with Sabra."

"What?" I said, my stomach filling with dread.

"There have been threats to sell stories and pictures. It seems like they don't have anything too bad, but we've had to bring lawyers in and make sure she understands the privacy clause in her employment contract."

I felt sick. "I don't want another assistant."

"Talia, I understand this was a bad experience, but there is work to do. Are you going to do it?"

"I can do it. I know how to take care of myself."

"What about one of your friends back home? Or family? A cousin?"

I thought of my young cousin, Jasmine. She was going to be turning eighteen soon. I wasn't sure what she wanted to do with her life since I hadn't been around so much in the last two years, but I thought she might be interested. "I'll ask around," I said.

"For now, I'll have my new assistant, Billy, help you."

"I don't want anyone around," I said, cringing at the way I said it.

"He'll work from my office."

"Okay," I agreed.

I felt shitty. I felt used. But I didn't have time to think about it. Laurie was calling. He never called anymore. I told Manny I'd have to call him back and picked up Laurie's call.

"Hello?"

"Talia," he sounded upset. "I'm really sorry to bother you."

"Are you okay?" I asked.

"I'm okay. It's Rooney. She's in hospital—"

"Oh my god. Is she okay?"

"We don't know what's wrong with her. Mom and Colin are in South Africa. They're trying to get back, but they don't know how long... I'm trying to get a plane. I know you're in London."

"Where is she?" I asked. He sounded terrified for his sister.

"St Mary's in Paddington."

"I'm leaving now," I assured him, collecting my things and moving to the door.

"Thank you," his relief was immediate.

"I'll call you when I'm there."

"Thank you, Talia," he said again. I hung up, rushed downstairs and got into the nearest taxi. It took half an hour to get to the hospital and another half an hour to find Rooney and to be allowed to see her. Laurie had to speak to the nurses and then Ryan, his mother, had to give permission over the phone before she got on the plane in Johannesburg.

Rooney's eyes were closed when they let me in to her room. She had a breathing tube in her nose and a drip in her wrist. She looked pale and yellow. I touched her arm as I sat down beside her. "Rooney," I whispered to see if she was awake.

Her eyelids opened slowly, heavily. She looked at me. Her eyebrows seemed to want to furrow. "Talia?"

I nodded. "I'm here."

"Why?" she asked.

"Your brother knew I was in town and didn't want you to be alone. He's on his way. So is your Mom and Colin," I assured her. She started to cry.

I knew the feeling. I knew what it was like to be alone in hospital, in pain, scared. But this was worse. She didn't know what was wrong with her. I stood up and reached over, hugging her as tightly as I thought I could without hurting her.

I stayed with her for hours. She slept on and off. She didn't feel well enough to do a lot of talking so I talked to her. I told her about my trip. I tried to tell her what had been going on with Laurie, but I didn't know much. I'd avoided most of it.

During one of her sleeps, my phone rang. It was Jasper. I stepped out and answered.

"Where are you?" he asked, concerned.

"I'm at St Mary's Hospital."

His voice filled with worry. "Are you okay? What happened?"

"It's not me. It's a friend."

"Who?" he asked, confused.

"Rooney Siler." I hoped he didn't recognise the name.

"Siler? As in…" Damn, I thought.

"She's Laurie Siler's sister."

His voice changed straight away. "Oh. I didn't realise you were friends."

"She's sick. Laurie is in the US and her parents are out of town so…"

"How did you know she was sick?" he asked, the slightest accusation in his voice.

"Laurie called me. He had seen that I was in London," I explained.

"Right."

"Are you bothered?" I asked, a little nervous though I knew he had no right to be.

"Not at all," he said, lighter. "Do you want me to come there?"

"You don't have to do that. Laurie and his parents will be here soon, and I'll head back to the hotel."

"Okay. Call me if you need anything."

"Okay," I said. He hung up.

I went back inside to find Rooney awake again and reaching for water on a tray by her side. "Let me," I said, as I rushed in to help.

Laurie's mother, Ryan, came minutes later.

"Roon!" I stepped back to make room as she rushed towards her daughter. "My baby!" she said, through her tears.

Colin, Laurie's stepfather, a tall rounded man with white hair, approached me and introduced himself, sombrely. "Colin Richardson."

"Talia Shaw."

"Thank you for being here." Ryan turned to me, hearing her husband.

"Thank you, Talia. It means a lot," she said.

"Of course, Mrs Richardson," I assured her. "I'll leave you alone."

"Ryan please, sweetheart. Laurie should be here soon." She went back to attending to her daughter. I stepped out of the room with a wave goodbye to Rooney.

I should go back to the hotel, I thought. Rooney had her parents with her. Laurie would be there soon. They didn't need me there. But instead I waited.

I was sitting out in the hall, willing my eyes to stay open but they were too heavy. I let them close. It wasn't long after that when I felt a hand on my knee. I opened my eyes to find Laurie crouched down in front of me. "Hi," he said, a little red-faced.

"Hi," I said back, waking up. "Is she okay?"

Laurie nodded. "They figured it out. It's an autoimmune disease. She's going to be fine."

I couldn't help myself but lean forward and hug him. He wrapped his arms around me and squeezed tightly. I felt myself relax into it and then remembered why that was a bad idea. "I'm so glad," I said as I pulled away.

"Do you want to get some coffee?" he asked as he stood up. I nodded and stood up to walk beside him.

We got into the elevator and travelled in silence down to the cafeteria. Laurie bought us a couple of black coffees and we took a seat by a window. I hadn't really looked at him since he'd arrived. I noticed the black circles beneath his eyes and the grease in his very short but untidy hair.

"What?" he asked, as he noticed my examination of him.

"You're a bit of a mess, Laurie."

He laughed a little, running a hand through his short crop. "I know."

"I don't blame you. You sounded terrified on the phone."

"I've been pretty scared. I felt useless over there," he said, taking a sip of his coffee and pulling a face. I left mine alone.

"You got here quickly," I said, hoping it would comfort him.

He reached over and grabbed my hand. "I can't thank you enough, Talia. I know I had no right to ask anything of you—"

I cut him off. "Hey. Don't be silly. You can ask me for anything... I'd do anything..."

I couldn't find the right words. I didn't want to say too much, give too much away, but I wanted him to know that he had me, if he needed me.

He rubbed the top of my hand with his thumb. I took my hand back and used it to pick up the coffee that I didn't want to drink. I pulled the same face as Laurie had and he laughed.

"Pretty shit coffee," he noted.

"Do you want me to go out and grab some? For your parents, too?" I asked.

"No," Laurie answered. "We'll make do."

A janitor was moving around the mostly empty cafeteria, clearing trash. I handed her my cup. "Thank you."

"Are you having a good trip? I didn't take you away from anything, did I?"

"No," I answered. "I mean, it's been a great trip. But, you didn't take me away."

"That's good. You're here with…"

He'd obviously been paying attention to the internet. I knew I shouldn't be, but I was embarrassed. I started imagining what he thought about me and Jasper. That we must be pretty serious to be travelling around Europe together. I hoped he didn't think I felt more than I did.

"Jasper Middlebrook," I answered. "It was very spur of the moment."

"You probably didn't see much of it when you were here last. It's hard when you're touring."

"Yeah," I answered.

He took another sip of the coffee and made the face again. "Why do I keep doing that?" he asked. I laughed. He set the cup out of reach.

He looked at me for a little while. Neither of us could think of what to say next. The sun was rising. I started to think it was time for me to go.

"I think I should apologise for last time," he started. "At the Met."

"No," I answered. "It's not necessary."

"I was drunk."

"I know," I stopped him. "It's honestly fine."

He stopped but looked as if he wanted to go on.

"I think I should go," I said, standing.

Laurie stood, too. "I'll walk you out."

We got to the door. The ground outside was wet but I couldn't see the rain. I looked at Laurie and moved in for another hug. In my simple flats, my forehead was right by his chin and he pressed a kiss to it.

"Thank you, Talia," he whispered.

He let me go. I looked up as if seeing to Rooney's level. "Will you say goodbye for me?"

He nodded. I gave him a small wave and stepped out into the light rain. I searched for a taxi and jumped in. I gave the driver the hotel address and looked back to see Laurie standing at the door, his hands in his pockets, his expression annoyed. He shook his head a little and said something to himself. He seemed to be berating himself. The driver took off.

I arrived back at the hotel a little after 8am. Jasper wasn't in the room. I texted him to tell him I was back, but never got a response. I caught up on some sleep but set an alarm for midday so we could salvage the day if he came back. I waited around for hours. He arrived back at the hotel in the afternoon with a group of guys, some of them his actor friends, others just friends. He welcomed me back flatly before inviting me to dinner with the rest of them. I guessed he was bothered about Laurie and Rooney. And, it bothered me.

None of them, his friends, were particularly interesting. They had plenty to say but none of it made much sense to me. A lot of 'you had to be there' kind of stories. And, Jasper didn't seem to have much to say to me either. So, I came out with some not so nice things. Including that the friend closest to me might appreciate an after dinner mint. They laughed, but I knew it was unkind.

We returned to the hotel room and Jasper was quietly fuming. Our first fight. Maybe a little too soon, but I knew I deserved it.

"You didn't talk half the night and the few times you did talk, you had nothing nice to say." He ripped his tie off and unbuttoned the first few buttons of his shirt. He fought very politely.

"You're right," I answered. I knew he was right. I had no point to argue. No amount of annoyance at his behaviour excused how rude I'd been. I moved toward him.

"I'm sorry. I was unforgivably rude."

He brushed the hair away from my cheek.

"Any particular reason?"

I shrugged. "I just felt a little ignored."

"Well, I'm sorry you felt that way. I don't get to see these guys very often," he explained.

"I know. It was stupid. I am sorry."

He wrapped his arms around me. "You're forgiven," he assured me. He kissed me quickly and smiled. That was easy, I thought. We spent one more full day in London. Seeing the last of the missed sights and shopping a little, before flying home the following morning.

Jasper and I kept dating back in LA. There seemed no reason not to. He slept often at mine, like Jack did, maybe because it was bigger than his house. He was in rehearsals for a film and I was still working on preparing for the tour.

We'd go to sleep together, but I never woke up with him. He would always be up early, running. He never asked me to go with him. I would've said no. Running was not at all something I enjoyed. But I didn't like waking up alone. At least he didn't have a dog, I thought.

I heard from Laurie a week or so after I got home. He sent me a text.

Laurie: Are you still in town?

Talia: I'm back in LA. How's Rooney?

Laurie: She's getting better. She said to say hi.

Talia: Say hi back from me.

Laurie: Will do. Thank you, again.

And, that was it.

In one of our final tour meetings, Manny sat me down before

everyone else arrived. He had his serious face on and I guessed it was again about Sabra. "What?" I asked.

"Katie and I have been discussing this. And, it is a problem. Jasper has been talking to the press."

Jasper? "What do you mean? Leaking things?"

"No, not at all. It's just, they ask him questions and he answers. He's a little too open."

I furrowed my brows, confused. "Why is that a problem?"

"It can be taken as... too much too soon. It comes off a little fake."

"Fake?" I asked, seeking clarification.

"Just because you've gone quickly from Laurie to Jack to Jasper..."

"Quickly?" I asked, offended.

"I know it doesn't seem quick to you but in the public's mind..."

"Why should I care about the public's mind?"

"You don't know why you should care?" Manny asked me, in a tone I was used to. That of a parent berating a child. He continued to forget that I wasn't a child and certainly not his.

"Can you talk to him about it?" Manny asked.

"Sure," I said, shortly.

"Great." The rest of the team came in and our meeting started.

I brought it up with Jasper the next day and he was mortified. "I'm so sorry. I didn't realise you wanted... I totally get it."

"It's not me," I clarified. "Manny is just a little..."

"I get it," Jasper said again. "I'm sorry."

He kissed me softly. We spent the night together before he left to shoot a Viking movie in Iceland.

We were both busy, but we tried to speak at least every second day.

Easton was in the news more and more as he continued his relapse. I was shocked to get a call from him late one evening.

"My girl. I need you in my video," he said.

"Wow, really?"

"Yes. Tell me yes, girl."

"Sure... If I can, I will."

"Imma take that as a yes."

"What is the plan? Do you have a treatment?"

"I emailed your assistant." Of course. I opened my laptop and went into my emails. "You got it?"

"I'm looking for it." There were over a hundred unopened emails there. I typed Easton's name into the search bar and it came up. I clicked on the PDF attachment. "Found it."

Oh my god. There were a series of photoshopped images of me, naked, walking around an apartment. "What the hell is this?" I asked, hoping it was some kind of bad joke.

"The director is just out of TISCH. He made this short film about a bipolar burrito."

"Easton, I'm not doing this," I said, firmly.

"Why the hell not?"

"I'm not going to go naked in one of your videos."

"What are you scared of? Your body's tight."

"Why don't you do it? Walk around naked in your video."

"You clearly didn't look at the whole treatment." I reached the end of the document and saw the Photoshop of Easton and I standing face to face, completely naked.

"I don't feel comfortable with being nude for the world to see."

"We'll get drunk and then you'll feel comfortable," he answered. I scoffed. He was not getting it.

"It's not going to happen," I said firmly.

"You serious?" he asked. "I thought we were friends."

"We are," I answered, though I didn't really believe it. "But, this is asking a lot and I'm not comfortable."

"This is fucked up," he said, raising his voice. "It's art. Why are you such a pussy?"

"Excuse me," I fought back. "Don't talk to me like that."

My fighting back seemed to make him even angrier. He started raging on the other end of the phone. "I'll talk to you however the hell I want. You'd be fucking lucky to work with me, bitch. To be in one of my videos. It'll help your shitty pop career take a step up to the next level. But, you don't want that, that's fine. You're a joker. You're a waste of my time."

"I'm not doing this with you, Easton. You need to get some help."

"Fuck you, bitch!" he screamed. I hung up.

I started crying. I knew he didn't deserve to make me cry, but I couldn't help it. My blood was boiling with anger and I felt humiliated. I tried to call Saffy, but the timing was wrong, she'd be asleep, I thought. I tried to call Teddy, but he didn't answer. So, I called Jasper.

He was on set, but he answered straight away. When he heard how upset I was, he quickly stepped away to calm me down.

"What did he say to you?" Jasper asked.

I could barely remember, I was so upset.

He told me I needed to buy a ticket and come to Iceland, insisting that I was stressed and needed a break. I knew I had only a week until the tour and I should've been in LA, but I convinced myself that a couple of days wouldn't hurt.

I flew out that night and arrived the next day at midday. Jasper was able to get the afternoon off and took me around the town where they were staying and shooting, showing me the few sights there were to see. We spent the night in his hotel room, ordering room service and watching 80s movies. He did comfort well.

He had to work the next day, but he invited me to the set to watch him. I was driven in by a hotel driver and then escorted to Jasper's trailer. "He should be in there," the PA advised me. I knocked on the door but didn't get a response. I stepped inside and heard him on the phone. He had it on speaker. I only had to listen for a few seconds before I realised it was his publicist on the other end. The man had the same rhythms as Katie. The same desperate yet self-assured tone.

"Her fans will go see it if she's on screen for more than 5 seconds."

"I'm sure I can get her to do it," Jasper answered. I moved closer to the door to hear better.

"Great," the voice said. "Try and get out and about while she's here. The public eat those images up. As do the studios. It's free publicity."

"That won't be an issue," Jasper answered. "I've already got our days planned. We'll be everywhere."

"Perfect. You've got some in person interviews on set next week so talk about her there, if you can. I'm sure the reporters will be bringing it up for you."

"You know I've got this," Jasper assured him.

"I know you do," the voice said. "If you can break 300 mil on this one then any project you want is yours."

They started talking about film projects after that and I zoned out. I didn't need to hear any more. All the public outings, all the sound bites he gave to every possible journalist. I was a fucking idiot.

It took another ten minutes before he finally stepped out of the bathroom. I was sitting on the lounge waiting.

"Babe!" He set his phone down and came toward me. "What are you doing here?"

He tried to kiss me, but I dodged it. "I'm breaking up with you."

"What?" he laughed a little.

"You heard me," I said, fuming.

"What's happened?" he asked, sitting down beside me.

I answered. "You're a liar. And, a fake."

"Woah," Jasper said, leaning back. "Where is this coming from?"

"I can't believe I fell for this crap," I said, becoming more angry with myself.

"Talia, calm down. I don't know what is going on here. What did I lie about?"

"That you care about me all."

"I do care about you. I'm in--"

I cut him off. I wasn't hearing that bullshit. "You care about your career."

"Why would you say that?"

"I heard you talking to your publicist."

"I don't know what you think you heard—"

"Save it," I said, not angry but exhausted.

He took an angry breath. "This is not the way I saw this working out."

"Me neither."

"You're barely giving me a chance to defend myself."

"There's nothing to defend. You were using me. Just admit it."

"That's absolutely untrue." I gave him nothing. "But, you've obviously made your mind up about me."

"I have," I said.

"Fine. Have a great life," he said, and stepped out of the trailer.

. . .

Another one bites the dust, I thought, as I boarded another plane to fly away from another man. I hated to admit it, even to myself, but I was starting to see the point the tabloids and the trolls had been making. But I knew I was chewing up these men and spitting them out. But I wasn't working through them for content. They were going through me. I was the one getting hurt. I hated myself for starting to believe their narrative. I determined to figure out a way to keep all of that noise out of my head. And, not just the voices of the tabloids or the trolls but Manny, too. I was going to live my life exactly how I wanted to.

TEN

Saffy had done all of the graphics work for the second tour. As a thank you, aside from her fee, I called to invite her and Peter to travel with me for whatever section of the tour she wanted to do. "Come see the sights. Stay in fancy hotels. Go out and drink and dance. We'll go shopping. You have to come this time."

"Thank you so much, Talia," she started. "But, I can't."

"Because of work?" I asked. She had her own graphics business which had been doing incredibly well in Australia. I understood if she couldn't leave it so new.

"No..." she paused.

"What aren't you telling me?" I pressed.

"Peter and I are engaged," she screamed.

"Oh my god, Saf," I wanted to cry. "I am so happy for you."

"Thank you," she answered.

"When did it happen?"

"Last month. The 22nd."

I stopped. It was the 14th now, I thought. It took her over three weeks to tell me. And, I had to prompt her.

"You know Peter's Mom has been in Europe and he didn't want to tell anyone before he could tell her," Saffy explained.

"Okay," I said, but why couldn't she tell me? Her best friend?

"You're not mad, are you?"

"Of course not," I said automatically, hoping it sounded true. "But, isn't that just a better reason to take a trip. Like a pre-wedding honeymoon?"

She laughed. "I have so much planning to do."

"I could help," I cut in.

"I kind of have to be here to do it," she answered. It felt like a million excuses. "My Mom is going to help me out and Peter's sister. I completely understand that you need to tour right now."

What did that mean? I wondered. I knew Peter had a sister, but I didn't think she and Saffy were so close that she'd be helping plan Saffy's wedding. Isn't that the maid of honour's job? Then I realised. She hadn't asked me. Had she asked Peter's sister?

"Okay," I said, when the silence grew awkward.

"But, I'll still need your help," she spoke up. "I'll need your opinion." That felt like my consolation prize.

"Sure," I said. "I really need to get packing."

We said our goodbyes and I hung up.

Most little girls plan their weddings. They describe them in detail to their very best friends and then the very best friends will ask, 'will I be your maid of honour?' That's how it was with Saffy and me. We were going to be each other's maids of honour. And, Ash and Kelly would be our bridesmaids. Even when thinking how ridiculous the rest of it was – hot pink dresses and hot air balloon weddings – I thought at least the maid of honour part was true.

And, then it wasn't. Was it my fault? I wondered, because I wasn't around anymore? There had been a time where we hardly spoke, but we had fixed things from there and spoke at least weekly. She was still my best friend. If I were to marry, I thought, I'd choose her to stand by my side. It hurt me deeply that she didn't choose me.

I called Teddy and he finally answered. I asked if he wanted to go out for drinks. He suggested we invite Crystal and then I figured, why not the whole crew? A little pre-tour party. It seemed to excite everyone that I was willing and even determined to do shots. One round became two and then three and then four. We were all considerably drunk and danced the night away. I felt immensely secure with them all and free to let go. Even Teddy was shocked, but he seemed glad to see me having fun. And, I was drunk enough that I was glad to see he and Crystal all over each other.

At the end of the night, I brought everyone back to my place to drink a little more before we all passed out. Only a few days later the tour began, and the party didn't stop. It was so unlike the first tour. I was so comfortable on stage. There was no writing due. And, I didn't feel compelled. I went out every night with the crew.

The tour was to run for five months from July to November. Teddy was only my opening act for the European portion and then I had an Australian act for the Australia Pacific area, a Korean boyband for Asia, and an up and coming female country singer for North and South America. Teddy and I recovered some of the closeness that we'd lost as he'd been busy building his career and I'd been busy with boys. He'd helped me get back to my room after a particular heavy night of partying and had stayed in the bed, too lazy to get back to Crystal and his own room. I woke up with my back against his, boiling from the body heat.

My mouth tasted off and my head felt like it had been beaten around with a baseball bat. I reached over for the phone to call room service, but I seemed to have picked it up just as they were putting a call through.

"Talia?" Manny's voice was clear and loud.

"Yeah?" I mumbled into the pillow.

"I just wanted to check in with you, and how you're handling this tour. Are you sleeping well? Eating well?"

"What?" I asked, rolling over onto my back. Teddy started to wake up beside me.

"Yeah. I know you've been going out much more this tour and some of the show pictures..." He hesitated. "You look like a little exhausted. A little heavy..." He said it lightly. My eyes shot open.

"Excuse me?"

"I don't mean to be rude. I hate that I even have to bring it up, but it's part of my job."

"Are you serious?" Teddy looked at me with a questioning expression.

"I only wanted to remind you that the world is watching."

I brought my hands up to my stomach. Yes, I had a little extra flesh there. I had been drinking a lot and subsequently eating a lot. Maybe I knew this was coming, I thought. Per sent me a paparazzi shot of me eating an ice cream in Rome. My costumer was huffy when she had to take out a corset which had been too tight before the tour even started.

"I'm growing up. I wasn't going to keep my 18 year old body," I argued.

"We can send Per on tour with you, if you like? Or another trainer?" Manny asked gently.

"No," I said. "Thank you."

Manny seemed to realise that was the end of the conversation and said his goodbyes. I hung up.

"What was that about?" Teddy asked, though he must have known.

"He thinks I'm getting fat," I said, exaggerating.

Teddy sat up, fuming. "What?"

"He didn't say exactly that. He asked if I wanted a trainer on tour."

"What a dick," Teddy said, falling back down onto the pillow beside me.

"We have been eating and drinking a lot." I pulled down the cover to show him my little food baby bump.

Teddy smiled and put a hand on my stomach. "This little thing?"

He turned onto his back and puffed up his stomach. I laughed. Teddy reached over me and grabbed the phone. "Hi, can we please get some room service?"

I shook my head at him. He only smiled and started ordering two of everything on the menu.

In Amsterdam, the crowd was so colourful. There were so many signs, I wanted to read them all. As I caught my breath from a particularly active song, I read a sign that stopped me. 'Easton Vane SUCKS. You're our QUEEN!'

When I got offstage I asked Teddy if he saw the sign and he hadn't. "What do you think it's about?" I asked.

"You don't think it's just about the Grammys?"

"But, that was so long ago." We headed toward my dressing room. "Can you have a look online while I get out of all this?"

He nodded and followed me into my dressing room. Teddy searched on the laptop as my dressers helped me out of my final look. "Oh shit."

"What?" I asked, walking over to him, closing up my robe.

He hit play on a video on a news site.

"It's been looking like you and Talia Shaw were able to become friends after last year's Grammys. Will there be any collaboration with her on this new album?"

"No way, man. She's spineless. A joke."

"Oh… Did something happen between you two?" the interviewer pressed.

"Yeah. We had a deal. She was going to be in my video. Maybe even on the track. And, she bailed."

"That is not true," I said to Teddy. "He wanted me to be in the video, but I hadn't agreed. I didn't know what the video was. He wanted me to be naked."

"Jesus."

Teddy slammed the laptop down. "Why did I even contact him? I should've just left it alone," I said.

"You're forgiving," Teddy answered.

"Do you think people believe him?" I asked.

Teddy shook his head. "Any reasonable person knows that Easton has issues. No one is going to pay any attention to this."

"Really?" I asked.

"Really," Teddy answered, certain.

Teddy stepped out as I changed into casual clothes and washed off the makeup. We got buses back to the hotel and I couldn't stop thinking about it. I got back to my room and went straight to the laptop.

"You ready?" Teddy asked, appearing at my hotel door an hour later.

"That wasn't the only interview. He's talking shit about me everywhere."

"He's an asshole. Forget about him," Teddy suggested. "Let's go out."

I had been thinking about what Manny had said. "I'm just going to stay home and write."

"Oh yeah? Album number three?" he asked.

"Maybe," I answered.

"Okay. Have a good night."

While Teddy and the others were out drinking shots, I sat at my laptop with a glass of red wine and my guitar on my lap. I played a few chords and took a sip. I tried to think of subjects, but there were only a few things on my mind: Jack, Jasper, wasted time, betrayal. I took a few more sips.

I kept trying but nothing else was coming. So, I got changed and caught up to the crew at a nearby club and got drunk. I'd write eventually, I thought. I always did.

Manny woke up me the next day, another call, another problem I didn't want to deal with, this time about Easton.

"We need to put out a statement now," Manny insisted.

"No," was my answer.

"If you have no comment then all the press is what he's saying about you."

"I don't care." I really didn't, I thought. Let him have it out on his own.

"Do I need to remind you of what he's saying?"

"Manny, I'm getting a little tired of arguing with you all the time." I also really wanted some breakfast.

"I can't always say yes to you, Talia. That's not going to lead anywhere good. I'm trying to advise you as best I can."

"Okay. But, I'm not being unreasonable here. I don't want to dignify the things he is saying with a response. You need to start to understand me. You need to be on my side."

"I am." No, he wasn't, I thought.

"You are. On occasion. But I need you firmly there. Or I'm

going to have to look for representation that will be." The threat wasn't like me. But I was losing all the patience I used to have.

He took a moment. "Okay."

"Please," I said, to soften myself.

"Okay," Manny said, more firmly.

After the next night's concert, I had a Skype chat with my parents that went too long. I missed the bus to the club, so I arrived late, again. I found my crew split awkwardly throughout the club. Some of the boys were tearing up the dancefloor. Most of the girls were gathered in a booth, seemingly comforting one girl. I looked a little closer to find it was Crystal. She was crying. I searched for Teddy and found him nursing a beer at the bar. "What happened?" I asked, taking the stool beside him.

He took a cursory glance over his shoulder at the scene and shook his head a little. "Did you know she slept with Adam?"

Adam was another of my dancers. He wasn't in the bar tonight, I thought. "I didn't know," I answered.

"She was drunk apparently," he explained.

"You broke up with her?" I guessed.

He nodded. I ran an arm up and down his back. "Sorry, Teddy."

He shrugged. "It's fine. We weren't that serious."

It was at least six months, I thought. "Do you want her off the tour?" I asked. It probably wasn't a great idea legally, but I wanted to have his back.

"No," Teddy answered. "But I do want another drink."

We ordered several rounds of shots. The girls went home early, but the guys stayed out. We went from that club to the hotel bar and finally back to my hotel room. I had no balance left as I shut the door behind the last of my male dancers, in the early hours of the morning.

Teddy was pouring himself yet another drink from my mini-bar. "You gonna pay for that?" I asked.

He laughed and made another drink for me. We clumsily clinked glasses and drank. The music from our hotel room dance party had turned from EDM to something slower. Teddy put an arm around me and took my hand, starting to dance us in a circle.

"How are you feeling?" I asked him.

"Bloody grand," he answered, moving us around and looking all around the room, lazily.

"You're not sad about Crystal? You can tell me," I insisted, bringing his eyes to look at me.

He laughed a little and then became serious. He was staring into my eyes. "Talia…"

"Yeah, Ted?" I asked, though I'd never called him that before.

He stopped dancing, let go of my hand and brought his up to my neck. I was too slow to realise what he was doing. I didn't stop him. He brought me closer and brushed his lips softly against mine, once, twice, and then closed the gap to kissed me, sucking gently on my lower lip before letting go.

He dropped both his hands and stepped back. My mouth was open in surprise. My heart was beating fast. He seemed to be sobering up, but I still felt hazy. I couldn't figure out what had happened or what I was supposed to say.

Teddy laughed a little then, surprising me. He turned clumsily and wandered back to my bed, kicking off his shoes and falling in to it. I smiled a little at the familiar scene. I had kicked off my shoes long ago. I exchanged my dress for a t-shirt and got rid of my bra and climbed into the bed beside Teddy. I pulled his arm out so I could worm my way under it and snuggle up beside him.

"I kissed you," Teddy said.

"I know," I answered, half asleep already, finding it all a little funnier than I had in the moments before.

He lifted my chin up so I would look at him. There was something in his expression, the tension between his eyebrows. He was waiting for me to say something. "I love you, Teddy," I said, honestly. I hadn't spoken to Saffy in all that time, touring. Teddy had been the one there for me. "You're my best friend."

The tension increased for a moment before releasing. He took a breath. He pressed his lips quickly to my forehead and tightened his warm arms around me. We fell asleep like that, the taste of each other lingering on our lips.

Teddy was gone when I woke up. A first. He never left before breakfast. I called his room, but there was no answer.

He stopped going out with us after that. Everyone assumed it was because of Crystal. Even her. I was glad he was finishing up at the end of the European leg. He needed to get away. I told him to go travelling. He could still get away without being recognised constantly. He needed to take advantage. We had our final show of the European leg in London and Teddy went to stay with his family before figuring out where he'd go. I told him to call me if he wanted to talk about Crystal or anything. He promised he would.

Lucy, who hadn't been able to come on the European leg because she was working on another album, something she was doing more and more as a writer, was able to join us on the Australia Pacific leg. We started in Perth and Lucy was shocked to discover the version of me who would party all night with the dancers and crew. We danced all night and drank our weight in booze. Lucy acted like she couldn't keep up, but I knew she was a veteran at touring and we were probably small potatoes compared to others.

Saffy was calling me again, as were my parents, constantly, ready to make plans, excited I was coming back to Sydney. But when I finally got there, I was too tired to do any of the things they wanted to do – hiking and fishing in Bondi with my parents and visiting wineries in the Hunter Valley to check out wedding venues with Saffy. I wanted to relax with my friends, the way I had been all tour. I had a new routine. I invited everyone to the Sydney shows and made sure to have dinner with my parents at least once before finishing up the leg in New Zealand.

We had a two week break before we started touring again in Asia, and I decided to bring the crew and the dancers with nothing else to do on holiday with me. We went on safari in South Africa and Zimbabwe. We stayed in big air-conditioned tents, glamping, they called it, and went out in roofless jeeps during the day to spot animals. One of the girls had the idea of making an amateur music video and it occupied a lot of our time. And, we maintained our partying streak.

The Asia leg was explosive. The crowds were bigger and louder than any others. And, had at least tripled since my first tour. And, the hospitality was kicked up a notch, too. We weren't just finding clubs and being offered the VIP section. Club owners were closing their night clubs down for us for our exclusive use. The hotel we stayed in in Tokyo, not only shut down their club, but threw us a huge party with circus performers, fire breathers, and an abundance of strippers. Lucy and I took photos and sent them to Teddy, so he knew what he was missing.

In India, I met a South African and told him all about my safari trip before asking if he wanted to go to my room. He readily agreed but we didn't get past the elevator. He was kissing and sucking on my neck and driving me crazy that I put the elevator on emergency stop and fucked him right there. Luckily, he had a condom in his pocket. It wasn't something I'd ever done before. I'd never done anything even close to it, but I had decided to stop caring and it worked. Maybe a little too well.

Somewhere around Bangkok, Lucy seemed to change her tune. "Don't go out tonight," she told me, as we drove back to our hotel after the show.

"Why would I not?" I asked in response.

"We can just chill. Maybe watch a movie. You're killing your liver," she insisted.

I laughed. "Are you serious? Would you say that to a male singer touring?"

She furrowed her brows. "Probably not."

I threw up my hands. "There you go."

"But, that doesn't mean it doesn't apply," she continued. "I know you, Talia. And, this isn't you."

"What are you talking about?" I asked, shocked. "I'm just having a little fun? What am I doing wrong?"

"Nothing," Lucy said quickly, seeming to think on my responses. "Just forget I said anything."

So, I did. I went out and had a brilliant time. Adam, the dancer who had made out with Crystal, even found some pills for us all. I had taken a pill only once before, in Sydney, at my first and only festival. I was too drunk to care where it came from. I only remembered the ten minutes after swallowing it. I remember grinding on Adam and screaming the lyrics to Cher's *Believe* at the top of my lungs. The rest was gone, I realised as I woke up. I was awake but my eyes were closed as I tried to recall how I got home. I opened my eyes for a second to make sure I was in my hotel room. I was. I had been attempting that for at least ten minutes when I heard that damn voice.

"Hello?" Manny. I reached for the phone and then realised that it wasn't coming from the phone. A banging sounded.

"Give her a sec." That was Lucy. They were at my door.

"Manny?" I called out.

"Talia," he answered. "Let us in."

I groaned as I climbed out of bed. I noted happily that I was still fully dressed and padded toward the door. I opened it up gently and Manny stormed in followed by a nervous Lucy.

"Morning," she said.

"Morning," I answered.

Manny looked around at my room. It was messier than it usually was. Or maybe messy was the usual now, I thought. "What the hell is going on?" he asked.

I looked at Lucy for clarification.

"There is a photo of you and that South African—"

Manny cut her off. "It looked like you were fucking in the elevator."

"What?" I asked, in disbelief. There was no one around, I thought. And, there was definitely no one in the elevator when we actually were fucking.

"Did you or did you not have sex with this guy in the elevator?" he demanded. The stress on his features, on his posture, was obvious. Even his outfit was haphazardly put together. I felt a little guilty.

"The best they've got is a picture of us making out," I answered.

"That's all it looks like," Lucy assured me.

"It looks really bad is how it looks," Manny said, taking a seat and pointing to the lounge across from him. "Sit."

I did. So did Lucy.

"I never thought I'd have to worry about you like this," Manny started. "Why didn't you say anything?" he asked Lucy.

"I told her she should slow down," Lucy argued.

"Not slowing down. Stopping. Stop the partying. Get your shit together," he looked at me intensely, insistent.

Fuck them. "You are both overreacting wildly."

"Talia—"

I cut him off. "I've had a shitty year."

"We know that," Lucy said, putting a hand on my shoulder. I shook it off.

"I'm not 'off the rails' and I'm not going to stop going out and having fun with my friends. So, you can give up on that. And, if you're going to try and make me, Manny, then I'll follow through on my threat."

Lucy looked at me with disappointment. I told myself I didn't care. "That's how it's going to be?" Manny asked me.

I took a beat and a breath. "I'm allowed to be young and have fun," I said.

"You are. But you also have a responsibility to your fans and your friends and your family and to me." He was right about that. I just didn't agree that my partying was in any way hindering that.

"I understand," I answered.

"I have a flight," Manny said, standing up and moving to the door. "I'll speak to you later."

He closed the door behind him. Lucy started moving toward it. "You've got to know that was an overreaction?" I asked her.

"You should shower," Lucy said and walked out the door.

Three months later and back home in LA, Lucy wasn't talking to me, Saffy had stopped calling, and even Teddy wasn't getting back to me though I knew he was back in LA. He had been promoting his album. I put it on all my social media as well, to do my part. Adam and his gay best friend, Sean, had become my party people. I had gotten into the habit of going out and getting drunk and dancing like no one was watching and I didn't feel like giving it up.

We had always gone to Poppy's. I'd become friends with the manager and the security guards, but Sean had a boy he wanted to meet at Ventura Lane, a very new bar that had opened up on Sunset Strip.

We pre drank at my house and the boys dressed me up in a little red dress that I'd been gifted by Ayperi and hadn't been brave enough to wear. The sheer material was very see-through, but since my talk with Manny I'd stopped with the room service and all the dancing had me thinner than ever. Adam called to let them know we were coming and secured one of their booths and bottle service.

We made our way there and got straight onto the dance floor. Sean had found his friend and Adam had started grinding on a girl, so I found myself dancing alone. I didn't care. The pre-drinks had gotten me tipsy and the music was perfect. A very handsome blonde boy with tattoos covering his whole body, including part of his face, tried to dance with me. I thanked him but insisted I wanted to dance on my own. Another boy, a pretty model type tried next and I decided to head back to the booth. I found myself alone, drinking vodka rocks and looking around the club. Movement in the corner of my eye brought my attention to a man, standing at his own booth. He was familiar. He moved past his friends and came toward me. Finally, a red light hit him. Laurie.

"Hey," he said, as he reached my table. My body tensed as he pulled me in for a hug and a kiss on the cheek. "What are you doing here?"

"Same as you, I guess."

He took a seat beside me. "You all alone?" he asked.

I shook my head and pointed to the dance floor. "The guys I'm with are dancing."

"That's not right. You've gotta come sit with us." I was shaking my head, but he pulled me out of booth and over to his. I recognised Jeremy, his assistant, and Rhys, from New York. There were two others I recognised - actors. "You know these two. And, this is Pierce and Davey. Boys, this is Talia."

"Nice to meet you," Pierce said, shaking my hand.

"Talia," Davey stood up because he was so close and kissed my cheek. Laurie pulled me to sit beside him. Sitting so close to him, his scent enveloped me.

"How was your tour?" he asked.

"Amazing," I answered. "Did you come?"

He hid his head for a second. "I did."

"Which one?" I asked. "London."

"Visiting family?" I asked. He nodded. "How's Rooney?"

"She's good. She loves you, you know?" I smiled. "My whole family does."

"That's nice," I answered. "My family does not like you."

I laughed, but he didn't. "I don't blame them."

I shook my head. "It's okay, Laurie." I gently tapped his cheek. "Have another." I picked up his glass and stole somebody else's from the table.

"Here's to Laurie. For being my favourite broken heart." His friends laughed a little and Laurie grabbed his chest in faux pain. We downed our drinks.

"Okay. Let's dance. Come on."

I pulled him up to his feet by his rough hands and lead him to the dance floor. Bad idea. Bad idea. Bad idea. The words seemed to pulse with each step and the music. We started to dance, and they drifted away.

We danced endlessly, as I knew too well how to do. He was getting sweaty. I realised I was, too. My hands were on his neck, my back to his chest, as we ground against each other, getting really dirty with the music.

The music and the darkness and the alcohol and the heat between us and the feel of his slick skin. There was a pulsing in my core. I knew what I wanted. What I'd wanted ever since I'd had it. And, I could tell he wanted me, too. There was no voice to say no. No one to stop us. I whispered in his ear. "Your place." He was breathing heavily. He nodded.

We rushed from the club - not saying any goodbyes - and into the closest taxi. Laurie gave his address and we took off. He reached for me, pulling me gently on top of him. It wasn't that long ago that I was making out with Jasper in the back of a taxi, I thought. But it was nothing like this. There was no awkwardness, no bumbling, only rightness and need. His arms wrapped around me and squeezed as I kissed him deeply, lapping at his tongue and running my hands through his hair, grown enough to hold onto. He smelt so good. So familiar underneath the alcohol and the sweat. I licked and bit at his ear and he bucked a little against me. Hard and ready.

He didn't have cash. I gave the driver a $100 dollar bill and Laurie and I ran to the top of his driveway. He had me against the door, pressing into me as I unbuttoned his shirt and he unlocked the door.

We weren't getting up the stairs to his bedroom. He carried me into the kitchen, moving to the stairs to go down into the living room but we only made it to the kitchen island. We tore at each other. His shirt was damp with sweat, it pulled off too slowly. I heard my dress rip as he yanked it up over my head, catching on my earring. I ripped it off, feeling my earring yank out, too. He lifted me up onto the table and pulled at my stockings. Why the hell had I worn stockings? He only got one of my legs out.

He rubbed me hard at my core and then dipped his fingers into my underwear. I arched into him, throwing my head back a little and almost losing balance. He held onto me. He rubbed his fingers against me. "Take them off," I whispered. He pulled them quickly off.

I rubbed and grabbed at his hard cock beneath his pants. He worked his belt off and brought them down. He tried to line us up, but it wasn't right.

"Move back," He demanded. I clawed my way back a little and he climbed up on top of me. I felt him pressed against me. I shifted so he fit me perfectly. I looked into his eyes and he looked into mine and then he thrusted in. I closed my eyes as I felt all the pleasure of that first moment go through me. I felt him stretching me out, filling me so well.

Laurie moved again, and I moved with him. We both grabbed the marble edge of the kitchen counter at the same moment to keep ourselves steady.

He kept going, moving in and out of me. The pleasure was steadily building, driving me crazier and crazier. Our slick bodies rubbed against each other. The cold tile was a relief as my skin overheated. He grabbed at my thigh, then at my ass cheek, putting us at an angle that made me want to scream. I reached out to my left and felt a pole. I grabbed onto it a little too hard. The tap started filling up the sink.

"Shit."

I turned it off. Laurie stopped and looked. Then started laughing. I laughed too until he moved just a little again and I couldn't think about it.

I grabbed onto his head, clutching at locks of his hair as he fucked me. I let go of everything as I came. He stayed on top of me, his weight comforting, as we caught our breath.

Finally, just as I was ready to fall asleep on the hard surface, he shifted off me. He lifted me off the bench top and carried me up the stairs to his bedroom. He'd carried me the same way after our car accident, I thought. His house, his bedroom, hadn't changed at all. He lay me in bed and pulled the covers over me. He turned the light out and got in beside me, spooning me tightly and falling quickly to sleep.

The orgasm had started to sober me up. I remembered those two words that had sounded in my mind hours earlier. I felt the beat of his heart on my back and remembered how my heart was broken by him. Brutally. Carelessly. I couldn't sleep beside him. I couldn't wake wrapped up in him.

I ordered an Uber, not wanting to bother Leif so late, and slid out from under the covers. I pulled off the stocking still left on my leg and pulled up my discarded underwear. He woke up. I wished he hadn't. "What are you doing?" he asked.

"I have to go," I insisted, grabbing one of his t-shirts from the floor. He got up and followed me from his bedroom.

"Talia, don't!" I rushed down the stairs and nearly slipped, feeling myself not completely sober yet.

"I'm fine," I insisted as I threw the shirt on. I didn't have my shoes.

"I'll drive you home," Laurie argued.

"You're drunk," I reminded him.

"So are you. Just stay the night."

"No." I couldn't say any more. I shut the door behind me to stop him from following me out onto his driveway. My Uber driver was there, waiting at the gates. I waved and rushed toward him, pulling at the bottom of Laurie's dirty t-shirt.

I counted my lucky stars that my driver was a much older man with a thick Russian accent. He didn't seem to recognise me. Laurie called but I ignored it. Before I even realised it, I was home and in my bed, warm and slipping into sleep.

I woke up, not to a sound, but just with the sense that I wasn't alone in the room. My eyes strained against the dark to make out a figure standing at my door. "Leif?" I asked. The figure was tall, but thin. Not Leif. My heart started beating.

The figure moved to the end of my bed. "What do you want?" I asked.

I could hear his breathing then. Heavy and muffled.

I was so scared. I wanted to believe it was all a dream. I wanted to scream. I reached over to the light switch at the side of my bed and flicked it on.

I screamed then, not a squeal but a small, fearful shout. The strange man smiled at me. "Hello," he said, his voice sickly high but quiet at the same time. His clothes were ragged and dirty. He had something in his hand.

"What do you want?" I asked again, my voice shakier.

"You," he said, plain and simple

I remembered him. Grey hair. Long beard. Ice blue eyes. He was in Las Vegas on my road trip with Laurie. The man who grabbed me in the casino. He had a small thin gun in his grip. He raised it then. The barrel was pointed right at me.

ELEVEN

"Please put the gun down," I pleaded.

"I'm not going to do that," he said. "I just want to talk to you."

"Okay. I'll talk to you. Just put the gun down first, okay? Please?" He shook his head minutely.

My phone was on my bed. I'd carried it with me, from Laurie's, in the Uber, into the house, into my bed. I moved my thighs a little to feel around for it. "I'm going to sit up," I said, wary of surprising him.

I started sitting up, trying to hide my search for my phone. I found it. I moved it beneath my fingers and toward me. "Okay. What do you want to talk about?"

"I want to talk about me and you," he started. I swallowed. I pressed my thumb to the home button and prayed it was on silent and there would be no unlocking tone. "I think you and I should be together."

Okay so he was obviously mentally unstable. Not just a stalker but delusional as well. I needed to call someone. But I couldn't see what I was doing on the phone. I tried to remember where to touch to get to the last calls section. I thought of the phone screen in my mind. "Talia." The man took a step forward, the gun shook a little.

"Yes. Okay. Why do you think that?" I asked. It was the far left, I thought, at the very bottom of the screen. I touched it. But, I couldn't see, I didn't know if it was working. I had to look.

"The way you look. And, the way you sing. The first time I saw you…" he kept on going. I couldn't keep paying attention. I lifted my legs, as if I were going to cross them. "Look at your house," he said, and turned around to look out my balcony window, down to my pool.

I took the opportunity to look. I was in missed calls. There was Laurie's name. I pressed it. I looked back up at the man, just as he turned around. I spoke loudly, silently praying Laurie would answer. "I have to tell you, I have security. And, they will probably be here any second. I'm sure you tripped the alarm."

"No," he answered calmly. "Your big Hawaiian security guard left at four. And, you don't have an alarm."

"How do you know that?" I asked.

"Because I've been inside before." I got chills. Had I been home? What did he do here?

"He comes back in the mornings," I said, not sure what time it was but it had to be after 5pm.

"You'll be dead by then." He started walking around the bed, toward the side I had moved toward.

"Please don't kill me," I pleaded. "I don't want to die."

"But, you don't love me," he said, a sadness creeping into his tone.

"Maybe I could," I answered, my voice changing a little as I started to cry.

"You couldn't. No one could love me." He was there in front of me then.

"That's not true," I answered. "You just need to speak to someone. Let me help you."

"Help me with what? You're the one that needs help," he pressed the barrel of the gun at my head. I closed my eyes, the tears falling down my cheeks. It seemed to prompt him to move his gun there, right where my tears had made a path for themselves.

"Why are you crying?" he asked.

"Because I'm scared," I answered.

"Don't be scared. I'm going to go with you." He brought the gun up to his head. Is he going to kill himself? Me first and then him?

"You don't need to do that. You don't need to do anything. I know you're hurting. Let me help you. I'll help you get a house like this one. Whatever you need."

He was shaking his head, he was bringing the gun back to my face. I couldn't let him do it. I was too young. I'd been through one near death experience. I wasn't doing it again, I told myself. I had to figure out a way to get out.

"Why don't we have something to eat," I asked. "A final meal."

He seemed to consider it but then shook his head. "Can I write a letter? To my family? To the public?"

He shook his head. "No. This happens now." His finger moved toward the trigger, but I moved faster. I hit the gun out of his surprised hands. I reached for it, but he kicked it away. I got out of the bed, reaching to get the gun but he tackled me to the ground. I screamed a little as my knee collided with the floor. The gun was within the reach of both of us. I couldn't let him get it first. I kicked wildly at him, getting his arms, but he got the gun. I kicked again and connected with his face. He cried out. I climbed to my feet and ran. I heard him get up behind me and follow.

I ran down the stairs and to the door. It took me too long to get it open. He was at the railing, his gun pointed at me. I hurried to undo the dead bolt. He aimed and fired just as I had the door open, as I was flying through it. I cried out again as I felt a bullet hit my arm. The spot felt on fire, a heavy scalding pain, but I couldn't stop running. The adrenaline kept me going. I couldn't look back. I prayed he wasn't following. That the next bullet wasn't going to end up in my back.

I got to the gate. It was open. As I moved through it, I remembered coming home. I remembered pulling it closed behind me. But not completely. Not so it locked. I had let him in.

I kept running. I screamed for help. My foot landed on a loose rock and I let out a yelp of pain, but I kept running. I saw a white car turn up my street. It sped towards me as I waved my hands and yelled for it to stop.

It stopped a few metres in front of me. I ran toward the driver's side. The car door opened. "Talia!"

It was Laurie. I ran into his arms, crying. I couldn't look back. I closed my eyes tightly. "Where is he?" he asked.

I couldn't turn around. I think he knew. He kissed my forehead and shushed me. "He's not behind you. You're okay." He touched my arm. "Oh my god."

The ambulance sounded in the distance. Another siren joined it. I could hear people coming out of their houses. I could feel their gaze on us. I couldn't stop crying. I felt my body shaking. Laurie just held me tighter, running his fingers through my hair, brushing it down, shushing me and calming me. I realised he wasn't wearing a shirt. Just his grey tracksuit bottoms.

The police arrived and the ambulance. Laurie walked me to the ambulance and told the EMTs that I was bleeding. The police were asking him questions. He sent them to my house. The EMTs sat me down on the gurney in the back of the ambulance and threw a blanket over my shoulders. My bare legs were freezing. I watched as the EMTs lifted the sleeve of Laurie's t-shirt to reveal the wound. Laurie sat beside me and squeezed my hand. I let out a yelp of pain as they washed some of the blood away. Laurie squeezed tighter. "Was she shot?" he asked.

"Just a graze," they answered. He let out a breath. I couldn't feel the relief. Only the searing pain.

"Sir?" A police officer approached the ambulance.

Laurie looked at me. "I'm just going to talk to him for a second. I'll be right back." I nodded.

He jumped out and spoke to the officer. The officer wrote down notes. Laurie was showing his phone. I had left mine back in the house. A police car came toward the ambulance from the direction of my house. Laurie watched it go by. I saw his expression become murderous. Was that the man in the car? I wondered. I had wondered what would happen when they found him inside. If he'd be waiting for them, gun at the ready. Or if he'd killed himself first. He would be alive, then. I didn't know how to feel about that.

Laurie looked back at me. I focused on the EMT cleaning my wound. "You're not going to need stitches. We'll just wrap it up nicely for you. Then we'll get you to the hospital."

"Why the hospital?" I asked. It wasn't my favourite place.

"It's just a precaution. You could be suffering from shock."

"I'm fine," I insisted. Laurie climbed back into the ambulance.

"What's going on?" he asked.

She answered me. "You can sign a waiver—"

I cut her off. "I'll do that."

"Wait, a waiver for what?" Laurie interjected.

"I'm not going to the hospital. I'm fine," I insisted.

"I'm sure you are. It's just procedure," the EMT repeated.

"Talia, I think you should go," Laurie agreed.

"No. I just want to go to sleep," I said. "Can I come to your house?"

Laurie thought for a second, deciding whether or not to insist on the hospital and then nodded. He wrapped an arm around me. The EMT found the forms and had me sign them.

The police wanted to talk to me next. A tall officer with dark kind eyes opened his car door for me to sit in as he asked some questions. I gave all my answers, all the details I knew. And, then I asked my questions.

"What happened to him?"

"They found him in your bed. He didn't give them any trouble, I'm told. Went quietly."

"What *will* happen to him?" I asked.

"It really depends on his criminal history. You'll be kept informed. You may need to provide testimony." I swallowed. Laurie was still beside me. "You too, sir."

He nodded. "Can we go now? She needs to rest."

The officer agreed, and Laurie walked me back to the car. It was a white tesla roadster. A new car, I thought. Laurie turned on the heater right away and directed it to me. I realised how cold he must've been, in only his track pants. I turned it back to him. We didn't speak as he drove.

We arrived back at his house. I realised it had been only hours since I left. As we walked to the door, I said, "If I had just stayed here…"

"Don't think about it," Laurie said, pulling me inside. He led me up the stairs and to the bedroom. My shoes and dress were still on his floor, just where I left them. He helped me into bed, taking care of my arm. "Does it hurt?" he asked.

I nodded, it did. But my fatigue was stronger. "Are you hungry?" he asked.

"No, thank you," I answered. Laurie climbed into bed on the other side. He looked at me and I snuggled into him, needing someone, him, to hold. He was cool, but he quickly warmed up. He smelled clean and like him, as if he'd showered after I left. I breathed it in. I tried to sleep. My body was screaming for it. But I couldn't. I could barely keep my eyes closed.

Laurie didn't sleep either. I could feel his uneven breathing, the little movements of his body.

When the sun came through the window, Laurie got up to use the bathroom. When he came back he asked if I wanted breakfast. I nodded and he left to make it.

Whether it was the empty bed, the sun streaming in, warming me, or just having waited so long, I quickly fell asleep.

I woke up an hour or so later with Laurie sitting up beside me. He had breakfast on his bedside table. Coffee, toast, yoghurt and some berries. "Hungry?" he asked when I looked at him. I nodded and sat up, feeling my arm still aching. I couldn't help but think of the last time he fed me in a bed. On the island. I thought he was thinking of it, too, as he handed the tray to me. I started eating, feeling my stomach rumble, from hunger and from the previous night's alcohol.

"How do you feel?" he asked, as I drank the coffee. "How's your arm?"

"It hurts," I answered. "I'll be fine."

"I can't stop thinking about. I was so happy you called and then what I heard... I've never been so fucking scared. I came as quick as I could. You know that, right? The second I heard his voice I was up."

"I know," I said, looking at the guilt on his face.

"When I saw you running down the street. Your face." He stopped and shook his head. "I wish I never let you leave."

"Don't think about it," I said, using his own words from the night before.

He gave me a short smile. "What are you going to do?" he asked.

"What do you mean?"

"With your house?" he asked.

I thought for a second. He had been in there before, walking around, doing god knows what. He was in my bed. I needed a new bed. And, new sheets. And, a new house. Or maybe that was too extreme. "I need to call Manny." Laurie grabbed his cell from his bedside table. I didn't know the number. It had already been programmed in my phone. "Do you have his number?" I asked.

"Um." Laurie took the phone back and searched his contacts. "I don't but my manager will."

Laurie shot away a text and the number came back in minutes. I dialled, and Manny picked up before it even rang once. "Are you okay?" he asked, fear in his voice. "Where are you? Are you at Laurie's?"

"I'm okay," I answered. "I'm at Laurie's."

"You didn't call me. I've been so worried. We all are."

Leif was in the background yelling, "let me talk to her".

"Tell Leif I'm okay," I said. Manny repeated it.

"We're at your house. Leif's been through it. Doesn't look like anything has been taken or messed with. I've brought the cleaners through. No more blood."

How much blood was there? I hadn't even thought of that. He'd gotten me at the door. It was probably on the porch and driveway. Maybe it was on the street, too.

"We've put in an advanced alarm system as well," he added.

"That's good," I said. "Thank you."

That made me feel like I could eventually go home. If Leif was there, too. Leif who had become like family. I could go home.

"Leif is staying there?" I asked.

"He'll be here all day and night until we find a night security guard. We'll have overnight security until we can get you into a gated community."

"What?" I asked.

"A secure gated community. We'll buy you a place there as soon as we find something suitable." Usually him talking like that, like he was making all the decisions, would have drove me insane. At that moment all I felt was gratitude. It felt like concern. Even fear, for me.

"I don't have my phone," I said, though I knew he probably knew. "Have my parents called?"

"They have. We told them you were at Laurie's. The police said he was the one who called."

"Yeah," I answered, looking over to him. He was sitting patiently, looking forward.

"I'll be home soon." He said it would be all set and then hung up.

"You're going home?" Laurie asked, as I handed back his phone.

"I'll need to go back eventually."

"Not really," Laurie said. "You could just sell it."

"It's not that dramatic," I said.

He laughed a little. "It's pretty fucking dramatic."

"I'm okay. These things happen a lot. I'm going to have overnight security from now on."

"Talia, you were shot," Laurie said, putting a hand on my thigh and looking at my bandaged arm. The blood had dyed the bandage brown.

"Grazed," I answered. "I just need to get on with it now."

"It happened a few hours ago. Let yourself recover." I was getting up, picking up my dress and my shoes.

"Can I borrow a bag?" Laurie got up and looked through his closet. He handed me a backpack and a pair of black track pants. I had to roll them around the waist a few times to get them to fit.

"I don't have any shoes that will fit you," he said, resigned to my leaving.

"That's okay." I put my things into the backpack. "Will you drive me home?"

"Yeah. Of course," he said, throwing a shirt on and following me down the stairs.

He drove me to the house. The paparazzi were swarming the gates. "I knew this would happen," Laurie said, stopping the car a fair way back. "Let's just go back home."

"This is my home," I reminded him. I texted Manny to open the gate. Leif came down the driveway. "Go on," I said to Laurie.

He crept forward and the paparazzi pounced. My heart started beating as the lights started flashing and the people started yelling. "Did he hurt you? Were you frightened? Did Laurie save you?"

Leif kept everyone back as Laurie drove up my driveway. He unbuckled his seat belt, but I put a hand on his to stop him. "Don't get out. You'll just give them a better picture."

"You don't want..." Laurie started and stopped.

"I'll talk to you later," I said and stepped out. I crouched back down to look at him. "Thank you."

He smiled at me. "I'm glad you're okay."

I waved then turned and walked to the front door. Laurie waited a moment before he started backing down the driveway and Leif helped him out. I walked through the door and was wrapped in a hug from Lucy followed by another from Manny. We didn't often hug but I squeezed him tightly. "I'm okay," I assured them both before they asked me.

Leif came up behind me and laid a hand on my shoulder. I turned around and opened my arms to him. He lifted me up a little, squeezing me tighter than anyone. "I should've been here," he said.

"No," I answered. "It's no one's fault but his." They all knew which his.

Manny gave me my phone and I dialled my parents. They were both in hysterics. My mom had already booked flights. I told them I was fine, but they were insistent. And, I realised I'd appreciate their visit.

Laurie called that night. I wasn't busy, just watching Netflix with Leif and Lucy, a good distraction, but I ignored it. I sent a text saying I was okay but busy, and I'd call him later. I didn't know how to tell him I was fine, that he didn't have to keep up any kind of charade of caring for me.

My parents came for a week. We spent the whole time in the house, watching movies and having barbeques and reminiscing about my youth and theirs. We didn't leave the house while the paparazzi were swarming. Leif was there during the day and a new guard, an ex-marine named Howie, was there during the night. I was sleeping fine, despite the lingering pain in my arm. Laurie kept calling, but I told him my parents were around and I'd call when they were gone.

Finally, I did. He deserved at least a call back. The conversation led to an invitation for dinner. As a thank you. I didn't cook. Just ordered some Lebanese food to be delivered. All was civil until he suggested I go and see someone and talk about what happened.

"I don't need therapy, I need alcohol. And my friends around me. I have Leif. I'm going to be fine."

"It was just a suggestion," he said. "But you can talk to me, too."

"Can I?" I asked.

"Of course," he said, furrowing his eyebrows, confused about why I would even ask.

This talking, this contact, the sex, it was too much. I wanted it to much. Still wanted him so much. And, I couldn't just be his friend. No matter the benefits. But…

I didn't want to ask it. I was sure I knew the answer. Sure, I knew him. But the part of me that would always love him had to ask. My voice was small. I hated that voice. "Do you mean… Are you saying that you and I can maybe be something again?"

He smiled but it became twisted. "I don't know." He knew, I thought. He knew what he wanted and what he didn't. I wanted to slap myself.

"Why then? Why do you keep calling me? Why did you sleep with me?" Why won't you let me get over you? I thought, trying to stay calm.

He searched for an answer. He shrugged but it looked painful. "I just miss you." That's just not good enough, I thought. It's selfish. "And, then everything that happened. I want to be in your life." He reached out for me. I moved my hand. No crying. Just anger, I thought. Just be angry.

"Well, you can't. You need to move on. And, let me move on." I just couldn't be that person. He wasn't just an ex-boyfriend to me. My body, my mind, my soul, was all in on him. I could never get over him like this.

Laurie took a sip of his beer. "I thought you had. Many times." Here came his anger, I thought. What right did he have to it? He was talking about Jack and Jasper. And, maybe the other boys I was rumoured to have dated.

"Then you know even less than I thought you did."

"Talia…" Laurie must have realised the mistake he made.

"I need you to leave, Laurie. And, stop calling. Because I'm not going to answer any more. Ever." I stood up, collected a few things from the table and walked inside.

Laurie gathered some things himself and took them inside. He followed me to the kitchen. He set them down. "I can clean this up," I insisted.

"If you change your mind…" he started. If I wanted to just be friends?

"If you change yours…" I countered. "It's gonna be too late."

Laurie nodded. He grabbed his phone and keys from the dining table and walked away. I watched him go, feeling some string attached deep in my chest stretching as the distance between us grew bigger and bigger. I thought it would snap. Maybe I hoped it would snap. But it didn't. It just hurt. A dull, lingering, forever kind of hurt. And, I wasn't surprised. I remembered this part. I had grown used to it. I'd grow used to it again.

TWELVE

Manny's assistant had emailed me a bunch of for sale houses in gated communities. There were plenty of lovely places, great big modern houses though they all looked a little similar. I had taken tours of a few of them, but I wasn't taken by any of them.

Sean and Adam had forced me to start going out again. They told me dancing would help me forget. But it was the drinking that seemed to help, and the dancing was just a consequence of that.

Howie went with us. He wasn't much of a talker or a dancer so he would stand menacingly in a corner watching.

One early morning, as he was taking us home, we went to In and Out. Laurie was there, in his car, in the drive-through, a friend I didn't recognise in the seat beside him. I didn't bring Sean or Adam's attention to him. Just sat quietly, hoping he didn't recognise my SUV. He didn't.

Adelaide Mills invited me to a dinner party and who should be there but Jack. He ignored me until I couldn't stand the awkwardness and walked straight up to him. He said, "how's it going?" with a snarl and then kept talking to his friend. No mention of what had happened to me. No questioning if I was alright. He'd surely heard. He probably also heard that Laurie was there. He was still angry at the way things had ended. All through the dinner he gave me death stares across the turkey. As soon as I finished eating I made an excuse that I had a headache and left.

All of that was to say that Los Angeles was starting to seem small. And, it wasn't because of the stalker, who'd been sentenced to four months in jail without Laurie or I having to testify but was quickly released on good behaviour and because the Los Angeles' jails were so jam-packed with prisoners. I needed a change. I missed James and his boyfriend, Fisher. I'd skipped out on a photoshoot for Vogue, but they still wanted me in New York to do a cover. And, Ayperi had an accessories team who wanted me to collaborate with them on a line, though I assured them I had no idea how to do such a thing.

I'd loved New York every time I went. Though there were still places that would remind me of Laurie, not that that was why I wanted to leave LA, but there were less of them in New York than in Los Angeles.

I asked Manny's assistant, Billy, to look at places in New York. Manny must've been with him that very moment because his call came straight away.

"I think New York is a great idea," he said. And, I was pleasantly surprised. He'd been so disapproving of so many things lately.

"I'm shocked."

"Why should you be shocked? I think seeing James would be great for an upcoming album. I know you've been having trouble writing." That's why he approves, I thought. Not for my sake but for a new album's sake.

After that call, I flew straight there. I had a dozen inspections in several days and secured a place within a week. My apartment, in one of the highest levels of a building in Chelsea, was newly built, and just over $10 million dollars. It thrilled and horrified me that I had that kind of money to spend, but New York City real estate demanded it. I knew I wanted a very secure building, with space for my friends and family. And, I had been spoiled by my pool, so I had to find one of those, too, though this one was inside and underneath a giant sky light. It had an expansive New York skyline view and came fully furnished and decorated by a prominent Dutch interior decorator and kitted out with all the kitchen, bathroom, and cleaning necessities. I wasn't renting out the LA place, so I only packed a few clothes and toiletries.

Sean and Adam were very disappointed to see me go and Lucy and Teddy were bothered by it, too, though both assured me they'd come visit. Leif and his girlfriend had split up in the months before, so he was actually excited to move with me. We were both getting fresh starts.

Since Howie had never warmed up to me, and maybe never warmed up to anyone, Leif had one of his cousins, Kevin, come over from Hawaii to do the night shift. I set them up with a two bedroom apartment in the same building.

On the first night I had a house warming party with James and Fisher and some other of their friends, Ayperi and her girlfriend, as well as Leif, Kevin, Sofie, my music video director, and some of her friends in the city. We had a classic Aussie barbeque with steak and sausages and ate out on the balcony looking out at the New York City lights. I could write here, I thought, hoping the inspiration would finally come.

One of the rooms of the house was a home office. I'd gone out and plundered a music store to get a few guitars, a set of drums, and piano, which filled up the space quickly. On my second day in the apartment I sat in that room for two hours willing some inspiration to arrive in my fingertips or my lungs. There was nothing. So, I left the room, closing the door behind me.

I asked Fisher and James to go out dancing and they were all too happy. Kevin proved himself to be a much more willing dancer than Howie, and both James and Fisher started to fall a little bit in love with the hulking Hawaiian.

My Vogue shoot was not just a cover but a ten page spread that would include two models and half a dozen locations spread across the city. I met the models in the makeup trailer on day one.

"Talia, this is Romina Ross," the production assistant pointed to the very tall, very thin, very pretty woman already seated. She had a short black bob and deep chocolate coloured eyes. "And, Christian Garcia," she gestured to the boy beside Romina. He looked like a young Spanish Brad Pitt.

"Nice to meet you both," I said with a small wave.

"You, too, babe," Romina said, looking me up and down.

I sat down and Christian kissed me on the cheek with his full lips. "Nice to meet you," he said, with a Spanish accent.

They got started on my hair. "I love your music, by the way," she said. I thanked her. "Especially that one song... *'I will never love a boy like you...'*" She was singing my lyrics.

"No, I like the one, *'Hit me like a red light...'*" Now Christian was singing and then the woman doing Romina's makeup began singing.

I laughed but my face grew red. "Okay, we're embarrassing her," Romina said, and the singing ceased. "How long are you in town for?"

"I've actually just moved here permanently," I answered. "Needed a change."

"That's so exciting," she said, spinning around. "Where are you living?"

"Chelsea," I answered.

"Oh my god, I'm in Chelsea, too," she explained. "I'll have to show you around. I know all the best places to eat and to go out."

"Sounds good," I answered.

"We'll start tonight," Romina continued. "You in, Christian?"

"Drinks?" he clarified. "Definitely."

The first day's shoot was on the roof top of an apartment building, very industrial, with all of us dressed in bright contrasting colours. It lasted as long as the sun did. Then Romy, as she demanded we call her, took us to a basement bar in Chelsea playing low slow R&B music. I texted Kevin where we were as we arrived.

"Shots!" she called as soon as we had ourselves a booth. Christian took off to the bar.

"You did really well today," Romy started. "You're a natural model."

"I wouldn't go that far," I answered. I still felt really uncomfortable in front of a camera. Especially without a guitar or a microphone in my hands. But she didn't seem to mind it at all. She was all confidence, so relaxed and assured.

"Is music what you've always wanted to do?" she asked me.

"Yeah, that's about it," I answered.

"I never wanted to model. I wanted to be a dancer for the longest time."

"Ballet?" I guessed.

"Exotic," she answered.

"What?" I asked, surprised. Did she mean stripping?

"Why not?" she continued. "But, I couldn't live this lifestyle. And, people are so judgey. God, my parents would freak."

Christian came back quickly with a tray full of shots. "We can't drink all of these," I assumed.

"I think we could find some friends to help us." Romy searched the room.

"I could call some friends..." I offered.

"That guy at the bar," Romy said as she sat down. "Do you see him?"

I looked. There were a few guys at the bar. "Which one?"

"Dark hair, blue shirt." I saw him. He was cute.

"You should go for it," I said, with an encouraging elbow.

"Not my type," Romy assured me.

"He's gorgeous! What is your type?" I questioned.

"Female," Romy answered with a quirk of the head.

"Oh," I laughed. "My bad."

"He was looking at you, anyway," she went on.

"Really? I'm not looking for anything--"

"Why not? Bad breakup?" she guessed. "Only one way to get over it."

"If you say by getting under someone else..."

"There is a reason it's a common saying. It's true," she insisted.

"No, thanks," I answered.

"Okay, we'll see if you change your tune after a few of these." Romy picked up two shots and handed them to me. Christian took two for himself and Romy took two for herself.

"To Talia moving to New York," Romy said, clinking her glass with us both before we downed one shot after the other. The shots were all alcohol, nothing sweet or sour or good. I stuck out my tongue and pulled a face.

"Dancing?" Christian asked, holding a hand out for us both. We took his hands and let him lead us onto the dance floor. It was all dirty dancing. I was glad of the two shots otherwise, I would've been too embarrassed to be grinding on these two strangers. Christian was definitely Spanish, I thought, as he confidently danced with both of us, twirling us around, lining us up in front of him and running his hands over our bodies. Romy put her hands on my hips and we ground it out to the dirty beats of the song.

Christian disappeared at some point and it was just Romy and me. My head felt a little fuzzy and the songs were so sexy, I couldn't help but give in to it. Romy loved it. I could see the part of her that wanted to be an exotic dancer. I could see the boys and girls watching her as we danced. Christian brought more shots out to us, another two each. We took them quickly and he disappeared with the glasses. A pretty South American girl had taken Romy's attention and the two started dancing on their own. I was about to leave the dance floor when Christian returned and grabbed onto my back.

A new song came on and he started dancing around me, looking at my body as I danced. It was like we were different people. Two characters. He started lifting up my shirt and running his hands over the skin of my stomach. I leaned back into his chest, I felt the hot skin of his face on my shoulder, his full lips tracing patterns on my neck. We were both sweating, with the alcohol and the dancing.

He started turning me around and I knew he wanted to kiss me. But we had three days of shooting left. Even through the haze, I knew it was a bad idea. I looked up and across the dance floor. I saw Romy and the girl she was dancing with moving through the crowd to what I guessed was the bathroom.

I turned my head and looked up to Christian, his eyes looked hungry. "I'll be right back."

I pushed away from him and through the crowd, following after Romy. It was dark and the crowd pushed back against me, but I finally found the door. Turned out it wasn't the bathroom, it was the emergency exit. It was dark out there, too. Then I made out their figures.

Romy had the girl pressed against the wall. They were making out, slowly. I could see Romy's hand undo her tight jeans and push her hand down, the girl grabbing onto her upper arm and guiding it further. She started moaning, just lightly in between the kisses. I knew I should've gone immediately back inside, but I was a foggy. I kept watching for a few seconds until I felt my phone vibrating in the back pocket of my jeans and I was shaken out of it.

I quickly walked back inside. I took out my phone. 'Teddy'. I knew I wouldn't be able to hear him. I ended the call and sent a text.

Talia: I'm in a club. Call in a bit?

He sent a response straight away.

Teddy: Sure. Have fun

I looked over to where I left Christian and he was making out with another girl. I laughed and started moving toward the exit. I stepped out into the cold and dialled Kevin's number.

I heard it ringing and realised he was standing a few metres from the entrance. He came toward me. "Are you okay?" he asked, looking to see if I was with anyone.

"Yeah," I answered. He led me by the elbow to the car parked on the other side of the street.

"I could've come with you, Talia. If you let me know earlier. Leif said—"

"I'm fine," I insisted. "It was too dark for anyone to recognise me."

"Still," Kevin added as he opened the car door.

"Thank you," I said, closing it behind me.

I called Teddy as Kevin walked around to the driver's side and took off. He quickly answered. "You didn't have to call me back that quick," he started.

"I was heading home anyway," I answered.

"Had a few?" he asked.

"A few," I answered. "How could you tell?"

"You're slurring a little." Was I? I didn't think so.

"What's up?" I asked.

"I just wanted to play you the intro of this song. It's not right…"

"Play it," I said.

"How about I call you back in the morning?" he asked.

"I'm fine, Teddy," I insisted. What is with these people? I thought. I'm not a child. I'm allowed to drink.

"I gotta go. I'll call you back," he said and hung up. I scoffed. Kevin eyed me.

"Do you guys know how old I am?" I asked.

"I think so," Kevin answered.

"Then can you get off my dick?" I asked, surprising myself with the language and the anger I was beginning to feel.

"You got it," Kevin answered. I immediately felt guilty. It wasn't his fault.

"I'm sorry," I said.

"Don't be, Talia. You get a lot of shit. I don't want to add to it," he answered.

I smiled at him. He took us home and got me in the door of my apartment before heading to his.

The shoot continued the next day. We shot in Central Park, out at a Hampton's house, and on a beach in Montauk the days after that. There was no awkwardness with Christian. He was too easy going. Romy asked where I ended up and I told her I went home. She was wildly disappointed.

Romy insisted we go out again the night after and the night

after that and the last night. And all of them were variations of the first but with a little pre-cocaine added in. I refused to partake, but I didn't begrudge them using it. I just asked her not to take it out in public with me around. You never knew who could be taking a photo. Just another reason to get the media and management on my back.

But I did drink. A lot. And danced. The last night, Romy came home with me. Kevin took us to buy pizza and we ended up watching movies in my living room with Leif as well.

"These are your security guards? Tell me you've fucked one or both of them," she said, within hearing distance of them both.

"Romy, no."

She laughed. "I would."

"You're gay," I reminded her.

"But, not blind," she continued. "They're both the Hawaiian versions of Thor."

That perked Leif and Kevin both up. We fell asleep before the movie ended and woke up in my bed. I figured the boys had moved us. Sweet of them.

Romy was starving. I wanted to order breakfast, but she forced me into the shower and then dragged me to brunch at a nearby Italian bistro.

"This is so cute," she said, looking at the dress she borrowed from me. "Why don't you ever wear it?"

"I do," I answered. I'd worn it to the Thanksgiving dinner from hell. The waitress came up to take our order.

"You have to have the Gamberi pasta. It is a taste sensation," Romy insisted after ordering a serve for herself. Pasta for breakfast wasn't what I'd hoped for. But it was the afternoon already.

"Okay," I nodded to the waitress and she took the orders.

"What are your plans this weekend?" I shrugged. "Come to

Singapore. It's my Dad's birthday and my Mom always throws the best parties."

"What?" I laughed.

"Why not?" Romy asked. "On me. Well on them."

"I can pay for myself…" I answered.

"Then what's the problem?"

I wanted to say 'I barely know you' but that seemed rude. It also didn't seem true anymore. I'd spent more time with Romy in the last week than I'd spent with any other friends for a long time. And, I'd flown to Cannes to see John after less time. And, I really didn't have anything to do. Well, besides writing.

"Okay," I said.

"Really? Amazing," she picked up her mimosa for a toast. We clinked and drank.

Two days later I was staring at a private plane. "Romy, I can't fly private."

"Why the hell not?" she asked.

"I don't know if you heard about my accident," I started.

"Oh shit. I forgot about that," she said, looking around as if she could see some other option.

"I already booked it," she said, like it wasn't obvious. I knew I should have bought my own ticket, but she insisted.

"I can just go get a commercial ticket," I shrugged. "Leif, can you grab my bags?"

Romy put a hand out to stop him. "No, come on. You're flying again, right? This is just a smaller version of that. It's safer than driving. We'll get you some booze and some drugs. Knock you out."

"It's fine, I'll just meet you over there," I assured her.

"Come on," she pulled at my arm. "I don't want to fly alone. How depressing."

Somehow, she convinced me to walk those four stairs onto the tiny little plane. My heart was beating something furious.

"Are you sure?" Leif asked me as he took the seat across from me.

"Give me two seconds," Romy insisted.

She poured me a vodka straight from the flight attendant's trolley and took out three bottles of various kinds of pills. She handed me two of each and told me to down them all.

"What is all of that?" Leif asked her.

"Happy night night pills," she answered.

Leif was shaking his head, but I downed them.

Minutes later, as we were taxiing to the runway, I felt myself falling asleep.

"Told you, babe. I'll wake you when we get there."

Leif looked nervous. I smiled at him as I started to doze off.

I was out like a light for twelve hours, but there was still eight more hours of flying. The flight took us back to LA where we refuelled and then we were off to Singapore.

"Are you okay?" I heard Leif's voice first.

"Do you want to double down or are you good?" Romy asked as I started to stir.

"Where are we?" I asked.

"Somewhere over Hawaii," she answered.

"Do you need anything?" Leif asked, pushing a water bottle toward me.

"I'm okay," I answered. I didn't want to talk though. I was still drowsy, but I felt my heart beat faster. I couldn't help but remember all those minutes, the last time I was on a plane like this. I couldn't help but picture Ashley where I was sitting and Kelly across from me. I couldn't help but picture Josie, the flight attendant. I made a mental note to check on her fiancé, to see if he needed anything.

Finally, we arrived. Leif could feel my hands shaking as he helped me down the stairs and into the waiting SUV. It was the middle of the night, but the city was lit up and the streets were lined with restaurants still overflowing with people.

"I have to take you to this place that makes the best duck rice you've ever had," Romy said.

"That'll be easy since I've never had duck rice," I answered.

"You don't know what you're missing. You've got to try Hainanese chicken rice, too. It's a Singaporean specialty."

We were taken to the Fullerton Bay Hotel, a huge Roman style building with columns going all the way round and five big red flags hanging over the entryway. It was lit up with gold lights that were reflected in the bay.

"I thought we were staying with your parents?" I asked Romy as they led us to our rooms.

"No way. They'd annoy the shit out of us," she answered.

"We have you just across from each other," the hotel receptionist said as she opened my door and then Romy's. Our porters took our bags into each of our rooms. Romy followed me into mine.

"I tried to get the presidential suite or even a Governor suite, but they were so heavily booked cause of this weekend," Romy explained.

"This is great," I assured her.

"Thank you," I said, giving a tip to the porter as he handed me my key and Romy hers.

Romy jumped onto my bed. "I hope my view is as good as yours."

The window from my bedroom looked out over the bay and part of the city.

"Food?" Romy asked. I wasn't remotely tired because of my drug induced nap but I was surprised at her energy levels.

"Sure," I agreed.

Romy and Leif and I went to three different restaurants in the early hours of that morning. The first for the Hainanese rice; a poached chicken with a gooey chicken flavoured rice and the second, a street vendor, for a green sponge 'Pandan' cake. Lastly, we found ourselves eating ice cream on deckchairs by the rooftop infinity pool at the Marina Bay Sands. Now, that was a view, I thought. The sun rose in shades of yellow and orange over the city that stretched out flat and quiet. I couldn't help but be grateful for this life that took me to such incredible places. Even if I needed a little chemical help to get there.

Leif was falling asleep on his chair, so we dragged ourselves back to the hotel and passed out.

The next day Romy had us both up at the ungodly hour of 11am to go shopping.

"Why shopping?" I asked. "I don't need anything."

"Of course, you do. You need a dress and shoes for the party, I need dress, shoes, jewels. Leif needs a new suit."

"I'm fine," Leif spoke up.

"You are certainly not fine. They won't let you in. Not in that old grey thing," Romy said, grabbing the lapel of his jacket.

She took us to a huge shopping mall filled with luxury brands and I couldn't help but be swept away with her, buying beautiful things. I knew I could afford it, but I wasn't sure how she could afford it. She bought half a dozen bags at least worth 5k each within the space of ten minutes. We got Leif three new suits, one black, one charcoal, and one navy. And, another three for Kevin.

Leif ended up needing the drivers to help him carry all the shopping bags.

"We need to go," I insisted. "I am starting to hate myself."

"You don't have a dress yet," Romy argued. She's already found a sparkly bright pink floor length gown which I didn't have the heart to admit that I thought was a little over the top.

"I brought dresses," I assured her.

"Oh my god," She was looking behind me. I turned around to see a blue sequin dress hanging in the shop window.

"It's nice," I agreed. "But maybe not for me."

"Not that one." Romy grabbed my hand and pulled me into the store. "This one."

She held up a bronze floor length sheath gown with geometric cut outs all around the bodice.

"That's way too much," I said, as she held it up against me.

"Honey, you have to look good. You can't show up in your average mini. I'm telling you. This is the one. At least, try it on." She shoved me toward the change room and forced the dress into my hands. I didn't bother fighting. I changed into it and stepped out.

"Oh my god, Talia," she said, looking over me. I looked past her to where Leif was standing outside the doors. He noticed me looking and ran his eyes over me. He mouthed the word, 'wow', and then threw up his thumbs.

"Really?" I asked Romy.

"Hell yes," she nodded. I turned back to the mirror and looked at myself. It was something you'd wear to the Grammys. Maybe I should save it for then, I thought, it was only a couple of months away. That's if I was even nominated. "I'm getting it for you."

"I can get it," I insisted, but I wasn't going to wear it to the party, I told myself.

Yet somehow, back at the hotel, as Romy had people doing our hair and makeup, I was somehow convinced to wear it. And, then I was glad I was.

It was not a simple birthday party. This was something else. Like New Year's Eve on crack.

"Are your parents royalty or something?" I asked her.

"Not royal. Just rich."

She explained all about her parents before she introduced me to them. Her father was Malaysian but lived in Singapore. Her mother was British. Both had come from money and together made even more of it. I just hadn't realised how much more. The party was held on a private estate. A house as big if not bigger than Buckingham Palace. There were thousands of people there, hundreds of waiters, dancers, jugglers, fire breathers, all kinds of performers on platforms throughout the house and through the backyard. The backyard was like Versailles. Endless gardens. I couldn't contain my awe. I wanted to explore, but Romy wanted to take advantage of the party, see all the entertainment, drink all the drinks, and of course, dance. She had half a dozen very handsome cousins who seemed very interested in me for some reason. They made wonderful dance partners.

I went to bed thinking that life as Romy's friend was maybe something special. There was no boredom, no tears, all fun all the time. And, it was exactly what I needed.

The next day her parents flew us privately to Macau, the "Asian Vegas" according to Romy. Her Dad was a gambler. She loaded me up with pills again and off we went. I realised this wasn't a great habit to start, but I also didn't imagine myself flying private any more than I absolutely had to.

Macau was a level like no other. I thought I was living the life of the rich and famous. I had no fucking clue. The hotel put us up in suites fit for kings and queens and took us to private gaming rooms where billionaires were spending $20 million a night. It was overwhelming. But god, was it fun.

We drank and danced and gambled. I found a love of Craps, the game where you stand around a long table with a dozen others, rolling the dice and betting on what number it will land on. It seemed to be the only table game where all the players were on the same side. They all talked to each other, cheered each other on. And, the table attendants, four of them at any given time, were hilarious. Like a comedy troupe. Or maybe I was just drunk.

Romy started sleeping in my room because it required less work to have our late night drunken feast and then breakfast together in the morning.

Romy had a lunch with her parents before we flew home, so Leif and I went to see some sights. I was hungover, but I didn't want to just stay in my hotel room in a city I'd never explored. I had Leif take me to St Paul's Church. It was more a façade than an actual church since most of it had long ago been destroyed by a fire. And it had about a million stairs to climb, but it was interesting. There were tonnes of tourists but whether they knew nothing about me or whether the big floppy hat and glasses I wore kept me well-hidden, we were only stopped a few times.

We walked down the stairs slowly as the sun seemed to be heating and worsening my hangover.

"What is going on with you and Romina?"

Leif never usually asked me those questions. I would tell him things, but he was much more aware of professional lines than I was.

"We're friends," I answered.

"You two became very close very quickly."

"She's fun. I need fun," I insisted, nudging Leif's shoulder with my chin.

"I know you do," he nudged me back. I thought he'd keep going but he didn't. I loved that about him. I realised he was worried, and I determined to make some effort to ensure he didn't need to be.

When we got back to New York, I finally got to see Romy's apartment. Her place was huge and had multiple levels. It was decorated to within an inch of its life, by someone else I was sure. She wasn't using her modelling income for this life.

Her closet was larger than my bedroom. It was completely disorganised. No colour coding or sections for pants and shirts. Everything was everywhere.

"Oh my god," she said, pulling out a pair of pants made entirely of sequins. Romy seemed to love anything shiny. "You'd look amazing in these."

She shoved them into my hands and started unbuttoning my pants. I stepped back, moving her hands away. "Really?" I asked. "They're a little… much."

"Try them on!" she moved back to the row and kept searching. "With this!"

I had my jeans off and the sequined pants halfway up when she started unbuttoning my shirt. I let her finish as I pulled the pants up.

I had come to learn that, coke or no coke, Romy had more energy than anyone I knew. And, no patience.

"No. Take that off. Try this." She threw a singlet to me.

"With these jeans?" I asked.

"No! It's a dress."

I scoffed, disbelieving, but changed into the barely there dress. "I am not leaving the house in this," I declared.

"Fine, but at least look at yourself." Romy turned me around to look at myself in her wardrobe mirror. "You look so good. So, fucking sexy."

I wouldn't have said the word, 'good'. I looked kind of trashy. But my body looked good. The dressed hugged my hips perfectly. My long legs looked even longer.

"You need to fix your hair and makeup though. Let me do it," Romy requested, pushing me onto her bed. She grabbed a makeup bag and got to work on me, taking out the bobby pins holding up my loose bun and styling my short caramel locks.

She started with my makeup, too, layering liner and dark shadows around my eyes.

"Oh my god. I am a genius. And, you look out of control." She ran quickly away. I stood up and looked back in the mirror.

Wow, I thought. I looked like a rock star. I looked almost like what the Ashley and Kelly used to do to me before our rock shows.

"Yes!" Romy came back with a camera in hand, pointed at me as I looked at myself in the mirror.

"Don't!" I complained, putting my hand in front of the lens.

"No, let me. Come on. Model for me!" she demanded. She had a way of making me do things I would never normally do. And, loving it. I started posing.

At some point Romy put on some grimy rock music and brought out a bottle of vodka. We started doing shots and I started being braver.

"Lift up your skirt a little," she called out. "Flash me!"

I pulled down my shirt, so quickly I couldn't imagine she could get the shot.

"Dance!" she called as I started moving to the music. I knew the lyrics to all these songs. They were Ashley and Kelly's favourites. I started spinning.

Round and round and round.

I fell back onto the bed and held my head. I was hazy from the shots, but the spinning had made me hazier.

"You have to see," Romy said, turning the camera to me.

I shook off the haze and looked onto the viewfinder with curiosity. I hadn't ever seen myself like that. Heroin chic. Then there were the pictures that made me blush. And, I had been the one doing the posing.

"You have to delete those," I pleaded, turning to look at her.

"You got it, babe," Romy assured me, looking back at me. She looked down at my lips and back to my eyes. She leaned in and pressed her small pouted mouth to mine. She pulled away smiling.

"What was that for?" I asked.

She shook her head and laughed before jumping off the bed and back to her wardrobe. She dropped onto the floor and began digging through her shoes.

"Here," she said, tossing a pair of spiky black boots toward me.

"I told you, I am not wearing this dress," I reminded her.

She rolled her eyes at me and then stood up and kept searching. Soon enough a trench coat was thrown at me. I put it on and did up the buttons before tying the sash tightly around my waist.

Romy finished her look with her own shiny purple coat. She came back to me and grabbed my sleeves, rolling them tightly to above my elbows.

"We're ready!" She called, to Leif, I guessed.

And, then we were out. Romy introduced me to some of her model friends, who loved coke as much as she and dancing as much as me.

Wednesday, Thursday, Friday, Saturday even Sunday, all we did was dinners, drinks, dancing, recover from our hangovers and repeat the cycle. We weren't letting anything stop us from having a good time. Even the paparazzi who seemed to become more and more aggressive. Romy didn't like them at all but didn't blame me. I figured she was followed herself regularly. But she did seem almost protective of me around them. Like a mother bear yelling at them to back off. Though they didn't listen.

The night after a new club opening, I woke up with a tired looking Leif shaking my shoulder and holding his phone out to me. "You weren't answering yours."

I picked mine up off the ground. It was on silent. I had a dozen missed calls and half a dozen texts and more coming.

"Hello?" I asked as I took the phone from Leif and started scrolling through my messages.

Manny had sent me picture after picture from TMZ and Perez Hilton. Pictures of Romy and I looking completely wasted as we left the club and climbed into a taxi, our eyelids half closed, makeup smudged, clothes askew, like Lindsay Lohan in her prime. I was too hungover to feel ashamed.

"Do you need rehab?" he asked.

I scoffed.

"We can spin this much easier right now than we could if you keep going and hit rock bottom. We don't know what that will look like and you might not be able to come back from it."

No, I thought. I'm not going to rehab. And, I'm not taking any more of these fucking calls. I had one thing to say. Simply, "Fuck off." I hung up.

Three days later, Romy and I flew, with a group of friends, to St Barts. We spent the lead up to Christmas laying in the sun, drinking copious amounts, and frolicking in the ocean. We had a Christmas banquet meal right there on the beach with a firework display over dessert.

On New Year's Eve, I floated out into the ocean by myself and watched my friends on the shore, dancing to the music of a Duran

Duran cover band and kissing at the stroke of midnight. I felt alone. I dragged myself back to my hotel room at 12:30am, determined to call my parents and wish them a Happy New Year. And, maybe see if they wanted a visitor within the next few weeks.

I had the phone to my ear and my fingers dialling the buttons when my door knocked. I hadn't turned any of the lights. The moonlight shone through the sheer curtains that brushed my skin as I walked past.

Another knock came as I opened the door. Romy stood there, a long cocktail glass in her hand, nearly empty of Pina Colada. She had a piece of pineapple sticking out of her mouth. "Hi," I said, stepping aside as she moved into the room. "What are you doing here?"

"The girl I thought I'd be fucking tonight went home with someone else."

She lay down on my bed and looked at me sadly. I gave her a pitying look and went to lay beside her.

"What are you doing here all by your lonesome?" she asked before pouring the last of her cocktail down her throat.

"I was tired," I answered.

She set her glass aside and turned over to look at me. "Really?"

I smiled and turned over to face her. "Not really."

"What?" she asked.

I tried to speak but I felt myself start to get upset. I pursed my lips to keep myself from crying.

"Aw..." Romy said as she wrapped her arms around me and brought me close. I let the few tears fall from my eyes. Romy squeezed me and wriggled a little. "Baby."

I laughed a little.

She loosened her arms and I took the space to move a little away. She brushed the fallen wisps of my caramel blonde fringe from my eyes, leaned in and kissed me. It was the second time she had kissed me on my lips. I wouldn't have thought anything of the first kiss, but this one was different. My body tensed and my heart started to beat a little faster. I tried uselessly to calm it. She kissed me again, deeper, opening my mouth and letting her tongue slip in just a little. My tongue rose tó meet her automatically. We kept going, kept kissing. I couldn't tell how I felt about it. I felt her hands roam down my back and grab onto my waist. Her fingers lightly travelled down my stomach and then climbed a little to my chest. She touched my breast, just lightly, feeling the shape of me and rubbing her thumbs against my nipple.

As her tongue probed deeper, her hand ran down my stomach again, lower and lower, until she was touching where I realised I had started pulsing.

I broke away from her kiss. My breath had grown heavy.

"What are you doing?" I asked, searching her eyes. She was smiling, still looking at my lips, her own breathing heavy.

"Trying to make you feel good," she said. She kissed me again. Her hand kept moving.

It did feel good. Maybe not right. But good. And, I didn't want it to stop.

THIRTEEN

I was lying awake questioning everything as Romy woke up beside me. She took one look at my face and groaned.

"What?" she asked, laying back down, resting her on her arm.

"Last night," I started.

"Obviously. What about it?" she questioned.

I tried to find the words. "I don't know…"

Romy shook her head a little. "Don't be so serious, Talia. Did you like it?"

I swallowed. I had to be honest. "Yeah."

Romy smiled. "Then that's it. It doesn't have to be a big identity crisis. We're friends." Romy leaned in and pressed a kiss to my lips. I wanted to argue that getting licked out was never a part of my other friendships. But was I being too serious? She was so casual about everything, I shouldn't have been surprised that she would be casual about this. Why couldn't I be the same, I thought.

We ordered from our favourite breakfast place, bacon and eggs and avocado toast, and spent the day watching funny YouTube videos.

That night, she wanted to go out again. And why not? I thought. It was becoming my mantra. She slipped a tablet between my lips in the Uber ride over and I didn't even think to argue. The dance floor was cramped and sweaty, but we forced our way through the bodies.

A strobe was the only form of light, I could only see every second moment.

Next thing I knew I was lying in a bed, grabbing the headboard, my body undulating as Romy ravaged me, her head between my thighs. She gripped my legs, holding me steady as she lapped at me with her tongue, nibbling on my clit, driving me closer to my orgasm.

I groaned with the ache she broke away. She moved herself up, bringing her leg over mine and joining us in a scissor.

I felt the slick wetness of her move over me, my head was fuzzy with the pleasure. My body moved on its own, friction, friction, friction, was all I could think or want.

Then just as quickly, she was gently pushing me down her body, bringing my face to her sopping cunt and I couldn't help but bring my lips there to taste her. I lapped at her the way she'd lapped at me, I brought my fingers to join my lips and brought her to the precipice of her own orgasm before she pulled me back up her body and joined us again at our cores.

There was something like torture in this driving to the edge just to pull back, over and over, our orgasms would build and then she would tear it away from both of us until finally she let me come and let herself come too. The orgasm ripped through me like something ferocious and we fell off exhausted. We gathered our breath and the sheets and finally fell asleep, dead to the world.

The next night was the same. The drugs made me carefree. They made everything beautiful. The lights, the drinks, her and the people dancing around us. The only thing ugly was the photographers who followed us from the car to the bar and back again. They seemed to be getting closer and more aggressive. Like a pack of angry dogs.

The next week I wore a pair of Romy's too high heels and fell leaving the club. The photographers swarmed, snapping their pictures, yelling and laughing. I felt someone grabbing me, grabbing my feet so I kicked out. One of the photographers fell back. His camera smashed. I heard Romy laughing into my ear as she helped me up.

The next morning, I seemed to have found the end of Manny's rope.

"I can't do this anymore, Talia. Unless you're going to calm down and maybe get some help, I can't represent you."

"You're quitting?" I asked, disgusted. He never cared about me, I thought.

"What can I do? You don't listen to me. You're destroying your reputation... You're supposed to be a role model to your fans—"

I cut him off, "My sales are increasing. There's no problem."

"It's not about sales—"

"Just hang up," Romy said, listening beside me. I was too hungover to give a shit. I hung up. It all seemed so absurd to me. All his reasons were ridiculous. I was fine.

Katie quit via email. The label sent another agent to talk to me, but I had no interest in listening to another Manny bitch into my ear every morning. I wouldn't let him in the door. Then I got a call from label threatening to kick me off.

I laughed. "I don't owe you anything anymore. Keep me on the label or don't."

Then came the worried calls and emails. Friends and family reaching out asking me if everything was okay. I couldn't keep telling people I was fine. If they didn't believe me, that was their problem.

We went back to LA for the Grammys. I *was* nominated half a dozen times. I didn't want to go but Romy said the after parties were worth it. Walking into that house made me feel sick.

"Where's your drinks trolley?" Romy called.

"Nowhere," I answered. "Might be something in the cupboards."

Romy was already pre-drinking for the coming night. She had plenty of friends in LA, too.

I invited Sean and Adam to come out, too. Strangely, Lucy showed up soon after.

"What are you doing here?" I asked as I hugged her. She eyed me wearily.

"You haven't been returning my calls. Or Teddy's," she answered. "Leif told me you were home."

I looked for Leif, but he wasn't inside.

"I haven't had my phone," I answered.

"The last few months?" she questioned.

"Things have been kind of crazy," I answered.

"So, it seems," she answered, looking past me to where Romy and the boys were doing shots. The sun had barely started to set. I could feel her judging me.

She reached out to touch my shoulder. "I'm worried about you."

"Seriously?" I asked. "If this is what you're here for then feel free to go back the way you came."

Lucy's brows rose as she blew air out of her mouth quickly. "What the hell is going on with you?"

"Nothing," I answered, feeling some guilt. "I'm having fun. That's it. If you want to have a little fun, catch up with your old friend, why don't you come out with us? You can see it's all innocent."

I heard a snort behind me and realised Romy had the coke out. Terrible timing. "Very innocent," Lucy answered.

"Like you've never done coke," I pushed back.

"Babe," Romy called out. She came running into the foyer. "Oh wow. Hi."

Lucy gave a polite smile. "I'm Lucy."

"Romy. Nice to meet you." Romy kissed her cheek. "Are you coming out with us?"

Lucy shook her head. "It's a big day tomorrow." She was nominated, too. I realised I'd never congratulated her.

"I guess we'll see you there," Romy said with a wave.

"I guess so," Lucy nodded and started to walk to the door.

"Congratulations. By the way," I said as she opened it.

Lucy looked back at me, a little sadly, a little like she didn't recognise me. "You, too."

She closed the door and walked away. I heard her phone ring. She answered it with a gruff, "Hey."

Romy pulled me back to the party. "Shots!" Sean yelled as he poured rows and rows of straight vodka. We didn't make it out that night. We barely made it to the Grammys.

The label, who had made the decision to keep me on, probably after the nominations came out, had sent someone to represent me for the night. Mary, as Romy called her, because she thought the woman looked like Jesus' mother, had Leif wake us up at 2pm to get ready.

By the time Romy and I stumbled out of the shower and into the spare bedroom to get ready, it was already 3pm. The hair and makeup artists were sitting down, starring at their phones as if they'd been waiting hours. I didn't tell them to get there at two, I thought.

Ari had sent an assistant to do my fitting in New York, so my dress and shoes and bag were all set. The hair and makeup artists had a million questions which I answered with a, "do what you want."

I slipped my feet into the black strappy sandals and finally looked at myself in the mirror. The dress wasn't the one I bought in Singapore. Ari thought that was a disaster. This one was a deep wine coloured off the shoulder satin mini dress with a deep thigh split on the one side. My hair was straightened and done half up half down with a few loose pieces floating around my face. The caramel had started growing out and I hadn't been back at the hairdresser to redye it. It started to look like balayage. My makeup was a simple eye with red lips to match the dress. I had small diamond studs on the ears, a simple ruby ring and a chunky choker necklace.

"Oh my god," Romy said, looking at me from the make-up chair.

"You like?" I asked. The assistant took photos to send to Ari for approval.

"I love," Romy answered. She eyed me hungrily. I blushed. I hoped the other women didn't notice.

Leif drove us and Mary to the red carpet. We were late so there wasn't so much of a wait. Romy wore a strapless hot pink jumpsuit with deep pockets that fit her phone on one side and a sizeable flask on the other. We took shots on the way to the carpet until Mary snatched it away from us. "At least until after the interviews."

I groaned. I had forgotten about the interviews.

"Just say as little as possible," Mary insisted.

"Rude," Romy said in my other ear. "Does she think you're stupid?"

It wasn't terrible advice, I thought, as I found myself lost for words. "You're getting a lot of flak for your partying, is there any reason to be worried?"

"No. Na-- None at all," I answered.

"Clearly it hasn't hindered your work. You've come back to the Grammy's with even more nominations than last year, and for a sophomore album, that's a rarity."

"Yeah... Thank you," I answered. The interviewer looked at me like I was useless.

"Well, we don't want to keep you. Have a great night."

"You, too."

As I walked away, I was sure I heard him say something to his cameramen and then heard them laughing.

"No more," I said to Mary.

"You have two more," She answered.

"I'm done," I said.

I could see she wanted to argue but something overcame it, maybe fatigue, and she shrugged. Romy and I were taken in to our seats in the very front row.

I recognised familiar faces around me but didn't get up to talk to anyone like I usually would. Romy was going on in my ear about a girl a few aisles back who she'd slept with and who then proceeded to throw up in her vintage Chanel ballet loafers the next morning.

Then there was Teddy and Laurie, both of them looking at me. I waved. Both waved back, but Teddy's expression was concerned. I couldn't tell what Laurie's was. But I knew he looked good. He always did. Breathtakingly so. He rose a little, as if he was coming to me, but the show started, and Teddy pulled him back. I realised

I hadn't congratulated either of them either. There was a reason I hadn't called Laurie, but I had no excuse for not reaching out to Teddy.

A rapper took the stage and gave a performance full of pyrotechnics. It was nicely distracting.

I could feel both Teddy and Laurie's eyes on me as the host made his opening monologue.

"And, there's Talia Shaw," he gestured to me. I smiled, as one is supposed to do when pointed out in the monologue. I didn't realise what he would say next. "It's nice to see your face rather than your..." he made a sound and looked down as if to look at my crotch. The crowd laughed. I gave half a laugh, too, though I wanted to cry. Fucking paparazzi, I thought.

"I'll just let you know, Easton Vane is not here tonight, but nevertheless, we've hired some security—" Two men in black shirts that said 'security' stepped on stage. The crowd laughed. "So, we won't have any of those same problems."

I smiled again, wide and fake. I couldn't look over at any one else. Especially Laurie and Teddy who I knew were still looking right at me.

"And, Laurie Siler is here..." The young girls in the arena screamed. The host picked up his microphone stand and hit back at the standing crowd below him. "Back, back!"

I looked over and Laurie was laughing. Teddy caught my eye. His smile was a little kinder, then.

The first two awards were best rap and best new artist. Teddy lost. But he seemed fine about it. I smiled at him as we clapped for the winner. The second the ad break came, Romy and I rushed to the powder room to powder our noses. And, by powder I meant coke up. "Are you sure?" Romy asked me. "What if you have to make a speech?"

"I'll be fine," I answered. If they were going to make more Easton or crotch jokes tonight, I wanted to not care. And, it always seemed to do the trick for Romy. I took the rolled up $50 from her hand and snorted as quietly as I could. I heard a giggle outside the cubicle and realised I would have an audience as I left. Romy and I drank from her flask and headed out.

"Romy!" The giggle came from a model friend of Romy's. That was a relief.

I left Romy to chat and headed back to my seat. James was there waiting for me.

"Talia, my love," James said in greeting and hugged me. "I called out to you when you arrived but…" He eyed my nose. He quickly cleaned his nose, eyeing me to do the same. I did.

"Thanks," I said quickly.

"Coke?" he asked me.

"Just a little."

"He was a dick," James said, gesturing to the stage and the presenter. I nodded. "Are you going to be okay to accept the award?"

"Yeah of course. We probably won't get it anyway," I answered.

James shrugged, but he seemed pretty sure. The show started again, and he rushed back to his seat. Romy came and sat beside me. After another performance, came best pop solo. I won. Romy squeezed me tightly. Laurie stood up and cheered as I made my way to stage. If anything, the coke improved my speech. I remembered all the people I should've thanked. I even thanked my family.

It all started moving quickly then, the performances, the awards, a sip or two from the flask, and then I won again. Best Pop Album. Song of the Year. Album of the Year. Record of the Year. James came up with me. Even Teddy came up. He hugged me. It felt good to be in his arms. I didn't have any speech left. I just

thanked everyone, over and over. James took over the speechmak-
ing. Romy looked up at me on stage with pride and something else.
Something kind of worrying.

And, then it was over. And, I needed a drink. Mary took home
the Grammys and Leif took us to the parties.

We made our way to the biggest one. Madonna's. But I saw
Teddy and Laurie heading in together and I forced Leif to turn
around.

Adelaide Mills was having an after party at her fiancé's property in the Malibu Hills, so we went there instead. The house was a
big modern block of buildings with heated polished concrete
floors and ramps instead of stairs.

Romy and I got separated when Adelaide found me and rushed
me away to meet her fiancé.

The man was an ex-footballer and as dull as anything. Or
maybe the coke was just wearing off.

I excused myself to find Romy. I got caught up with an old
band I used to like who wanted to congratulate me. I offered
congratulations in return for their win in best pop group performance. As they kept talking I found Romy standing in the kitchen
with a bunch of girls. They were picking at a tray of fruit. She met
my eyes. We smiled. I liked the secret. I liked that no one in the
room had any idea about us. About the things we did to each other.

She stood up and walked toward me.

"Do you have a tampon?" she asked me.

"Yeah," I said, reaching for my clutch. She grabbed my hand and
pulled me away from the band and toward the bathroom.

"Sorry, emergency," she said to the boy about to go in, as she
brought us in quickly in front of him.

"It's buried in here," I said, searching the depths of my clutch.
She pushed me against the door and dropped to her knees. My

dress came up next and then she was plunging her tongue inside me. I yelped. She stopped to shush me before hitching one of my legs over her shoulder. I held on to her head with one hand and covered my mouth with my other arm.

I rode her face, gripping onto the counter and the shower wall beside us. I felt out of control and unsteady as waves of pleasure rocked through me. I bit down on my arm to keep from screaming and hit my head back against the door. Romy grabbed my waist to hold me still. I almost collapsed as she moved away. She kept me still. I looked at the bright red bite mark on my arm. "Fuck."

"You're so beautiful when you come." I looked down at Romy, on her knees in front of me. She was looking at me with that same look she had while I was on stage. I was even more worried then. It was almost like... love. "What?" she asked me, furrowing her brows. She must have seen the concern on my face.

"Nothing," I said quickly.

"Are you okay?" she repeated. I shifted my underwear back in place and dropped my dress. She stood up.

"Yeah," I answered with a smile. She moved in and kissed my lips, softly.

She pulled away and I tried to hide the concern that was only growing. She smiled at me and I smiled back. "We should get back to the party," I said, we'd already been in there too long and there was no time to return the favour. She agreed. The look faded. I told myself it was nothing.

I woke up to the shrill sound of the home phone. I didn't have a home phone in New York. I didn't miss it.

I answered without thinking. My father's voice was slow and low.

"I wanted to say congratulations."

I smiled, my eyes still closed. "Thanks Dad."

"How are you doing, kiddo?"

"I'm good. Things are good." Romy shifted beside me.

"Yeah? You taking care of yourself?" They were the usual questions I got from him, but they sounded different now.

"Why do you ask that?" I asked.

"'Cause I care about you," he answered. It was something I rarely if ever heard from my Dad and it stopped me.

"What have you heard?" I asked. "It's all bullshit."

I realised I had never sworn in front of my Dad like that. It took him a little while to respond. "You just seemed a little out of it last night."

"When?" I asked.

"When you went up for your awards," he answered. Apparently, I wasn't as put together as I thought.

I felt that anger rise up in me, but I pushed it down. "I'm really okay, Dad." I hoped he believed me. I didn't want them worrying. I knew it couldn't be avoided with my mother, but my father wasn't the type. "I promise," I added, and then felt guilty like it was an immediate lie. I reminded myself that I was okay, and it wasn't a lie. He accepted it and assured me he would tell my mother as well.

Once we hung up, I wanted to look at the internet and the news and see what was being said, but I knew that would only make me feel worse. I decided to strip off and jump into the pool. A little cold therapy.

We spent another two days in LA, Romy had a job and I had interviews. I called in sick and had them all over the phone from the comfort of my bed. I made sure to be sober for them and tried to clean up the image that I had assured Manny was in no need of cleaning.

The day we were supposed to leave, Teddy came to visit. Leif asked if I wanted to see him. Of course not, I thought. I knew exactly what he'd have to say. Especially if my display at the Grammys was as bad as Dad had made it out to be.

"Tell him I'm not here," I instructed Leif.

Leif went back to the door. He mustn't have realised I was still at the balcony.

"She wants you to go."

"Just let me in, Leif," Teddy demanded.

"You know I can't do that," Leif answered.

"James said she was doing coke on Grammy night? Are you just gonna let her get out of control like this?"

Leif fought back. "She's an adult. She's my boss. I don't tell her what to do."

"She's also your friend, isn't she? Are you one of those fucking people? Those 'yes' people? You're just gonna let her get away with whatever she wants? Are you gonna start buying drugs for her?"

"Back off, man," Leif said, his voice low and scarier than I'd known it to be.

"She needs people looking out for her," Teddy pushed.

Leif's voice softened. "I am."

Teddy seemed to give up and left. The door closed, and I returned to my room. Finally, Romy got back from her shoot and we headed to the airport.

FOURTEEN

My 22nd birthday took place on a Wednesday. The days leading up to it had gifts upon gifts being delivered. My entire hallway became filled with flower arrangements. I barely knew any of the people whose names were signed on the cards. Nothing came from the people who were supposed to be my best friends, until Saffy showed up at my door on the Tuesday morning.

"Who?" I asked Kevin in disbelief.

"You can't have forgotten your best friend," Saffy called from the doorway. I ran to see her standing there, a rolling luggage case at her feet, a big Saffy smile on her face.

"What are you doing here?" I asked as I hugged her.

"It's your 22nd birthday," she said, like it was the most obvious thing in the world. I remembered then why it had been so long since we'd spoken. I saw the ring on her finger. "Are you gonna invite me in?" she asked.

I stepped aside. She walked through. She looked around the apartment in awe.

"You want me to take this?" Kevin asked, gesturing to Saffy's bag.

"I can do that," Saffy said.

"The blue room, please," I said. Kevin took the bag and headed up the stairs.

"The blue room?" Saffy repeated.

"The biggest spare room," I answered.

"How many spare rooms do you have?" she questioned.

I laughed a little. "I'm still a little shocked to see you."

She smiled brightly. "We wanted it to be a surprise."

"Who is we?" I asked.

Saffy took a breath. "Your parents booked me the flight. With the miles you gave them."

"That was nice of them." It seemed a little strange, like they had planned this all together. Why wouldn't they come out, too, I wondered, like last time. Though I wouldn't have wanted it. Romy had planned a party in the apartment and had ordered a whole lot of coke. Shit, I realised, how would I explain that to Saffy. Distraction, I thought. Distraction was key.

"Well since you're here, let me take you out. We'll go get some lunch and do some shopping. You'll need an outfit for my party."

"Your party?" Saffy questioned as I called out for Kevin.

"Yes, tomorrow night," I answered. "You'll still be here, right?"

"My flight home is Friday," she answered.

"Great! Kevin, we're going out," I announced as he reached the bottom of the stairs. He grabbed the keys to the escalade and we got moving.

I realised Saffy was exhausted when she started sitting down at every store we entered. "You're jetlagged," I said, texting Kevin to pull up the car to take us back home. "I'm sorry."

"No," Saffy shrugged. "I slept on the plane. I thought I'd be fine."

Kevin took us back to the apartment and I gave Saffy the barest of tours before leaving her to her sleep.

Romy came over early the next morning and jumped onto my bed to wake me up.

"Good morning, babe!" she said, peppering my cheeks with kisses. She smelt like mint and vodka. There were more and more signs from Romy that casual had become something more for her, but I hadn't found the courage to discuss it with her yet, so I just ignored it. I realised with Saffy here, I'd have someone to talk to about it. "How do you feel?" she asked me.

"Twenty-two," I answered. She laughed. She dropped a box on my stomach. It was black velvet, about the size of a necklace or bracelet. I opened it up to find a sapphire tennis bracelet. I sat up, immediately awake.

"Romy, this is too much," I insisted.

"No, it's not," she argued.

"It definitely is. Way too much." I handed it back to her.

"What are you doing?" she furrowed her brows, pushing it back to me.

"I can't accept that. It's…" I couldn't explain it. It was not a casual friendly gift.

A knock sounded on my door. "Go away," Romy called out, guessing it was Leif or Kevin.

"Talia?" It was Saffy.

"Who is that?" Romy questioned.

"My friend," I answered. "Come in, Saf!"

Saffy opened the door cautiously. She took in the scene quickly, Romy sitting up on the bed beside me, but acted like it was nothing.

"Happy Birthday," she offered.

"Thank you," I answered. "This is my friend, Romy. Romy, this is Saffy."

"Nice to meet you," Saffy waved.

"Likewise," Romy answered, in a decidedly unfriendly tone.

"I'll see you downstairs," Saffy said before quickly closing the door.

"Why is she here?" Romy asked, confused.

"She came to surprise me," I answered. "What is your problem?"

"I'm a little offended you don't like your gift," Romy said, taking the bracelet back.

"It's not that I don't like it," I started to explain. "It's just too much."

"What does that mean, 'too much'. I don't know what that means," she jumped off my bed.

"Just, it must have cost a lot and…"

"You know I can afford it," Romy shrugged.

"I know…" I couldn't keep going, I thought. It was the day of the party, that she had organised, this wasn't the time for the conversation we needed to have. "Maybe I'm being silly."

"You are," Romy said, assuredly.

"Can I have it back?" I asked. Romy shrugged and tossed the box back to me. "It's beautiful. Thank you."

Romy gave in, smiling and jumped back onto the bed. She knocked me over and planted a kiss on my lips. "Happy Birthday," she said, as she licked at my lips to open them to her.

The decorators arrived at 10am to start turning my modern apartment into a discotheque. There were disco balls and silver streamers hanging all over the place. Anything expensive was moved into a storage room as well as a few extra lounges to make space for a dance floor, DJ booth, photobooth, and bar.

Leif and Kevin were joined by three other security guys and a female security guard to provide a little extra muscle. Romy and I really hadn't discussed a guest list, but at 5pm people started showing up and more than half of them were strangers.

"Who are these people?" Saffy asked me as we waited at the Bar for my birthday cocktail. It was a bright blue martini cocktail called 'the 22'.

"I have no idea, honestly," I answered, grabbing the drink and sculling it. "Sofie!"

Sofie arrived with a great big box in hand. "Happy Birthday, Talia."

I introduced my friends and was glad to see Sofie was extremely friendly to Saffy, unlike Romy had been. I took my gift into my bedroom and made sure to lock the door straight after. It reminded me to check that my music room was locked, too. There was an awful lot of money in there.

I crossed the hall and opened the door. Not locked. Good catch. I was going to simply lock it, but I found myself entering. I expected to see a layer of dust but of course there wouldn't be, I had cleaners. I imagined them coming in here and dusting the guitars and the drums and the keyboard. What must they think of me, I wondered. Maybe they think someone else writes my music, I pondered unenthusiastically.

I walked to my desk which still held half a dozen empty notebooks.

"Talia!" a shrill voice called from downstairs. I rushed from the room and locked the door.

I made my way downstairs to find Romy standing with James

and Fisher. I crashed into their arms. "Happy Birthday!" They shouted into my ears.

"Thank you," I answered, grateful that I now knew at least four people at this party. "Let me get you drinks!"

I had every intention of getting them drinks, something other than the sour blueberry thing that was my birthday cocktail, but I was pulled in every direction. All these strangers had birthday wishes for me and it felt impolite not to hear them. There seemed to be a pile of gifts growing in one corner of the room, but as I became overwhelmed at the growing number of strangers in my house, many of them staring endlessly at me, the gift that made me happiest was the little bag of white powder that Romy slipped into my hand around 9pm.

I rushed back upstairs to my bedroom bathroom and got myself nice and happy again. I came downstairs with an extra bounce which led me right to the dancefloor. I danced until my silver birthday dress was sticking to me with sweat. Leif brought out a giant chocolate birthday cake with 22 red candy roses running around the edges. 'Happy 22nd Birthday Talia' was written in cursive in white icing in the centre. There were 22 candles underlining the words.

The crowd sang happy birthday to me. I met their faces. I found Saffy's. She was taking video on her phone. Maybe to send to my parents. I suddenly felt embarrassed. Finally, the song was over, and I blew out my candles. The crowd roared. The cake was removed to be cut into tiny little pieces. I left them to that and returned to my beloved dancefloor. Romy joined me and then James and Fisher, too, until they seemed to have a lover's tiff, and both stormed off in opposite directions. I didn't see Saffy for the rest of the night.

I didn't remember sleeping. The first thing I remembered was my head in a toilet bowl, pressing my cheek against the very cold porcelain.

"Can I get you anything?" I turned to find Saffy standing over me in a fluffy blue robe.

"Water?" I asked.

Saffy pointed to my knees where a tall glass of water was waiting. "Thanks."

I drank from it, washing away the vomit still on my mouth. I shivered in disgust.

"What time is it?" I asked.

"About eleven," Saffy answered.

"Only?"

"Eleven AM," she reiterated, guessing what I had begun to guess, that I seemed to have lost twelve hours somewhere.

The sun was creeping through the bathroom curtains, obviously high in the sky. The house was all quiet. I struggled to stand and Saffy helped me to my feet.

"Do you want to shower?" she asked me, in a way that made me think I didn't smell great. But since I was struggling to stand, I shook my head and headed toward my bed. She helped me over. I was glad to find it empty, hoping Romy had taken someone else home, but the second my head hit the pillow, my door flew open and there was Romy, in all her naked glory.

"Morning Sunshine!"

I groaned and closed my eyes. "She just threw up a bunch," Saffy explained. I opened my eyes to find Saffy looking anywhere but at Romy.

"Why are you naked?" I asked Romy.

"We all went skinny dipping," she answered in explanation. There were still a bunch of strangers in my house I gathered.

"Can you make them leave?" I asked.

"Why?" Romy scoffed. "The party is still going."

Saffy furrowed her brows.

"Just tell them I'm sick."

"That's not a great reason to kick people out of your house," Romy argued. It seemed to be to be a perfectly good reason.

"Romy!" I said, in the most demanding tone I could muster.

"Jesus, fine. We'll go." I wanted to argue that I didn't mean her, but it had a two birds one stone quality that I was grateful for.

Saffy left the room, too. I could hear the ruckus return downstairs as the stragglers came into the living room from the pool. I could hear Saffy and Romy's voices. They seemed to be arguing. Suddenly there was silence. I slipped back into sleep.

"Hey," A quiet voice woke me again, I imagined a few hours later. Saffy was there with a big tray in her hands. I could smell bacon and pancakes and syrup, and coffee!

"You're an angel," I said, as I turned over and sat up. She brought the tray into my lap. "Thank you."

"You're welcome."

Saffy made for the door but I wanted to talk to her. "Saf, stay," I asked. I couldn't get out of the bed but Saffy got in. "How is the house?"

"A mess," Saffy confirmed. I stuffed a crispy bit of bacon into my mouth. I got out my phone and texted the building's on-call cleaners. I noticed all the messages I'd missed. Manny had sent one. The simplest two words. Laurie and Teddy had sent theirs, too. Teddy demanded a call back. Laurie hoped I was doing well.

"So, how is the wedding planning?" I started.

"Not great," Saffy answered, taking a breath. "Honestly, we've done so little of it. And, it's only two months away."

"I didn't get my invite," I clarified.

"It's with your parents," she answered. "I wasn't sure of the new address."

"Oh," I answered. "Where is it happening?"

"Doltone House," she answered. It was a big ballroom right on the harbour in Sydney.

"Nice," I answered. "Do you have a dress?"

"No," Saffy laughed. "I can't believe I don't have a dress yet."

I smiled at her, sadly. "You should get one here. New York is the best place for that. Let me take you."

She shook her head, "I don't think you're quite in shape for that."

She was right, I knew. I huffed a little, disappointed in myself. "Sorry Saf."

"It's fine," she shrugged. I drank my coffee, hoping it would give me a little energy. Maybe I could be ready in the afternoon. Maybe I could call in a few favours and have the shops stay open late. "I have a few dress appointments back home."

I nodded. I cut into my pancakes and offered a piece to Saffy. Saffy took it off the fork, dipped it into syrup and ate it.

"God, this is good."

"Did Leif tell you about this place?" I asked.

"Romy actually," Saffy clarified. "Apparently it is your usual hangover food."

"It is," I answered, my own mouth full of pancakes.

Saffy nodded. "That Romy is an interesting character."

"Is she?" I asked.

"She's the one in all the pictures, partying with you?"

"Yeah," I answered. "She knows all the good spots."

"Does she?" I nodded. "So, what is the deal between you two?"

"What do you mean?" I asked, becoming a little warm.

"Some of the pictures out there…"

I scoffed. "Why are you looking at all these paparazzi photos? You're just helping their careers."

She raised her voice to match mine. "I don't go searching for them. You're all over the magazines and the internet."

I didn't answer.

"I don't mean to put you on the spot. I'm just wondering... It seems like you two have a little more than friendship happening." Saffy's voice came down and she eyed me patiently, like I could tell her anything.

"We've been hooking up," I answered.

She started nodding and let out a breath of air. "Wow."

Suddenly, the fact that she now knew about this meant that I could tell her all of the stuff I'd been bottling up with no one to talk to. "It started really weirdly, I was super sad and lonely, and we'd become really close friends and it just happened, but then it kept happening. I thought it was just casual, just exploration, but she has become really intense and I don't know what to do."

"You don't like her as much as she likes you?" Saffy questioned.

I shook my head. "I like her as a friend," I answered. "Only a friend."

Saffy nodded. "You need to tell her then, before it gets worse."

"She's gonna flip," I said quickly, though I hadn't admitted that to myself before. I had seen her flip out on the paparazzi and on other friends who had done her wrong. I knew how it would be if I ended things with her.

"Still," Saffy pressed. "It will be worse the longer you leave it."

"I just figured she'd find someone else," I said, shaking my head.

The doorbell rang. "Fuck," I groaned, imagining it was Romy returned.

"I'll get it," Saffy offered.

Saffy ran for the door. She came back a few minutes later.

"A cleaner is here."

"Oh right." I sat up. "I should probably shower so she can..." I gestured to my sheets that probably smelled as bad as me.

Saffy nodded. "I might go out exploring."

"On your own?"

"I'm a big girl," she answered.

"Okay," I nodded. She left then. I thought she'd be a few hours, but she was gone all day. I thought we'd have more time to talk, but she didn't come back til late at night. I was watching Netflix on my lounge. Leif was passed out on the other end of it.

"How was your day?" I asked.

"Good. I saw the high line. And, I walked all the way around the Met. That place is massive."

"It is, right?"

"How are you feeling?" she asked me, sitting between Leif and me.

"Better," I answered, though my stomach still rumbled, and my head was still pounding with a headache that no amount of paracetamol could fix. "Are you hungry?" I asked, though Leif and I had eaten two pizzas between us only an hour or so before, I would've eaten again with her.

"I ate," she answered. "I'm knackered."

She pulled herself up and headed to the stairs. "You're going to bed?"

"I have to call Peter, but then yeah, I'll probably just sleep."

"What time is your flight in the morning, I'll drive you."

"Yeah? It's 12."

"No worries. I'll drive you," I assured her. She smiled brightly at me.

I kept watching Netflix. Leif's quiet snoring seemed to be making my headache worse. I didn't want to wake him and kick him out. I went to the kitchen, where a mountain of leftover alcohol had taken up residence. I poured myself a little glass of whiskey, imagining a little hair of the dog would ease my headache. And it did, so much so that I poured myself another glass and then another.

I stumbled off to bed with a lovely warm buzz.

The next morning, I wanted to drive Saffy to the airport myself. I wanted to talk to her alone. I wanted to ask why she had demoted me from best friend/maid of honour to nothing at all. But I realised I was probably still drunk from the night before. Leif drove instead.

"I thought you were driving me yourself," Saffy questioned as we got in to go.

"I know," I answered. "But I thought this was safer. We can still talk."

I pressed the button to put up the wall between Leif and Saffy and I.

"So, yesterday was weird," she started.

"I'm sorry about her," I answered. "I'm not sure what I'm going to do about her."

"I'm pretty shocked you never told me about it," Saffy continued.

"Well, we haven't spoken in a really long time," I answered, feeling myself becoming defensive.

"I have tried to reach out," she argued.

"Have you?" I questioned, not remembering when.

"You probably don't remember. Just like you don't remember your 22nd birthday."

I furrowed my brows. "What?" Was she going to tell me off for drinking on my birthday?

"When was the last time you were sober?" Sober... that word

sounded so serious. It didn't apply to me. But I couldn't remember. My mind ran back over the last few days, few weeks, it had been a while.

But I wasn't telling her that. I jumped right on the defensive. I'd been in this position enough times in the past few months. "What do you care?"

"What? You're my best friend!" She was looking at me like I was crazy.

"Not really. Not the kind of friends we used to be." Leif turned a little in his chair. Even through the glass divider, he must have heard us.

"We've both been busy. I don't blame you for that." Saffy reached out for my arm.

"Well maybe I blame you!"

Saffy sat back. "Where did all this anger come from?"

"It's not anger! I'm hurt. I'm hurt that you're getting married and waited weeks to tell me. And, then I find out that you don't want me to be your maid of honour and stand beside you—"

"Wait." She cut me off. "Why would you think that? Of course, you're my maid of honour."

"What?"

"Who else would it be?" she demanded.

"I thought Peter's sister…"

She was shaking her head. "I'm so mad at you right now. And, scared for you. But you're the only person I want there beside me. Who I have always wanted to be standing there with me on my wedding day. Since we were little girls. How could you possibly think that would change?"

"You didn't ask," I answered.

"I didn't know I had to." I started to cry. Saffy reached for me. "What is going on with you?" It was a question I'd been asked so many times up until that point, but I always had an answer. Nothing. I didn't have that answer any more. I couldn't keep lying to myself. I was making fucking horrible decisions. I was drinking and doing drugs and doing no writing at all. I hadn't sung or picked up an instrument in so long. And, I was in this relationship that I never wanted and couldn't find my way out of.

"I don't know," I answered.

"Why don't you come home with me?" she asked, earnestly. I shook my head. "Why not?"

"I can't just pick up and go," I answered.

"Of course, you can," she said. "You can do whatever you want."

I shook my head. "I can't just run away from all of this."

We pulled into the drop off zone at the airport.

Saffy reached for the door. "I'm sorry we fought. I'm just worried. So are your mom and dad."

"I know," I nodded. "I'm sorry. I don't want you to be."

Saffy hugged me tightly. "Can I do anything?"

I shook my head against her cheek. "I'll be okay," I assured her. She looked at me then and seemed to believe me. "I'll see you soon."

She nodded and stepped out of the car. Leif helped her with her bags. We watched her walk into the airport. She turned at the doors and waved at us. I remembered doing the same thing with my mother, when she had dropped me off for that first fateful flight. Never would I have imagined in that moment that my life would be like this. It was a fucking mess.

I had to get my shit together. I had to end things with Romy. I had to go home.

I arrived back at the apartment and took out my travel bag. I started packing. Romy arrived soon after, dressed up and ready for another night out.

"Hey!" she greeted me and then took in the scene. "What's going on?"

"I'm going home," I said, organising my clothes.

Romy half laughed. "What? To Australia?"

"Yeah," I answered, seriously.

Romy grabbed my arm. "For how long? Am I coming?"

I turned to face her. "I don't think that is such a good idea."

"Why the hell not?" There was the first hint of it.

I tried to be gentle. "I think that we need to spend some time apart."

"Are you fucking serious? You're breaking up with me?" Her eyes went wide and black.

"Well, we were never really…"

Her eyes became wider and darker than I thought possible. "We practically live together. Don't tell me we're not together."

I argued. "But, we never talked about anything like that. I'm not even sure this is something I want."

"What does that mean?"

I liked her as a friend, and I'd liked the things we were trying, but when it came all the way down to it, I wasn't attracted to her in that way. "I… I like men."

"Fuck you!" I thought she was going to slap me, I realised I probably would've deserved it. She stormed from the room. I heard the front door slam moments later.

I told Leif I was going home, and he could come with me or stay. He smiled, seemingly proud of my decision. "I'll come," he agreed. Kevin would be given work with the label.

I packed up as much as I could into one big suitcase, I left all of Ari's clothes behind. All the shoes and bags and jewels. I took the jeans and the t-shirts and the things that had always made me feel so comfortable.

I took my guitar, too. Just in case.

I couldn't wake up in the morning without thinking about Romy.

I sent her a text.

Talia: I'm sorry, Romy. I want us to stay friends.

Romy: Get fucked

As I was organising the house, considering whether to sell it or lease it out, I got a call from Manny. I was nervous to answer it. I felt all the guilt from the way I'd treated him. But he was reaching out.

"Hello?" I answered.

"Hi," he said, his relief immediately obvious.

"How are you?" I asked.

He almost laughed. "I'm good. How are you?" I suddenly realised that this was a question I hadn't asked him in maybe years.

"I'm so sorry," I said straight away. "I'm so, so sorry."

Manny let me ramble apologies and explanations and assured me that he understood I was going through something, but he just wanted to be there for me. "Sometimes, I feel like I have to cover personal feelings with professional responsibilities. I realise it makes it seem like I only care about the professional part." That made sense, I thought.

We talked for hours then, with me reminding him of the awful things I'd been doing, and him assuring me that everything passes. I wanted to ask if he would represent me again until I remembered that he would have nothing to represent. I hadn't written anything in the longest time.

"So, you're going home?" he asked me. The label must have told him when I was calling to find work for Kevin.

"Yeah," I answered, my own relief palpable.

"That's good. You need a break."

"I've been having a break," I reminded him.

"A different kind of break," he clarified. "Make sure you take all the time you need. Only come back if and when you're ready."

I took a breath. "Thank you."

I decided to sell the house. I was done with New York. It took a couple of weeks to organise it all, packing it all up, shipping the things I wanted from the New York house to the LA house. I stopped going out at all. I swam in my pool and watched Netflix with Leif. I started reading all the books waiting to be read on my kindle. The time flew by.

On the day of my flight, I got into the car and we took off through Chelsea. We passed by Romy's house and my stomach dropped. I couldn't imagine leaving things with her that way. We drove a little further, to a street side florist and bought a dozen white roses then went back to her apartment. I rang the bell a couple of times before her voice came over the speaker. "What?"

"It's me," I said.

"I know." I looked up to see a camera overhead.

"Can I come in?"

"No," came her quick answer.

"Please. I'm flying home today." It took a few moments before I heard the click of the door unlocking. I assured Leif I'd be right back. He nodded.

I climbed the stairs and reached Romy's level. She had left her door open. I walked inside to find her sitting on her lounge, a big blue glass bong in her hands. Her eyes were red rimmed.

"Hi," I said, walking over to stand in front of her. "These are for you." I held them out, but she wouldn't take them. I sat them on the table in front of her.

She looked up at me with a scowl. "What are you doing here?"

"I need to apologise."

"For what?"

"I treated you badly. I was... a fuck boy. A fuck girl. I knew we felt differently, and I let it keep going. I don't know what I was thinking. I wasn't thinking. There's no excuse but I am sorry."

Romy started to cry. I sat down beside her. I felt my own tears rising up.

"Romy, please don't cry. I hate that I hurt you. You were a friend to me when not a lot of people were. And, you didn't deserve to be used like that."

She only cried harder. She wouldn't say anything. I moved in to hug her, but she stiffened up and I back away.

"What can I do?" I asked, getting down on my knees in front of her. "Please talk to me."

She looked at me, something sad in her eyes, something like guilt. "I did something."

"What?" I asked. "It's okay." I brushed the hair away from her eyes and wiped the tears from her cheeks.

She shook her head. "No."

"What is it?" I asked her, just wanted to alleviate some of the pain I could see in her shaking hands. I reached for them. She pulled them away. I started to become nervous. "Romy?"

She shook her head again. It was something she couldn't say. "What did you do?"

"It's really bad," she said.

"Romy, what did you do?" I yelled, my own fears getting the better of me. There were so many things that could hurt me. She cowered a little and I felt another sweeping wave of guilt rush over me.

"I'm sorry," I said, reaching out for her again. She pulled away, obviously not wanting any comfort from me. I wanted to know what it was that she had done but I didn't want to cause any more pain.

"Do you want me to go?" I asked.

Romy's face hardened. "Yes," she said, firmly.

I nodded and walked toward the door. "Goodbye Romy."

Romy didn't say anything as I walked out. I was sure I'd never see or speak to her again. She was the only person I had in my life as a constant for the last three months, I thought. How could someone go from a constant to nothing at all to you? It seemed unimaginable.

Leif and I got to the airport and checked in quickly. We found ourselves in the lounge staring out at the ginormous airplanes through the wall to wall windows. I heard a few quiet footsteps approaching from beside me. I looked over to see a young girl standing a little distance away, a small first-class menu in her hands with a little American Airlines pen.

"Hi," I said, welcoming her over.

"Hi," she answered, nervously. "Can I please have an autograph?"

"Of course, you can. You're so very polite," I said gratefully, taking the menu and the pen from her. "What's your name?"

"Allison," she answered.

I mocked shock. "That's my middle name."

She smiled brightly. I wrote a quick message and handed it back. "Did you want a photo?"

She shook her head, "I don't have a camera."

"Well, I can take it for you and send it to your Mom. Is she around?" I searched a little and saw an older man watching from a distance. He had a little pink carry on by his feet. "My dad," Allison explained. I waved. He nodded politely back. I thought I could sense a little bit of disapproval.

"Do you know his mobile number?" She nodded. "You're so clever."

I took out my mobile and took a selfie of us both. I gave the phone to Allison to type in her father's phone number. I heard the message tone as he received it. He smiled at me then. I didn't worry about what he'd do with my number. They seemed like nice people.

"Thank you," Allison said as she started to walk away.

"You're welcome."

She turned around for one last thing. "I really love your music."

I smiled brightly at her and she gave me one her brightest smiles back. She walked back to her dad.

I lay back down on the day bed beside Leif. I wanted to cry. I imagined that little girl seeing the pictures of me in the state that I'd been in for all that time. I hated myself. Leif reached over and took my hand. I didn't need to look at him or for him to tell me what he was thinking. He was good that way.

We got on the plane and were home in 19 hours. Leif and I were staying in an Airbnb in Cronulla, one of the beachy suburbs further away from the city, with long stretches of sand and very few people walking it.

We recovered from our jetlag by taking long walks and ordering in good food. Leif fell in love with the local Mediterranean restaurant and it's mezze plates.

I had been in Sydney for three days before I went home. I think I was waiting to look into the mirror and see more of the girl I used to be. I realised that probably wasn't going to happen. I had changed immeasurably. But Dad opened the door and looked at me like I was still his little girl, and everything would be okay. I melted into his arms.

"Missed you, kid."

"Missed you, Dad."

Mom arrived home from the supermarket to find Dad and I engrossed in conversation about a book he was reading about the history of humanity. He was telling me about how far from primal living we are and that beneath our imagined civility, we are still animals and this life doesn't suit us.

"God, what got you started?" she said, with a groan.

"Hi, Mom."

Dad could be relied upon for his steadiness, but Mom burst into tears the moment she heard my voice. She turned as I stood and within seconds I was tightly clutched in her arms. "You're home," she said.

They wanted me to stay in my old room, but I was sure I'd be best to stay where I was. I didn't think Leif wanted to be living with my parents either. But I promised to return for dinner, maybe take them out now and then. Dad even convinced me to play a round of golf.

Once I knew my parents didn't loathe me, I had to make myself brave enough to face Saffy. Last time a rift had grown between us, she was the one to show up for me. Because I was cowardly. I wasn't letting that happen again.

But it wasn't the same as with my parents. They had seen from a distance, what I had been up to. Saffy had been there, had witnessed it first hand, up close. I was ashamed. But I also knew, because she had told me enough times, that she would never judge me. I knew it intellectually, I just had to know it.

Instead of calling Saffy, I called Peter. He was surprised to hear from me until I asked him when and where Saffy's next bridal appointment was. He guessed what I was planning. Inconveniently, the appointment was that very afternoon, but Peter had no idea where. He had to call his sister to confirm the address. I hoped his sister wouldn't spoil the surprise.

As soon as I got the address, I rushed over there, buying champagne on the way and assuring Leif via text that I was perfectly fine.

I arrived at the boutique before the others. There were two storekeepers, both young women, whose faces turned to shock as I was through the door, but quickly and admirably hid it. I explained the situation to the two of them and just in time, was hidden behind one of the change room curtains.

"Wow," a voice broke the quiet. "This place is so nice." I didn't recognise it.

"Anna told me about it," Saffy said, her voice sparkling with joy.

"Welcome. You must be Saffron Tavares," the shopkeeper confirmed.

"Saffy," Saffy insisted on her nickname.

"Why don't you all take a seat on these lounges and we'll bring out some of the dresses in your size," the other shopkeeper offered.

"Thank you," Saffy answered.

I could hear them moving to the couches in front of the change rooms.

"Do we get champagne?" one of the girls asked. Her low voice sounded a little like Peter's.

"Hell yes, you do!" I shouted as I jumped out from behind the curtain.

Saffy jumped up. "Talia? What are you doing here?"

I bounded into her arms. "You thought I'd miss this?"

"Seriously, what are you doing here?"

"I'm home. Indefinitely," I answered.

Saffy half laughed, half cried. She hugged me again, tightly. "Thank you."

"Thank you," I said just as quietly. "I'm sorry I haven't been here for the everything else."

"You're here for the important stuff," Saffy answered. She pulled a little away and looked me up and down. "You look amazing."

I knew she meant healthy. I'd started eating vegetables and going out in the sun since I'd been home. But it was nothing compared to Saffy's glow. She was in love and getting married. I should've seen that glow when she came to New York, but she all she was doing was worrying about me.

"Sit down!" I instructed. I handed out the champagne glasses and went around to the rest of the girls, introducing myself to the ones I didn't know and hugging the ones I knew. I poured their champagne and went off to the help with the dresses.

I found the shopkeepers bringing a clothes horse from the backroom, dresses already pulled. "Is that it?" I asked. There were only five or six there.

"Within Ms Tavares budget."

I smiled. "Throw out the budget. It's my treat. Bring her everything beautiful in her size."

The two women smiled brightly and nodded.

I returned to the girls. Peter's sister, Reese, offered me a glass of champagne. Saffy looked over as I was politely declining. She smiled gently at me. I didn't think I was any kind of addict and I didn't think Saffy thought I was either, but I didn't need it at that moment. I wanted to be as present as possible.

"Oh my god," one of the other girls saw the dresses arriving first. A rush of awes and sighs came over the group.

"They're so beautiful," Reese said.

The ladies took out one dress at a time, showing them to Saffy and getting her opinion. They made a separate clothes horse for the dresses she liked. Around ten options out of the twenty. And, then came the trying on.

Saffy looked so beautiful in all of them. She looked so confident wearing them all. So sure. It made me happy.

"I love this stitching through the bodice."

"But how can you not go for the *Ava*? It is unlike anything else I've ever seen."

The girls were arguing about the dresses, all of them with different female names, as Saffy tried the last one on.

"But which do you like?" Reese asked me as Saffy stepped out.

"That one," I answered, as I looked at my beautiful best friend in a *Megan*, an off-white mermaid shaped gown.

It was so intricate and so delicate looking, but she looked so fierce and beautiful at the same time. The colour went so well with her warm skin and the shape flattered her curves like it was made just for her.

On all the other dresses there was a pin here or there. Something needed to be brought in or hemmed up. The girls didn't touch this one. It fit her like a glove.

Saffy was looking at herself in the mirror. None of us said a word until she turned and looked at us for our thoughts. She found my eyes.

"Talia?"

I shook my head, I was speechless. Reese had a few though. "You have to get that dress."

"If she won't, I will," another girl said. We laughed. It was impossible to think of it not being that one.

"How much is this one?" Saffy asked.

The shopkeepers looked to me. Saffy followed their gaze, confused.

"It's on me, Saf."

She scoffed. "Don't be silly."

I stood up and walked over to her. "You know I can, easily. Please let me."

"You've done so much already. You don't need to do any of it. You don't…"

"But, I want to. It would make me so happy to be able to do this for you," I pleaded.

Saffy shook her head. Was it too much? Was it not my place? Maybe her mother had wanted to pay for it. "Okay," Saffy said, finally. I smiled. "I love you," she said then.

"I love you, more," I answered.

"Can you be my best friend?" One of the girls asked from behind us. The others laughed.

"So, this is the one?" the shopkeeper asked.

Saffy nodded and looked at me. I nodded in response.

Another bottle of champagne popped behind us. "Let's get it wrapped up then," the woman said, rushing Saffy back behind the curtains before the bubbly made its way onto the dress.

I picked up my soda water and gave Saffy her champagne as she returned dress.

"To my very best friend and the love of her life." She raised her class, clinked mine and drank.

We all went back to Peter and Saffy's for dinner. I invited Leif to join us and he came right over. Though he stood out physically, he seemed to fit in pretty immediately. The boys wanted to go out after dinner, but we spent most of the night around a laptop looking at shoes and jewels to go with the dress. The boys, including the groom, wanted to see the dress, but Saffy stayed strong. She wanted it to be a surprise.

I went home with a full belly and full heart.

The next morning, I asked Leif to teach me to surf and he was very willing.

We spent a few hours and I was able to catch one baby wave. It was enough to leave me feeling accomplished.

In the afternoon, I finally felt able to turn on my laptop and look online. There was plenty of vitriol. From the media and from supposed fans. But there was also support. Plenty of, "leave Talia alone." I checked in with the boys and girls who I had gotten to know on social media in the beginning. Most of them were still fans. One or two had chosen to dedicate their love to Sebastian Stan. I thought that was perfectly understandable.

Then there was a Sydney girl named Jade. She was thirteen when I first spoke to her. She must've been fifteen then, I thought. The most recent picture was a tray of hospital food. I scrolled further back and saw that Jade had been in hospital for a month. A week before that she'd shaved her head. Three months before that she'd been diagnosed with a type of Leukemia.

It could only be so many hospitals, I thought. I called all of them looking for her. None of them could tell me where she was. I messaged her online friends, hoping they could tell me. Most of the replies I got were freak outs but no answers. Until one of those freak outs was prefaced by the hospital name.

Leif was out surfing. I wrote him a quick note and took the keys.

The hospital was only an hour or so away, but I drove quickly and got there in 50 minutes.

"Holy shit." The receptionist looked at me like I had three heads.

"The Leukemia ward?" I asked her.

"Level Four."

I made my way. The level was buzzing. A woman in scrubs met along the hallway.

"Good Morning. My name is Lorraine. Can I help you?"

"I'm looking for a young girl named Jade."

"Jade Denton?" An older woman was sitting in a row of chairs by the nurse's desk.

"A fifteen-year-old girl?" I asked.

"That's my granddaughter," she confirmed with shock.

"Can I see her?" I asked. The woman laughed a little. She took me slowly down the hall and to the further room. She knocked gently and opened the door.

Inside the room, an older man sat beside a thinner paler looking Jade. She had needles in her arms and bandages around her chest. She looked up at me and furrowed her brows. "You're not real."

"I know you," the grandfather said. "That Shaw…"

"Talia Shaw," Jade answered.

"Hi, Jade," I said, coming to sit beside her. "I'm sorry to disrupt," I offered to her grandfather.

"I'm sure I know who she'd rather visit with," he said, sitting back.

"How are you?" I asked Jade.

"I'm dying." I froze. "I can't believe you're here." I suddenly realised she was using the expression rather than speaking literally. She seemed to realise it at the same time as I did. We both started laughing. Her grandparents looked at us both like we were insane.

"We'll go get some snacks," the grandmother said, pulling her husband up beside her and leaving the room.

Jade had a million questions. About my music. About becoming a pop star. I answered them all enthusiastically. Even the ones that started coming about Laurie. He was beloved by 15 year old girls all over. Jack and Jasper didn't have the same kind of fanbase. I'd forever get questions about Laurie, I thought. I told her everything, honestly. She asked for photos and we took a thousand. She called all of her friends and had me speak with them. Her grandparents brought back chocolate and candy and chips, and we had a feast.

But soon she grew tired. I could tell, though she wouldn't admit it.

"I've had such a nice day with you," I told her.

"Me, too," she said.

"You're so strong and beautiful. I'm sure you can get through this."

"Thanks, Talia."

I left her with her grandparents and got on the phone immediately. "I know you're not my manager anymore, but would you help me with something?"

Of course, Manny said yes. I wanted to know if her parents needed financial help. Manny told me he'd look into it right away. I wanted their medical bills paid, but I also wanted to make sure Jade had everything she possibly wanted in that room. I drove from the hospital to the electronics store to do that part myself.

I bought a laptop, a DVD player, dozens of DVDs. I passed a girls clothing shop and decided to go a little wild with clothes as well. When I returned to the hospital Jade was sleeping. I gave over the things to her grandparents to organise. They kindly and gratefully assured me they would set everything up for her and let her know that it was my doing.

I visited her again the next week, but she was out for a procedure. I determined to go back again, but then my commitment to helping with the wedding planning took over and I couldn't find the time.

Saffy was underestimating when she said that barely anything had been done. They had the church and the priest and the vows, but no method of transport to and fro. They had a venue but hadn't confirmed the catering menu. We had her dress, but none of the bridesmaid dresses, not to mention accessories. There was no entertainment booked. No cake. They hadn't even confirmed the design of their wedding bands.

It was a tiring, but fun three weeks as we ticked all of the things off the list. And then finally the day arrived.

I'd booked a hotel suite for the night before. Saffy was just going to get ready at home, but as the hair and make-up artists arrived, the nail technicians, and the whole bridesmaid party, it was clear the hotel suite was the right choice.

The bridesmaid dresses were the same classic pinky blush colour, but different shapes to suit the differing bodies. My dress, the maid of honour dress, was a deep v bodice, backless to the waist above an A line skirt in a blush champagne colour. I felt like a princess in it. My hair was curled and done up in a loose bun, a few curls floating around my face.

We were taken to the church in chocolate coloured Rolls Royce Wraiths.

The ceremony was only the tiniest bit long and their vows were silly and romantic. The kiss was sweet and we all roared and cheered as they walked back down the aisle.

Then there was the reception in a beautifully decorated ball-room overlooking a sparkling harbour. There were chandeliers and blush coloured roses everywhere you looked. The cake was a seven-tiered white chocolate masterpiece covered in the same, but edible, blush coloured roses. The band was a fourteen-piece orchestra with an older male singer with a Nat King Cole rasp.

We ate and drank and danced and talked. There were speeches and tears and I had started to picture myself in Saffy's dress. Living these moments. I tried not to picture the guy who'd be in Peter's suit.

Saffy came to my table as cake was served. She had a pleading kind of look in her eyes.

"Will you sing?" Saffy asked me, grabbing hold of my arm tightly.

I coughed a little on my champagne. "Really?"

"Please? I didn't ask before because you had already done so much, and I didn't want to put pressure on you," she explained.

"I don't want to take anything away from your day," I answered.

"You could only add to it."

I knew the song I'd sing. It wasn't even my own, but one of Teddy's. A song that was only a year old but had, I was certain, been played at thousands of weddings by this point. He'd written a beautiful ballad about a love that would last forever. I could play it on the piano already up there on the stage.

"Will you?" Saffy asked again.

"Of course," I answered. She smiled wide and her shoulders hitched up.

"I told the band already," she said. "They're waiting for you."

I laughed a little. "Gimme a minute?"

She nodded. I rushed to the bathroom to take a few minutes to myself. I was going up there, but I just needed to remember how to do it. I took some water and splashed it on the back of my neck. I took a few deep breaths. And, then I was ready.

As I walked out of the bathroom, I saw the vibe of the room

had changed. Peter was looking over the shoulder of one of the groomsmen, to his phone, his brows furrowed.

Saffy stood with her parents, laughing, seemingly unaware of whatever it was.

A girl I'd know from school was rushing around the room, talking to the other guests our age. All of them were going for their phones, reading, shocked, looking at me.

Suddenly, there were guests taking photos of me on their cameras as I moved across the room, back to my table. As I tried to find my own purse amongst the bridesmaid's purses, to get my phone, Saffy approached.

"Talia…" she sounded nervous.

"What is it?" I asked. As she explained to me what had happened, what was online, I lost my breath. As she spoke, I looked up to see half a dozen men, their giant cameras pressed against the darkened windows, their flashes going off. How had they found me here?

Mom and Dad were looking at me, embarrassed and in pain. That was enough to have me crying.

Saffy rushed with me to the back of house areas. I was trying to control my crying, but it made me sound sick.

"It's okay," she assured me.

"I have to go."

"I know," she nodded. Peter came quickly towards us.

"Leif is bringing around the car."

"I'm sorry," I said, a sob wracking my chest.

Saffy held my hands. "It's okay. It's not your fault."

"Yes, it is," I insisted. "I ruined your wedding."

"It's not ruined," Peter piped up.

"It's not. And, you're not to blame," Saffy repeated.

Yes, I am, I thought. I ruin everything. Leif pulled the car up. He opened up an umbrella despite the sunshine.

"I'm sorry," I said again, hugging Saffy and Peter.

"I'm sorry you have to leave," Saffy said, real sadness in her eyes.

Leif sheltered me, and we ran together to the SUV.

He slammed the door behind me and ran to the driver's side. We took off and the flashes faded away.

"Are you okay?" Leif asked, looking back at me in the rear view.

I just shook my head. I couldn't speak. I heard my phone vibrating. It was constant. Blowing up. I took it out and looked over the messages.

Manny: I'm sorry, Talia. Katie and I tried to stop it. Call me when you can.

Lucy: That piece of shit motherfucker. I'll kill him. I'm sorry I haven't been around. Please call me back.

Mom: Are you okay, sweetheart? Call me. Dad and I are here for you. We love you.

Saffy: Thinking of you.

Teddy: Are you okay? Call me? Where are you?

There were more, from James and Vinny and dozens of others repeating the same sentiment.

There were a tonne of calls, most of them from Laurie. It wasn't surprising, he liked to pop in at trying times. But he hadn't left any messages.

Then there were the social media notifications. I told myself not to look, but I did anyway. There were the pictures and the video.

"Don't watch it," Leif said.

There were theories that it was a lookalike. More ridiculous theories were that he'd paid some kind of spy to break in and take them. The commonly accepted story was that a hacker had taken them off my computer or hers. I knew the truth. I knew it as soon as I saw the pictures. I remembered what Romy had said. She was sorry. She did something. She did this.

Easton had dropped a full length album out of nowhere. And, one of the songs was called *Tales*. The lyrics were all about a drug addicted closeted lesbian pop star who'd tried to convince him to have a three way with her lesbian lover. The video was half a drama production, half video, and photos. The drama portion had three characters, one who looked like Easton, one who looked like Romy, and one who looked like me. The video and photos were of me and Romy. Some of them naked. Some not. Our faces were mostly obscured. I was dancing. We were fucking. There was even some footage of me in my shower in New York. I didn't know she was filming.

I wasn't ashamed of my relationship with Romy. I wasn't ashamed of my sexuality. I was heartbroken at the invasion of privacy. Another betrayal. Another public humiliation. It made me want to scream. So, I did. I screamed. Over and over. Louder and louder. I just screamed.

To be continued in Book 3: Happy Endings